SECRETS AND SPURS

HOLLIE LUCKIE

PLAYLIST

Ghost Town by Sam Barber
Nicotine by Ella Langley
Somewhere Over Laredo by Lainey Wilson
May Be by Vincent Mason
I Ain't Going Nowhere Baby by Cody Johnson
When She Comes Home Tonight by Riley Green
Closest to Heaven by Ella Langley
10-90 by Muscadine Bloodline
Fall This Way by Braxton Keith
Dear Rodeo by Cody Johnson
There's the Sun by Zach Top
I Wish You Would by Mackenzie Carpenter and Midland
Forever Ain't Long Enough by Max McNown
Frost on the Pines by Joe Jordan
Call A Cowboy by Lainey Wilson
Big Enough Mountain by Joe Jordan
Hope That I'm Enough by Parker McCollum
One Night Dance by Randall King
Ain't Nothing 'Bout You by Brooks & Dunn

Blue Eyed Constellation by Max McNown
Wildflowers and Wild Horses by Lainey Wilson
Cowgirls Like Me by Mackenzie Carpenter

AUTHOR'S NOTE

Thank you so much for reading *Secrets and Spurs*. Lucy and Colton's story is so much fun, and I'm so excited to share it with you. This book is full of farm chaos, spice, and all the banter you could want. However, there are a number of heavier, more serious topics that are discussed throughout the book.

Secrets and Spurs contains mature content that may not be suitable for all audiences. For a full list of content warnings, flip to the content list at the back of the book. Please note that both of these may contain spoilers.

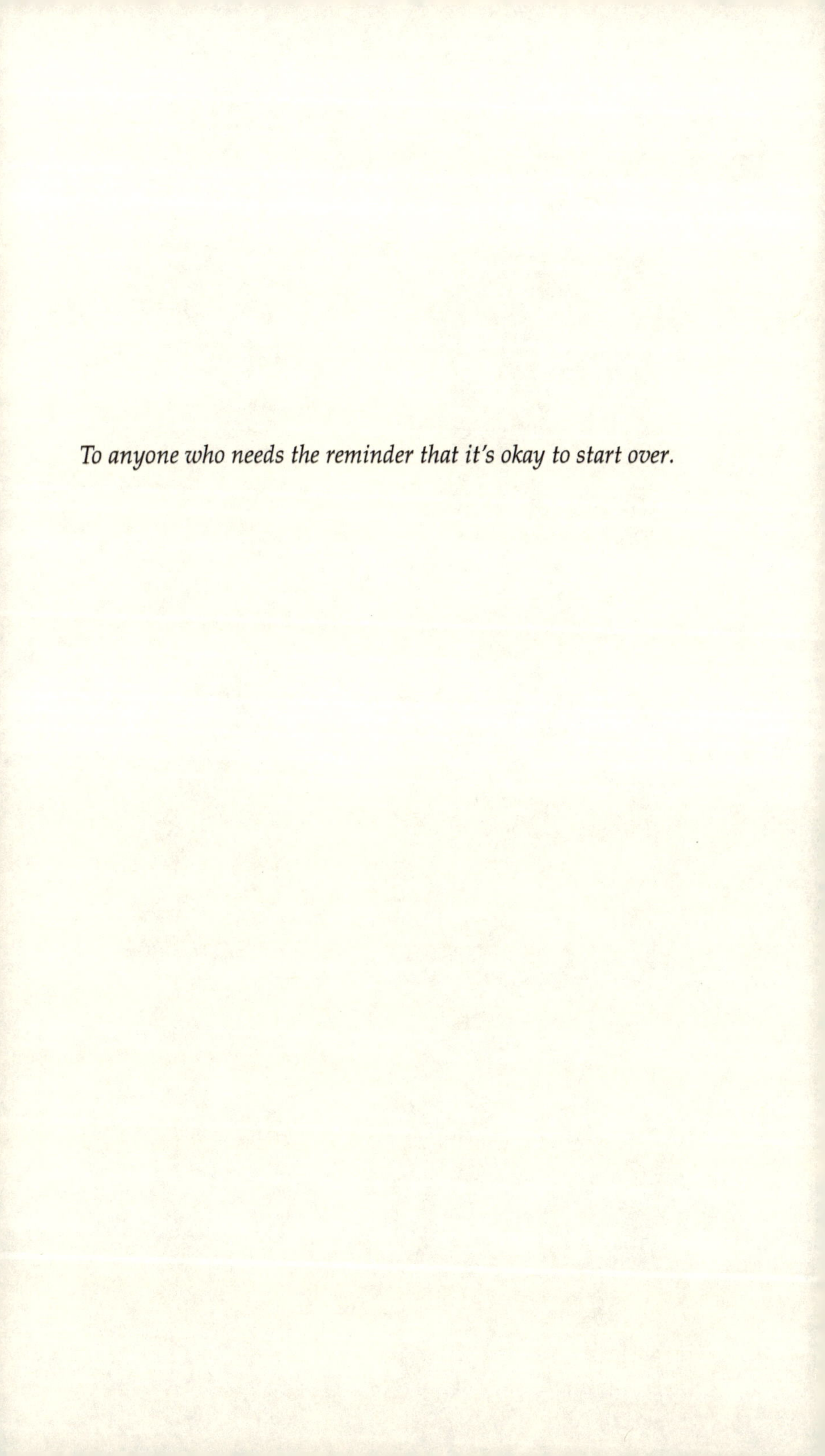

To anyone who needs the reminder that it's okay to start over.

PROLOGUE

COLTON

"Eight seconds, Colton," Sam, my coach, reminds me as he pulls my rope and watches me get settled onto the back of Diesel, the large, old bull I pulled for today's ride. "You just need eight fucking seconds and then you're the six-time world champion."

"Really, I must have forgotten," I mumble under my breath, pulling the rope tighter around my hand.

"Nobody needs your attitude," Sam says, smiling as he looks down at me. "Now go out there and show these rookies how it's done."

Diesel grunts and snorts beneath me, rattling the sides of the chute, but I ignore him, refusing to focus on anything except staying on his back for the next eight seconds. But whether I want to think about it or not, it doesn't change the fact that Sam is right. If I nail this ride, I'll finish out this season on top and get a nice paycheck before spending the next few months getting recharged for next season.

Sam motions for me to make sure I'm set, and after taking a deep breath, I nod at the gateman before letting the world slip away as the gate swings open. Diesel immediately takes off into the open arena, and I focus on shifting my hips with every buck of the bull beneath me. He's strong, but I worry he's not bucking hard enough to give me the points I need.

Just as I have the thought, Diesel spins hard to the right, and I dig my spurs in, focusing on keeping my balance as he throws one of the hardest bucks I've ever felt in my life. I stay on as he thrashes and writhes beneath me just as the buzzer goes off, signaling the end of the ride. I resist the urge to let out a whoop because I know I just fucking won the damn thing, reminding myself I still need to get off this damn bull before I go too crazy.

I lean back, preparing to throw myself off the side just like every other time I've ridden, as Diesel throws a sharp turn to the left.

Fuck. I think, preparing to hit the ground hard. But instead, the tough rope tangles in my legs, trapping me, and I'm left dangling upside down from an angry bull.

Shit.

I tug at the rope, feeling panic set in as I swing closer to the body of the bull as he rears up on his back hoofs before the ground rushes back to me.

If I can just get loose…

I continue to tug, but I'm out of time. A hoof rushes toward my face, and the world goes dark.

"Are you going to tell him he can't ever ride again, or are you gonna make that my fucking problem too?" I hear Sam yell as

I struggle back to consciousness. "I mean the kids in the prime of his career, and you mean to tell me it's gone just like that?"

Cracking my eyes open, I look around, quickly piecing together the fact that I'm in a hospital. The monitors beep loudly around me, drowning out the voices in the hallway for a moment as I try to piece together everything that happened. One minute I was riding, and the next I wasn't. After a moment, I focus back on the conversation outside, as a voice I don't recognize tries to calm Sam, and I feel myself fighting a smile despite the fact that my head hurts like hell. Sam's never been anything close to even-tempered, and I can tell that whoever he's talking to doesn't have a clue how to handle him.

I close my eyes, desperate to stop the splitting headache, just as Sam's words hit me. "Can't ever ride again," he said. Everyone in this damn hospital has to know he's talking about me. Blowing out a breath, I try to decide how I feel about it, just as a doctor walks into my room.

"Oh, look, you're up. I guess, even with all you've got going on, you can't sleep through the racket your friend was causing in the hall."

"Yeah, he likes to make sure everyone can hear him," I say with a small laugh, grimacing as my head feels like it's been split open. "How long was I out for?"

"Around three hours," the doctor says, making his way into my room. "But, Mr. Harris, I'm gonna be honest. I don't know how you're still alive. From what we were told happened to you, you're lucky that bull didn't trample you," the old doctor says, sitting back in the chair beside my bed and rubbing his eyes. "But after looking at your scans, it looks like you've had a pretty significant brain bleed. We're closely monitoring it, and for now, it looks like you won't need surgery. But I'm afraid to tell you that your bull riding days are over. After a traumatic brain injury, your risk of reinjury is significantly higher. There's also a good chance that your reflexes and coordination will be impacted. And next time, you might not be lucky enough to walk away from it."

The doctor finishes speaking, and I take a deep breath, trying to keep up with everything he's saying. Every time I've gotten on the back of the bull, a little part of me has known it could be my last ride. I always knew I wouldn't be able to ride forever, but the finality of this moment still stings a lot more than I thought it would. When I turned thirty-six earlier this year, I tried to start preparing myself for the day I couldn't ride anymore. But I'm fairly certain that nothing could prepare me for the rush of emotion I'm feeling right now.

I open my mouth to argue, before I think about the fact that he's right. I've seen many of my friends push this dream of ours until they had injuries they'd never recover from, and I always promised myself that if I were in that situation, I'd know it's time to hang it up. A lone tear threatens to well up in my eye, but I blink it away before nodding.

"I understand," I tell him honestly. "So what's the treatment look like from here?"

"Right now, we're just monitoring you closely. You have a broken arm from where you were dragged, and I'm afraid it'll need surgery in the next day or two. But as long as there aren't bumps in the road, you should be able to be discharged before the end of the week."

I nod, now vaguely aware of the pain in my right arm. "Can't wait. Thanks, Doc."

The doctor nods before turning to leave, and as the door closes, I shut my eyes and take a long, deep breath.

Fighting the wave of emotion I'm feeling at my career coming to such an abrupt halt, I blink back tears for the first time in years. This wasn't how it was supposed to end. But, like the doctor said, I know I need to be thankful that I'm able to walk away from this one at all.

I'll spend the next few days getting checked over by the doctors, and then after that, I guess it's time to figure out what I want to do with the rest of my life.

CHAPTER 1
COLTON

"And with that, I think all that's left is to say welcome to Mills Corner," my realtor, Bruce, says as I sign the last page in the stack of paperwork in front of me. "Congrats, she's all yours."

I feel my lips slip into a ghost of a smile as I take in the forty-five acres of farm land in front of us that I just purchased, and I let myself relax with the knowledge I'm finally home.

"You know, I was beginning to think this place wouldn't ever sell," Bruce says, looking over at the old farmhouse from where we're standing on the porch. "I know she needs a lot of work, but something tells me this place might be exactly what you need right now."

"Yeah, I think you may be right. Thank you again for all your help," I tell him as he hands me the keys to the farmhouse before waving and heading off toward his old truck in the driveway.

"Sure thing. Feel free to call if you need anything," he

yells over his shoulder before taking off, stirring up a pile of dust behind him.

I can't help but smile as I look around at the broken boards on the porch and the screen door that's hanging just a little off its hinges. Weird? Maybe. But it's been almost six months since my rodeo career ended, and the idea of finally having a purpose and a project makes me feel like everything is right in my world again.

Grabbing the keys, I get ready to head inside and start a mental list of everything that I need to fix just as my phone rings.

"Hello," I answer, pushing the front door open.

"Hey, man," Hayes, my best friend and mentee of the last three years, greets me. "Are you officially a homeowner now?"

"Hell yeah," I respond with a laugh. "All those years we spent on the circuit, but I never thought we'd end up as neighbors."

"Yeah, yeah. I should've known you wouldn't be able to stay away from me for long," he teases, and I roll my eyes despite the fact that he can't see me.

"Whatever you say," I say, bending over to look at the massive hole in the hardwood floor.

"Anyway, I'm sorry I'm not there to celebrate your first night in town, but go have a drink at The Watering Hole on me tonight. When I'm home tomorrow, plan to come by the house and grab dinner."

"You know, most of the time when people say have a drink on them, it implies they're the one paying for the drink, right?"

"Listen, asshole. Not all of us are million-dollar bull riders, okay. I think you can afford the two-dollar beer in Mills Corner," Hayes points out, and I shake my head.

"Yeah, yeah. Just pointing out the fact that you're full of

shit, as usual. But regardless, dinner tomorrow sounds great," I tell him honestly.

"Perfect, I'll let Mama know you're coming. And I'll tell her your favorite food is poppy seed chicken too."

"Hayes, that's your favorite food, not mine," I point out.

"Yeah, but she doesn't know that. And I'm fucking tired of eating food out of a bag."

I chuckle, continuing to make the rounds around the living room. Buying this place sight unseen may not have been my smartest idea, but it's already the closest thing I've had to a home in the last ten years, and something tells me the work will be worth it. Plus, it's not like I have anything better to do now that I'm officially done riding.

"Are you still there, man?" Hayes asks, pulling me from my thoughts.

"Yeah, sorry, I got distracted. You know, it's kind of wild to me that as long as we've been friends, tomorrow will be the first time I meet your family. You're always talking about them, but until a few weeks ago, I wasn't sure they even existed."

Hayes lets out a laugh, "Yeah, they're real. A real pain in my ass most of the time, but they mean well. And with you moving in next door, something tells me you're about to get more than your fill of the Phillips family."

"You do remember there's at least a mile worth of farmland between us, right? Pretty sure your mom won't be walking over to borrow a cup of sugar anytime soon."

"I'm afraid you're drastically underestimating the determination of the Phillips women. Once they put their mind to something, they're pretty damn stubborn. If either of them decides to develop an affinity for baking in the middle of the night, don't think they won't throw on their boots and make the trek."

I laugh at Hayes's animated response just as I hear something shuffling in the direction of the bedroom. Confused, I listen to my best friend ramble on as I make my way down the hallway, the noise growing louder with every step.

"Colton, did you hear me?" Hayes shouts, just as I start to push open the door.

"Yeah, uh, give me just a— holy fuck!" I yell, taking in the chaos in front of me. Across the large bedroom, there's another smaller hole in the wood floor, and next to it, there's at least ten squirrels, scampering around and trying to hide from me. After a pause, one runs straight toward me, and I panic, running out of the room and slamming the door shut. It hits the door with a loud thunk a second later while I fight to catch my breath.

"Dude, what the fuck is going on over there?" Hayes asks, clearly alarmed.

"Squirrels. Lots and lots of squirrels," I breathe out, the fear evident in my voice.

My best friend bursts into laughter through the phone, but I ignore him, still trying to catch my breath.

"Wait, wait, wait. You mean to tell me that you spent the last fifteen years of your life riding on the back of a bull, and you let out a scream like that at some woodland creatures?"

"The bulls aren't in my fucking bedroom, asshole," I breathe out, just as a large rat runs across my foot, causing me to yelp in surprise and Hayes to laugh even harder.

"Fuck, I didn't know I was moving onto a set for *National Geographic*," I mutter. "I think ol' Bruce left a few things out of the information packet he emailed me last month."

"Dude, I told you. I'm happy to have you in Mills Corner, but that place is a dump. I know you're excited to work on it, but I think you might have bitten off more than you can chew with this one."

Adjusting the cowboy hat on my head, I blow out an

annoyed breath before responding. "It's gonna be fine. It may just be a little more work than planned."

"Whatever you say, man. Anyway, I've gotta get ready for my ride tonight, but I'll see you tomorrow."

"Sounds good, I'll see you then," I tell him, hanging up and turning to look back at the house. I feel the small pang of sadness that usually comes when Hayes mentions riding, but I push it aside and center myself by focusing on what's in front of me.

"All right," I mutter. "We're gonna get this place organized, but first I need a fucking beer."

"Just a Michelob, please," I tell the bartender as I settle in at the bar of The Watering Hole later that evening.

She nods and heads off to grab my drink as I take in the scene in front of me. According to Hayes, this is one of the only restaurants in town, and it's packed for a Friday night. The large room has one of the biggest square bars I've ever seen in the middle of the room, and there's at least thirty tables squeezed in the space behind me. Toward the front of the room, there's a large dance floor and stage. The stage is empty, but it's still kind of early, and it hasn't stopped a group of locals from line dancing to an old Brooks and Dunn song coming through the speakers.

"Thank you," I say to her as she slides my beer in front of me.

"Sure thing, Sugar. Do you need a menu?"

"Yes, please," I respond, and she pulls an old laminated piece of paper out from under the bar.

"I'll give you a bit, and then I'll be back to check on you," she tells me before she walks away.

The waitress hasn't been gone for more than a minute before a woman slides onto the barstool beside me.

"Hey there, Cowboy," the woman teases, and I look over to see her gesturing to the brown cowboy hat that's pretty much a permanent fixture on my head.

I open my mouth to respond, but find myself staring at her instead. She's by far the most beautiful woman I've ever seen. Her long brown hair is curled around her face, and her brown eyes hold just a little bit of mischief as she stares at me. And not to mention the fact that her jeans and tank top point out every dip and curve of her perfect, tanned body.

Before I can say anything, the lights go out and everyone around me cheers. My face must show my confusion because she laughs before leaning in to whisper, "After eight, they kill the lights and let the band take over."

Sure enough, the stage lights come on, and the room fills with a hazy glow between the neon signs and the small smoke machine on stage.

"So, Cowboy, what brings you to Mills Corner? Something tells me you aren't from around here," she says, taking a sip of her drink.

"What gave me away?" I ask, fighting the urge to smile.

"Well, if you haven't noticed, every woman in this place has been drooling over you since you walked in. Pretty sure we'd know if you were from around here. Plus, I've lived here my whole life, and I know everyone," she answers as the band starts to play on the stage in front of us.

"That's fair," I admit. "Anyway, I must have missed your name."

"Nope, I don't think you did," she says, staring at me for a moment before breaking into a fit of giggles. "But since you asked, I'm Lulu."

"Nice to meet you, Lulu. I'm Drake," I say without thinking. Over the years, I've gotten used to giving people my middle name to avoid the rodeo girls who just want to say they took me for a ride. I realize it's not necessary anymore now that I'm retired, but I guess old habits die hard. "Are you here by yourself?"

Lulu rolls her eyes before gesturing to the dance floor, where a girl is standing in the middle of the line dancers, making out with a guy in a backward ball cap. One of the dancers knocks into them, but they ignore it, continuing to kiss in the middle of everything. "I wasn't supposed to be. My cousin dragged me out to dance with her, but she ditched me when she saw her on-again, off-again boyfriend here."

"Oh, well, I'm honored you picked me to keep you company then," I tease, and she rolls her eyes.

"Don't let it go to your head now, Cowboy. You just happened to be sitting next to the only empty barstool in this place, and the boots I let Amelia talk me into wearing are killing my feet."

I take a sip of my beer before I say, "Hmm, I guess that really worked out for me then, huh?"

"I guess we'll have to see how lucky you'll get tonight," she shoots back, and I can't help but smile. Looks like there might be more surprises than I thought in Mills Corner.

CHAPTER 2
LUCY

God, what the fuck am I doing? I think to myself as I look across at the hottest man I've ever seen in my life.

I didn't want to come out tonight when Amelia called and told me to get my ass ready, but I have to admit, I'm not mad with how the night is going so far.

I usually don't find cowboy hats hot on a guy. In my experience, at least 90 percent of the ones wearing them end up being wanna be's from the city who couldn't rope a calf or ride a horse if their life depended on it. But something tells me Drake is different. The boots on his feet aren't shiny, and I can tell he's spent more than his fair share of time outside. Combined with his dark curly hair, his piercing brown eyes, and the fucking sexy as sin mustache on his face, I'm a damn goner.

"So, Lulu, tell me more about yourself," Drake says, and I refocus my attention on him, trying to decide what to tell him.

Amelia and I agreed to use our nicknames and silly made-up stories about ourselves tonight if we came across any out-of-towners as a fun way to take her mind off her recent breakup, but judging by the way that she and her asshole boyfriend, Mitch, are kissing like long lost lovers, I guess that plan went out the window.

Deciding to keep it vague, I say, "Well, I've lived here my whole life, and my family has a farm here in town. My cousin and I run a business together, which I really love. What about you?"

"Honestly, I'm still figuring it out," he says with a shrug, and I can't help but giggle at his honesty.

"God, I feel that. I don't know who decided that we're supposed to have our shit together the day we get a diploma, but honestly, I think they should be fired," I tease, taking a sip of my Crown and Sprite.

Drake nods and opens his mouth to say something just as Sandra, one of the older waitresses, walks up and gestures to the menu on the bar. "So, Sugar, did you decide on anything to eat?"

As he looks down at the menu, Sandra gestures between the two of us, then winks at me. I roll my eyes at her, just as Drake says, "Uh, we'll take some loaded fries and another beer, please. You want another drink?" he asks, turning his attention back to me.

"Sure, Cowboy, why not. Thank you," I answer as Sandra turns to grab our drinks. "So, what brings you to Mills Corner? It's not like there's a whole lot to do around here. Wait, wait, wait. Let me guess. You're either passing through on your cross country road trip designed to help you find your life's true purpose, or you forgot to book a hotel room in Smith's Valley for the first football game of the season this weekend, and this was the next best thing." I guess, referring to the college that's about an hour from here.

"Nope, I'm more of a Poplar Springs guy," he says, and I cringe. The Poplar Springs Bulldogs are our biggest rivals, and after spending four years at Smith's Valley University, I consider myself a pretty loyal fan.

"God, just when I was starting to think you were all right," I groan dramatically. "I thought you would have better taste than that."

Drake chuckles before his eyes rake over me. "Hmm, I don't know. I think my taste is just fine," he murmurs, making me blush just as Sandra returns with our drinks and a large platter of fries.

"Here you two go," she says, sitting everything down on the bar in front of us. "Just holler if you need anything else."

Drake snags a fry and pops it into his mouth as I reach for the new drink. "Want one?" he asks, holding out a fry that's covered in cheese and barbecue meat.

"Sure," I answer, before reaching out to grab it from him. Instead of letting me take it, he surprises me by guiding the fry into my mouth. As he does, his thumb grazes my lip, and I swear the bolt of electricity almost knocks me off my barstool.

He smiles at me as I adjust in my seat, feeling a little dazed, before I remind myself to chew before taking a long sip of my drink.

"Oh, come here. You've got a little something…" he says, reaching out and brushing my lip for a second time. I'm pretty sure he's full of shit, but I certainly don't mind the fact that he's looking for another reason to touch me.

We're quiet as he eats, reaching out every once in a while to feed me another fry. Each time he does, he brushes a part of my face, and by the time he's done with his food, I feel like I'm going to combust if he doesn't touch me.

God, Lucy, pull it together, I remind myself, trying to get a grip on the way my mind is running wild.

We sit for another moment in silence, before I look over at

the dance floor and ask, "So, Cowboy, what's it gonna take to convince you to spin me 'round the dance floor?"

Drake laughs, running a hand around the back of his neck. "I may need a few more drinks for all of that," he teases, gesturing to the quick-paced line dance going on in front of us before leaning in to whisper in my ear. "But the minute a slow song comes on, I can't say I wouldn't mind having an excuse to have my hands all over you."

I blush at his words, his face so close I can feel his warm breath grazing my ear. *God, I want this man.* Pausing, I weigh my options before and decide there's no reason I shouldn't step up the flirting between us. Since Amelia abandoned me, I'm alone for the rest of the night. Besides, he's probably only in town for a day or two, so there really isn't anything to lose.

Turning, I look at him and take a big sip of my drink before I ask, "Who told you that you needed an excuse?"

His eyes widen in surprise as he lets out a chuckle, and I bump my shoulder against his playfully.

"God, I should've known you were trouble," he murmurs, and I don't miss the mischievous look on his face.

We lean in closer to each other, our lips centimeters apart from touching. My whole body hums in excitement at the thought of having his mouth on mine. Our lips graze, just as the sound equipment on stage makes a horrible noise. Startled, we jump apart from each other, and the lead singer grabs his microphone to apologize.

"So sorry about that, guys. Clearly, we still have some kinks to get worked out. But now that we have your attention, we're gonna slow it down just a little bit. Grab your favorite girl or guy, and take them for a spin."

Drake and I stare at each other for a moment before he chuckles. "So, Darlin', you up for a dance?"

CHAPTER 3
COLTON

The silence before Lulu agrees to dance with me is heavy, and I can't help but feel like I'm back in middle school for a moment. Am I—a thirty-six year-old retired bull rider—actually this nervous asking a girl for a dance? Apparently so.

I've never really enjoyed the bar scene, and with how busy I've been the last few years, I've pretty much avoided it completely. unless it was work related. But tonight? I think it's safe to say I'm having a really fucking good time, and I don't want it to end just yet.

Finally, Lulu nods before reaching out to grab my hand, and I let her lead us out to the wooden dance floor. As soon as her body curves into mine, I immediately know that, at least for tonight, I'm a goner. The thrill I get wrapping her small body in mine after spending the last hour desperate for a reason to touch her is almost as good as the high I get from riding. As the music plays in the background, I can't help but feel like this is the start I need in Mills Corner. A reminder that, while my riding career is over, that doesn't mean my life is. I can find new hobbies and a new purpose—I may just have to look a little first.

"So, Cowboy, now it's your turn. What's your story?" Lulu asks, pulling me from my thoughts.

"Well, like I said, I'm kind of in a stage of new beginnings, and I'm trying to decide where I want to go from here. I just bought my first house, and I'm excited to get started working on it. Other than that, I'm just really glad you decided to come sit beside me tonight."

"Oh yeah? Why's that?" she asks, running her fingers through the back of my hair as we sway to the music.

"Because you're possibly the hottest girl I've ever met, and you've managed to make me laugh, despite the fact that it's been a pretty wild few weeks," I say honestly, and she leans closer to me until her mouth is hovering just below mine.

"Do you want to talk about it?" she whispers, her breath hot against mine.

"I'd rather do this," I murmur, pulling her mouth to mine. The moment our mouths clash, I know this girl is trouble. She tightens her fingers through my hair, desperate to be as close as she can possibly be, and I reach down to grab her leg and wrap it against me so she can feel how badly I want her in the darkness of the crowded dance floor.

Our tongues tangle, and both of us pull each other closer. As we kiss, I try to remember the last time I was this attracted to a woman, but nothing comes to mind.

I don't know how long we kiss—both of us lost in the feeling of our mouths on each other after the tension we've managed to build over the last hour or two—when the lights come on around us, startling us both.

"All right, y'all. We're gonna take a quick break, but we'll be back shortly," the lead singer announces. Lulu takes a quick look around, blushing when she realizes the eyes of half the bar are on us.

"Fuck, my mama is totally gonna hear about this tomorrow," she mumbles, and I can't help but laugh at her outburst.

"Joys of a small town, I guess?" I tease, and she nods.

"God, I love Mills Corner, but there's a reason I usually make it a point to avoid even a little flirting in this place. If we aren't careful, Mrs Audrey will have a wedding announcement in next week's edition of *The Mills Corner Chronicles*."

I chuckle again, trying to distract myself from how bad I want the girl in front of me. "What made you change your mind tonight, then?" I ask, brushing her hair back from her face.

"Hmm, I'm not sure. Must've been the hat," she teases, reaching up and putting my hat on her head.

"Oh yeah, that must be it," I agree, shaking my hair a little at the loss of my hat. "You know Darlin', I really only take that hat off for one thing, and it's not dancing."

Lulu's eyes blaze with desire, and she leans back into me to whisper, "Is that right, Cowboy? Let me guess, you take it off to fuck?"

"Not quite," I murmur, immediately hard again at the sound of that word coming out of her pretty mouth. She moves closer to hear what I'm gonna say next, before I whisper, "Sometimes I leave it on to fuck, but I always take it off to eat."

Her eyes flash with confusion, motioning to the bar. "Wait, that can't be true. We just ate over there a minute ago, and you didn't take it off."

"Not the kind of eating I'm talking about, Darlin'," I whisper, resisting the urge to laugh as her eyes widen in alarm.

"Oh, I—I didn't realize," she stammers, and I pull her in to drop a kiss on her lips.

"I've gotta say though, it looks sexy as fuck on you," I murmur, between kisses, causing her to chuckle.

"Okay, seriously, if we don't get out of here, I'm never gonna hear the end of this," she tells me, and I look around again to realize how many eyes are still on us.

"That's all you had to say, Darlin'," I say. "Let's go."

CHAPTER 4
LUCY

feel like I'm floating as I lead Drake out of the bar, before he directs me in the direction of his truck. Sure, I had my share of hookups in college, but it's been over five years since I graduated. Between the stress of the farm and the lack of options in Mills Corner, I'll be the first to admit that my love life has been a bit... slow. But now? I've never felt this wild and free in my life.

"Come here," Drake whispers, pulling me beside a large gray Ford truck. I expect him to open the door for me to climb in, but instead, he pushes me against the side of his truck and kisses me hard. The fear of knowing that anyone could find us here shoots through me as his lips graze down the skin of my neck. I groan as he pulls my shirt to the side, feeling like he's lit me on fire as his mustache trails closer to my exposed chest.

"God, yes," I groan, throwing my head back to give him better access.

"So. Fucking. Sexy," he mutters, continuing his path. After a moment, I can't take it any longer, and I pull his face back to mine, rolling my hips against his obviously hard length through his jeans.

"Need—you—now," I pant, desperate to feel him everywhere.

"Slow down, baby, we've got all night," he mumbles before adding, "And I intend to take my sweet time learning every inch of this sexy-as-sin body."

My cheeks flame, and I lose track of time as we continue to kiss in the darkness of the parking lot.

"Please, Lulu, can I touch you? I can't wait any longer to feel your hot cunt wrapped around my finger," he begs.

I have the sudden thought that I wish it was my full name coming from his lips. I never thought I'd be into dirty talk, but holy shit, that's hot.

I nod before teasing, "God, I thought you'd never ask."

Drake chuckles, and I resist the urge to cry out as his finger reaches under my skirt and grazes my clit through my panties. Just as he tugs them to the side, the ringer of my phone cuts through the night, and I nearly jump out of my skin.

Pulling back, Drake looks at me in concern. "Need to get that?"

"Hell no," I mumble, pulling him back to me. "They'll leave a voicemail if it's that important."

Drake nods, and our mouths clash frantically again, before my phone rings again.

"You sure you don't need to answer that?" he asks, and I pause.

Amelia was more than preoccupied when I left her in the bar a while ago, and the only other person who would be calling at this time is my Mama. She knew I was out with Amelia, so if she's calling, it's because something's really wrong.

By the time I've decided to at least see who it is, the ringing's stopped and started again.

"I think you should probably get that," Drake says, and I nod, feeling my concern rise when I see my mom's name on the phone.

"Hello? Mom, what's wrong?" I ask.

Through the line, my mom groans before saying, "Listen, I told your Aunt Martha not to call you, but I'm on the way to the hospital."

"That sounds like a pretty fucking good reason to call me," I say, already looking around for my things.

"Language, baby," she scolds, and I roll my eyes at her usual antics. "I'm pretty sure your Aunt Martha is overreacting," Mama says with a groan. "But I fell trying to get Daryl and Denise back in their pen, and my hip is giving me more trouble than I'd like."

"I'm on my way," I tell her. "How did the pigs get loose?"

"Oh, you know those silly things are always looking for a new adventure. And I'm not quite the spring chicken I used to be."

"God, okay. I'll be there in a few minutes. See you soon," I tell her, hanging up before turning back to Drake.

"Everything okay?" he asks, and the obvious concern on his face makes me smile.

"Yeah, but there's been a family emergency and I have to go... My mom hurt herself trying to get the pigs back in their pen. I'm so sorry," I whine, running my hand over my face and grabbing his hat to set it back on his head. "But if you're in town for a bit, I wouldn't mind staying in touch," I say, before I can stop myself.

"I'd love that," he mumbles. "Because I'm nowhere close to being through with you."

A thrill runs through me at his words as I nod. Grabbing his phone, I type my number in before giving him a quick kiss on the lips. "Perfect. Text me, Cowboy," I say over my shoulder, already calling an Uber to take me to the hospital.

"Yes, ma'am," he says from behind me, and I can't help but smile before turning my focus back to making sure my mama is okay.

"HEY, Lucy. She's down the hall to your left. Room 102," Kasey, one of the nurses at Mills Corner Hospital, who I went to high school with, tells me, gesturing down the long hallway of our small hospital.

"Great, thank you, Kasey. Are your boys doing okay?" I ask over my shoulder, already heading down the hall to my mom's room."

"Oh, you know, just growing like weeds," she yells with a laugh. "You'll see when I bring them to the pumpkin patch next month."

"Sounds good. Tell them and Mike I say hello," I tell her, inwardly cringing at the reminder that our season at Cedar Creek Farms is less than a month from starting. There's so much Amelia and I have to take care of before the pumpkin patch and other activities are ready to go, but I can't think about that right now.

Pushing the stress from my mind, I knock quickly before pushing open the door to Mom's hospital room.

"Listen, Mama, if you wanted me to stay home with you tonight, you could have just asked," I tease, wincing as I see the cast they're wrapping around her foot.

"Oh, you hush, baby girl. You know you didn't have to come check on this old clumsy woman," she says, reaching up her arms from her place on the bed for me to lean down and give her a hug.

"So, what's the damage?" I ask, sitting down next to her bed and grabbing her hand.

"Well, I don't know that we could call it damage. Just a bruised hip and a broken ankle. Nothing an old woman like me can't handle," she says, waving me off like she doesn't have a care in the world.

"God, Mama, I'm so sorry. I should have double checked on the pigs before I left," I tell her, feeling the guilt settle in at her current predicament.

"Baby, it could've happened to anyone. It's fine. Luckily, I don't need surgery, and I'll be good to go in a bit."

As soon as she finishes her sentence, my Aunt Martha bursts through the door, waving frantically.

"Hey, baby girl, I'm so glad you're here," she says, running over and wrapping me in a hug. "This sister of mine just insists on keeping things interesting around here, huh?"

"I'll say," I mumble, rubbing my eyes as the events of the night catch up with me. "But wait, Mama, how are you gonna get around the house on crutches? Your room is on the third floor," I remind her, thinking about the renovations to the house my mom had done after my dad died several years ago. She couldn't stand to stay in the room they'd shared for most of her life, so she turned the attic into a huge master suite. It's been a great change for her, but now? The idea of getting her up and down is a bit daunting.

"Oh, your aunt and I were just talking about that. I'm gonna plan to stay with her for the next ten weeks. She just finished her downstairs renovations, and that'll make all of our lives easier," Mom explains, and Aunt Martha nods.

"Yep, I'm kinda excited. Your Uncle Bryce has a few business trips coming up this month, so it'll be like old times," she says with a laugh.

"Mama, are you sure? If you want to stay at home, we can figure something out," I tell her, worried she'll feel like she's being kicked out of her own house.

"I'm sure, baby. Plus, I'll still be around during the day if you need help getting ready for the season. Oh, and while I'm thinking about it, do you have plans tomorrow night?"

"No, I don't think so," I answer, feeling my phone ping in my pocket.

"Good. Don't make any. I'm coming back to the house and we're having dinner. Your brother will be home, and his friend Colton just moved to town, so we invited him over too," she explains.

"Mama, I love you, but you're the only person I know who would be worried about hosting dinner for someone while you're sitting in a hospital bed," I tell her, shaking my head in her direction.

"A little hospitality never killed anyone, Lucy," my mom says with a laugh as they finish her cast. She and my aunt launch into a conversation about the state of my aunt's garden, and I pull out my phone to see if Amelia finally realized I was gone. Instead, I'm momentarily surprised to see a message from an unknown number until I remember that I gave Drake my number. Scrambling, I hurry to see what he said.

Unknown: Hey Lulu. It's Drake. I had a great time with you tonight. Hope your mom is okay.

Smiling, I stare at my phone for a second, trying not to fidget with how giddy I feel. On the ride to the hospital, I overthought every moment of our interaction tonight, and I managed to convince myself I'd probably never hear from him again.

Lulu: Hey Drake. I had a great time too. And she's doing all right. Just some bumps and bruises for the most part.

Drake: Glad to hear it. Listen, I've got plans tomorrow, but I'd love to see you Sunday if you're free.

Lulu: Hmm… I don't know… I'll have to think about it ;)

Drake: :(

Drake: Don't think I won't beg.

Lulu: Well, I do love a man who begs…

I laugh as the bubbles indicating that Drake is typing pop up, then disappear. Deciding to put him out of his misery, I add.

Lulu: I'm just kidding. Sunday sounds great :)

"Lucy Lu, what's got you grinning like a little schoolgirl over there?" my mom asks, bringing me back to the moment. Shoving my phone back in my pocket, I turn to her, knowing that if I even hint about having a little crush on a new man I met at the bar, she'll have the gossip chains and the group texts going in under an hour. Honestly, she and her friends could probably have his social security number and his full dating history by the end of the night if they really wanted to. And while I know if things keep going with Drake and me, I'll have to tell her eventually. For now, I want to enjoy keeping him to myself for a little longer.

"Oh, just checking in on Amelia. It looks like she and

Mitch are back together again," I say, knowing that'll distract my mom.

"Ugh, again? I love that girl with all my heart, but when is she going to realize that boy is nothing but trouble? Every time I turn around, he's finding a new way to break her heart before swooping back in to save the day again," my mom complains, and Aunt Martha nods in agreement.

"Yes, and my girl is way too pretty and smart to be crying all those tears the way she is," my aunt adds.

"I know, I know. But y'all know as well as I do that nothing we can say is gonna change her mind. Maybe he'll finally get his shit together, and if not, we'll be here to help her pick up the pieces again," I tell them with a sigh. "I just want her to be happy."

"Me too, my sweet girl," my mom says, pulling me in for another hug. "Now, what do you say we go see if we can't get out of here?"

CHAPTER 5
COLTON

God, I'm officially too old for this shit. The thought crosses my mind as the early Saturday morning sun pours through the window of my truck. When I got home last night, I decided sleeping here was my best option, since I still haven't figured out the best way to handle the squirrel situation in my bedroom yet. Not to mention the fact that I still don't have any furniture yet. I've spent more than half of my life on the road and done my fair share of nights sleeping in my truck when I was first starting in the rodeo circuit, so I figured it wouldn't be too big of a deal. But judging by the way my body is aching and my entire body is covered in sweat, those days are probably long behind me.

"All right, I guess it's time to get up," I say, pushing the door open and forcing my stiff legs to straighten. After rounding the truck and making my way up the walkway of my new house, I turn back and smile at the view. The entire morning sky is lit with pink and purple clouds as the sun continues to rise, making the farm land in front of me glow.

Pushing open the door, I try to convince myself that yesterday's first venture into the house hadn't really been as bad as I made it in my head. Surely, it'll be fine. The squirrels are probably long gone, and the rest isn't anything that some paint, new floor boards, and a few mouse traps won't fix.

By the time I make it inside and head toward the bedroom to grab a shower, I've talked myself into thinking that nothing's going to jump out at me. Relaxed, I start humming one of the songs the band played last night, thinking about how incredible Lulu looked under the low lights of the bar.

I'm so mad at myself for agreeing to have dinner with Hayes and his family, but there's no way I can cancel. I've never met his mom or the rest of his family, and despite the fact that I would much rather spend the evening learning every inch of Lulu's body, it won't kill me to wait a night.

I step into the bedroom, which is thankfully squirrel free. Blowing out a breath of relief, I look around and make a mental note of the repairs needed there before moving to take a shower. I shrug out of my shirt and shorts, and pull back the old shower curtain I definitely need to replace before looking down and letting out a loud yelp.

"Oh, for the love of Christ," I mutter, my plans of a shower completely interrupted by the damn family of squirrels that have taken up residence in my bathtub.

Just like yesterday, they scamper the moment they see me, running in every direction until I stop trying to keep track of them. "Go, get away," I yell, the fear I felt yesterday magnified by the fact that I'm fucking naked. Is this what the people on *Naked and Afraid* feel like? Because absolutely the fuck not.

"Just let me open the door," I mutter, more to myself than anything, kicking myself for trapping myself in this damn room when I knew there was wildlife on the loose. I mentally pat myself on the back for managing to mostly keep my composure this time, swinging open the door wide for them to exit.

Relieved, I let out a whoop of victory when they start

running out the door one at a time, ignoring the fact that they'll still be loose in the house. That's a problem for another day. Just as I'm about to close the door and celebrate the fact that it kind of feels like I won that round, I feel something on my foot.

I let out another yelp, looking down to see one of the damn things trying to scamper up my leg. I feel its sharp claws slice my skin, and I scream, jumping and shaking as hard as I can to shake the animal loose. It looks at me with wide eyes, both of us frozen in shock before it finally comes loose and flies halfway across the room.

It lands with a thunk and stands running out of the room, as I blow out a breath of relief. *God, this is a fucking disaster.*

"I guess I'd better try to get an idea of where they went," I mutter, wanting to have enough information for the pest control whenever I make it around to calling them later today.

Peeking around the door frame, I see that most of them are huddled in the corner of the hallway. Just as I'm about to blow out another breath of relief, satisfied the animals are going to leave me in peace, two of them dart at me from their spot down the hall. Panicked, I sprint down the hallway, and briefly wonder if I run outside if they'll follow me. Since I don't have anything to lose, I decide to try it, determined this will be an act of pure genius mixed with a little desperation.

But as soon as I step out on the porch, the old door catches behind me and slams shut, locking me out. Naked.

"God, can this morning get any worse?" I mutter, running my hands through my hair. The words are barely out of my mouth when I hear the sound of a truck pulling down my driveway.

Fuck, fuck, fuck. I instantly recognize Hayes's truck stopping right in front of the house. I try to hide myself, but I know by the whooping laughter I can already hear coming out of my best friend's truck that it's no use.

"Damn, dude. Am I interrupting something?" Hayes calls out with a laugh, making his way up the walkway. "I mean, I can come back later if you're busy."

I flip him off before using one hand to cover as much of myself as I can and the other to point at the inside of the house.

"Squirrels. Fucking squirrels," I mutter, and Hayes collapses into himself in laughter.

"The squirrels are your explanation for why you're outside naked, and I'm guessing locked out of your house?"

"Hell yes, they are! They're evil, evil little creatures. I was trying to get in the shower after sleeping in my truck last night, when the little fuckers decided to ambush me."

Looking down, I gesture to my leg. "See, one tried to climb my leg like a fucking tree and managed to scratch the shit out of me."

Hayes continues to laugh, tears threatening his eyes as I continue my rant.

"Then, I thought it was safe to poke my head out just so I could tell pest control which way they went, and the damn things rushed me again. So I ran outside to get away, not thinking about the fact that the door was locked from the inside. Plus, I wasn't exactly expecting any visitors," I finish, ignoring the way my supposed best friend is howling with laughter at me.

"Dude, I'm sorry, but that's fucking hilarious," he groans. "Please tell me your rabies shot is up to date, though."

"Yeah, yeah, I'm all good on that front. But now I've gotta figure out what the hell I'm gonna do about all this," I say, gesturing to the farmhouse.

"Is this the part where I say I told you so?" Hayes gloats, and I flip him off again in response.

"Okay, fine. Let's do this. I've got some clothes in the truck. You put them on because I can't take you seriously with your junk hanging out, and then we'll see what we can do with the squirrels."

"Fine." I gesture for him to bring the clothes to me.

He shakes his head, turning and running to his truck before coming back with a pair of gym shorts and a T-shirt.

I make quick work of putting them on before straightening and gesturing to the farmhouse in front of us. "All right, let's break into my house."

"Jesus, what a fucking day," I mutter to myself as Hayes pulls down the driveway a few hours later. It took us almost three hours to get the damn door unlocked, but even then, neither of us were brave enough to face the squirrels again. Now, I only have about an hour before I need to head over to his house, but after the stress of the day, I've been dying to just relax for a while.

Sitting down in the old rickety chair on the porch, I pause and pull out my phone and start looking for a few pieces of basic furniture. As much as I've moved around and lived on the road over the last few years, I haven't accumulated many belongings of my own, and the idea of having something that's actually mine feels really fucking good.

After picking out a chair, a table, and a bed frame, I switch over to messages to send Lulu a quick text.

Drake: Hey, Lulu.

> Drake: Just wanted you to know I can't stop thinking about you, and I'm excited to see you tomorrow. I hope your day has gone better than mine.

Lulu: Oh no! What happened??

Lulu: And hello to you too Drake :)

I feel a momentary stab of guilt over seeing the name on my screen, promising myself that I'll fix it tomorrow when I see her again.

> Drake: Squirrels. Lots and lots of squirrels.

Lulu: ???

Lulu: Are you sure you're okay?

> Drake: The house I just bought? Yeah it's infested with ten of the most vicious squirrels I've ever met.

Lulu: Aww, squirrels are so cute though!

> Drake: Not when you're naked and they're crawling up your leg…

Lulu: STOP

Lulu: YOU'RE LYING

Lulu: I'm pretty sure I'd pay thousands to see that…

> Drake: I won't charge you anything for the naked part ;)

> Drake: But the squirrels? Fuck no.

> Drake: Never doing that shit again.

Lulu: *eye roll*

Lulu: Okay enough of the jokes… are you okay?

Drake: Yep, I'm good now. But it looks like I'll be sleeping in my truck another night or two until they can get this figured out.

Lulu: Oh no!!

Lulu: Wait, is your house in Mills Corner? I didn't even ask you last night.

Drake: Yeah, it's about 10 minutes out of town.

Lulu: Oh, wait. Really?

Lulu: I guess you're not feeling the Mills Corner Motel?

Drake: As tempting as that is, I think I'll pass.

Lulu: I don't blame you. That place gives me the creeps.

Lulu: Hmm

Lulu: Let me think about it tonight. I'll have a solution for you by the time I see you tomorrow.

Drake: Oh really?

Drake: Let me guess, you're friends with pest control here in town, and you're gonna help me get in touch with them? I tried their on-call number a time or two today and never got any answers.

Lulu: Yeah, Andy isn't known for being the best at getting back to anyone.

Lulu: I'm assuming selling the house and letting them have it to themselves is out of the question?

Drake: Unfortunately yes…

Drake: But don't think I haven't thought about it.

Checking the time, I groan when I see it's time for me to head next door. I'm grateful to his family for inviting me to dinner, but right now all I want to do is sit here and talk to Lulu.

What the fuck has gotten into me? I've never enjoyed texting and I've definitely never wanted to cancel my plans to stay home and talk to a girl. But I guess there really is a first time for everything.

Lulu: I promise we'll figure something out.

Drake: I'm holding you to that.

Drake: I've gotta go, but I'll text you tomorrow.

Lulu: Sounds good Cowboy.

CHAPTER 6
LUCY

"Earth to Lucy," my mom chimes, waving her hands at me from across the kitchen. "Honey, I've been talking to you for the last five minutes, and you've hardly said a word. What's got you so distracted this afternoon?"

"Oh, nothing," I promise her, tucking my phone in my pocket and mentally kicking myself for zoning out the way I did. I love my mom with all my heart, but if she even gets the slightest clue that I'm developing a crush on this new man in town, I'll never hear the end of it.

"Okay, well, come give me a hand with dessert. Can't you see I've got my hands full over here?" she whines, before winking at me.

"Mama, I've been waiting for you to give me something to do for the last hour," I remind her, and she laughs.

I'm about to ask her how she's feeling when my brother Hayes walks in the door.

"Hey, Mama. Hey, Lucy Lu," he says, his eyes widening when he sees the cast on her foot and the crutches under her arms. "What the hell happened here?"

"Oh, I'm fine, honey. Just had a little fall yesterday, but it's nothing that these old crutches and some rest won't fix," Mom reassures him.

"And you didn't think to call?" Hayes asks, the exasperation evident in his voice. Ever since Dad died, my brother has become over protective of me and my mom. I know he has good intentions, but sometimes he can be a little suffocating. And I have no doubt that not knowing about our trip to the emergency room is going to send him into orbit.

"I knew you were busy riding last night, and I didn't want you to have any distractions. But don't worry, Lucy Lu has taken great care of me today, haven't you, Sweetheart?"

I nod, and Hayes shoots me a look of disapproval. "So. can someone fill me in on what happened?" he asks, and I don't miss the lack of patience in his tone.

"Daryl and Denise," I mumble, preparing myself for a fight.

"How in the hell did the pigs break Mama's ankle? Damn it, I can't stand those fuckers," my brother explodes, and I remind myself that fighting with him won't help anything.

"Honey, it's fine," my mom reassures him. "The pigs managed to get out of their pen, and I fell when I was trying to get them back in. It's not their fault. Plus, look at how cute they are."

All three of us turn to see both of my pigs splashing in the mud puddle I filled for them earlier today.

"Yeah, see. How can you be mad at something that cute?" I ask, causing Hayes to roll his eyes.

"I don't care how cute they are. How in the hell is Mama gonna get up and down all the stairs for the next couple months?" my brother asks accusingly.

"I'm staying with your Aunt Martha for a while. So it'll just be you and Lucy for a while here at home," Mom tells him, and he cringes. I can tell he's out of questions to throw at me, but I still have a feeling this isn't the last I'll be hearing about this whole situation. *Great.*

"Actually, I was coming to talk to you about that. Colton is having some issues with the old place next door, and he needs a place to stay. He'd never ask for help, but it doesn't seem right, letting him sleep in his truck until he gets everything settled. Do you care if I offer him the guest room for a bit?"

Wait, that's so weird. Drake's having to sleep in his truck too, I think before refocusing on Moms's answer.

"Oh dear, I was worried that would be the case. The poor boy, sleeping in his truck! And in this heat? Absolutely not! I think that would be wonderful, as long as Lucy's okay with it," my mom says, and both she and my brother turn to look at me.

I cringe inwardly at the thought of living with someone I've never met for the next few weeks, but I know there's not really a reason to say no. Hayes would never consider bringing someone into our house that he didn't trust, so I just shrug.

"Fine. Can't wait to spend the next month or two with not one, but two annoying old men," I tease, and Mama laughs.

"Hey, I'm only thirty-one," Hayes argues. "Now, Colton on the other hand…he's an old man"

Mom and I giggle at Hayes's joke, and I hold up my hands in surrender.

"Fine, fine. Y'all aren't old. You know I have to give you shit, though," I concede. "But wait, how old is Colton?" I ask, my curiosity piqued. I've never met my brother's best friend, and all I really know about him is that he bought the place next door to us when his rodeo career ended suddenly a few months ago.

"Don't I know it. And maybe thirty-six. I'm not sure, but I know he's several years older than me."

"What's wrong with the house?" Mama asks, gesturing for me to pour the cake batter I just finished mixing into the pan in front of her.

I pour and lose myself momentarily in thoughts of last night while my brother rambles on about his best friend. But my attention is piqued when I hear the word "squirrels" come out of his mouth.

Wait. There's no way in the world. Drake's name is not Colton, and there's no way the man I spent last night with was as old as my brother's best friend. Plus, not that age really matters, and I know it was dark most of the night, but I'd say he was closer to my age of twenty-seven than almost forty. It must just be a weird coincidence.

"Anyway, now that that's settled, how's everything here at Cedar Creek coming?"

"Ugh, we're so behind schedule this year," I groan, thinking about everything Amelia and I will need to take care of before the season starts at our pumpkin patch. "The pumpkins are not growing quite as well as they have in the past, and we still have so much organizing to get done for the hay bale obstacle course fundraiser."

"Well, I'm sure it'll be fine. You and Amelia always manage to pull everything off just in time," my brother reminds me.

"Yeah, but just once I'd love to be a little ahead of schedule," I mumble, and Mom laughs.

"Baby girl, I hate to break it to you, but you've never been early for anything a day in your life."

I roll my eyes, but silently acknowledge she's right. I'm never actually late, but being chronically pressed for time is one of my most consistent personality traits.

"Fine, I guess you're right," I mumble as my black lab, Knox, runs into the room, barking like crazy.

"Oh, it looks like Colton's here," my mom points out, and

I pause to look out the window as a gray truck rolls down the driveway.

I stare for a moment before I realize I know that truck. I'm almost certain I spent several minutes pressed against it last night, begging for the man inside it to fuck me.

Holy shit, this is gonna be a disaster.

CHAPTER 7
COLTON

'm humming along to the song on the radio as I pull into the long driveway leading to the Phillips' family farm. A large white farmhouse with a green tin roof sits at the bottom of the hill, and it looks out over a property that's almost as pretty as the view from my house next door. There's more pumpkins lining the path than I've ever seen in my life, and I smile at the orange pickup truck sitting at the end of the drive that matches the color of the pumpkins and the fall leaves perfectly. In the yard, there's a pen where two rambunctious pigs play in the mud, causing me to pause.

Lulu told me that her mom fell trying to get the pigs in the pen last night, but surely it has to be a weird coincidence, right? I'm sure lots of people around here have farm pigs.

Shaking away the thought, I throw my truck in park and head up the walkway to knock on the large front door. A moment later, Hayes comes out on the porch, followed by an older lady on crutches.

Shit, there's no fucking way. My mind races to piece together all the coincidences, just as Lulu walks out on the porch.

I freeze, taking in how gorgeous she is in the late afternoon sun. Last night, I knew she was attractive in the glow of the stage lights. But now? She's fucking radiant.

Shaking my head and forcing myself to keep my composure, I paste on a smile as Hayes comes over and slaps my back.

"Look who bothered to put clothes on this time," he jokes, and I resist the urge to flip him off as he moves us closer to his mom and sister.

"Oh, you stop that," his mother tells him, shooting him a look of disapproval before turning a smile toward me. "Colton, it's lovely to finally meet you. Welcome to Cedar Creek Farms. I'm Hayes's mom, Charleen. We're so happy you're here. This one never stops talking about you."

"Thank y'all so much for having me," I say with a genuine grin. "And is that right, Hayes? That's so sweet."

My best friend flips me off from behind his mom's back, and I struggle to hold in my laughter before turning back to Mrs. Phillips. "It looks like you took a bit of a tumble. Are you feeling okay?"

"Fine as wine," she responds, brushing away my concern with a flick of her hand. "I'm just a clumsy old hag that lost her balance looking for those stinkers out there," she says, pointing to the pigs.

I smile at her again before getting the courage to turn my attention to Lulu.

We stare at each other for a moment of awkward silence before she reaches out her hand. "Nice to meet you, Colton," she says, adding extra emphasis to my real name before shooting me a look of betrayal. "I'm Lucy."

Hm, no more Lulu, I guess?

"It's nice to meet you, Lucy. You know you're much older than I was expecting. The way Hayes always talks about you, I was expecting someone fresh out of high school," I say with an awkward chuckle.

Lucy rolls her eyes, and their mom chuckles. "God, it's so annoying when he does that. I'm fucking twenty-seven, you asshole," she says, pointing her attention to her brother. "Apparently, time stood still for him since our dad died, and I'm permanently thirteen in his mind. He's a little overprotective, and it drives me nuts."

Everyone goes quiet for a second, and I inwardly cringe. Age doesn't really mean shit to me, but I have a feeling the fact that there's nine years between us isn't going to help my case if anyone finds out what almost happened last night.

And the worst part? I really want it to happen again.

"Well, enough of that, now that we all know each other, let's get inside. We're letting all the bought air out," Mrs. Phillips says, leading the way back inside on her crutches. "Hayes told me that poppy seed chicken is your favorite."

I shoot my best friend a look as he smirks, following them inside. "You really didn't have to do that, but it sounds wonderful. Thank you, ma'am."

"Of course, it's the least I can do for our new favorite neighbor. How's it coming over there at your new place?"

I cringe before I can catch myself, causing all three of the Phillips to laugh. "Admittedly, Hayes may have been right when he told me I was biting off more than I can chew. But it's gonna be great when everything's finished."

"I have no doubt. But in the meantime, I expect you to make yourself at home here, do you understand? There's no way anyone in this town is gonna let it rest when it gets out that you're sleeping in your truck, and you'd much rather have Lucy and Hayes as your roommates than Miss Audrey or Miss Earline. You'll never get a moment of peace with either of them. We have several extra rooms in this place, and you won't even have to put up with me. This leg of mine is gonna have me staying with my sister for the next ten weeks."

I freeze, trying to figure out how to politely decline. Yes, sleeping in a squirrel-free bed sounds like heaven, but becoming roommates with the woman I can't get out of my head and her brother—who also happens to be my best friend—doesn't sound like the best decision I've ever made.

"Oh, I can't do that. I really appreciate the offer, but I can't impose on y'all like that," I tell her, hoping she'll drop it.

"Why not?" Hayes asks, sounding exasperated.

"Yeah, why not?" Lucy repeats, and I don't miss the challenge in her voice. *Yeah, I was right last night, this girl is definitely trouble.*

I continue to stare at her for a moment before deciding there's no way out of this one. Do I even want out of it? I don't know, but either way, I guess I might as well go with it.

"Okay, fine. Thanks, roomies," I tell them, putting extra emphasis on the last word.

Hayes lets out a whoop and Lucy winks just before Mrs. Phillips interrupts. "Come on, y'all. Dinners ready."

And as I watch Lucy lead the way to the old oak table in the middle of the kitchen, I can't help but wonder what the hell I've gotten myself into.

CHAPTER 8
LUCY

"Colton, can I get you a beer? Tea? Water?" my mom asks, hurrying around the table on her crutches.

"Sweet tea would be great," he says, taking a seat and taking his cowboy hat off. When he does, he looks at me and shoots me a quick wink. I feel myself blush at the gesture, remembering what he said last night. "I hit my two beer limit for the week last night at The Watering Hole."

"Two beer limit?" I ask, sure the confusion is clear on my face.

"Yeah, apparently alcohol isn't the best way to heal from a brain injury," he says, running his fingers through his curly hair.

"Oh," I whisper, putting together that Colton is Hayes's friend who was hurt earlier this year. My heart pangs at the thought of him being so badly injured, but I push it aside to focus on what Mama is asking him.

"Goodness, Darling, I can't believe I haven't asked you yet. How are you feeling? You look great," she says, and I have to admit she's right. If I didn't know he'd suffered a career-ending injury just a few months ago, I would have never guessed that he had gone through something so traumatic.

"Wait, Lucy didn't Mom say you were at The Watering Hole last night too when she called you? Y'all probably saw each other and didn't even know it," Hayes says with a laugh.

Colton and I make eye contact before I laugh awkwardly. "Oh, yeah, probably."

"So, Colton, tell me more about yourself," my mom says, taking her usual seat at the table while Hayes and I grab the poppy seed chicken, rice, green beans, and rolls off the stove.

"Oh, well, to be honest, I came to Mills Corner looking for a fresh start. You all know I had a little excitement about six months ago with the accident, so when Hayes told me about the place next door, I jumped on it. I've got some calls out for some animals I've had my eye on, and then I decided I'd figure the rest out when I got here," he explains.

"And how's that working out for you?" Mom asks.

"Well, we've had some ups and downs already, but I don't have any regrets," Colton says, looking directly at me.

I smile, understanding the double meaning of his words. Now that we know who the other is, the fling we had going probably can't continue, but it feels good to know he doesn't regret it.

We settle into a comfortable silence, the four of us filling our plates and eating quietly. I try to keep my eyes from drifting over to stare at Colton, but, god, it's hard. He's by far the most attractive man I've ever seen, and just like last night, the sight of his mustache and cowboy hat has me feeling a little desperate for him. My face flames a little at the reminder of what we almost did last night. Truly, only I could get myself in this position. In hindsight, I guess it seems a little obvious that he and Drake are the same person, but honestly, the idea never crossed my mind.

"So, Colton, I know you've spent a fair share of your time riding bulls, but that's about all Hayesie here has told me about you," my mom says, and Colton laughs.

"Oh, Hayesie, I'm hurt," he starts to tease, causing my brother to groan.

"Really, Mom? I've told you for years to quit calling me that, and now this asshole is never going to let me hear the end of it," Hayes complains, and my mom shoots me a wink across the table.

I stifle a laugh, and Colton continues, "Well, Mrs. Phillips, to be honest, the rodeo has been pretty much my whole life the last fifteen years. I started riding when I was a teenager, but my mom was adamant I needed to finish college before I started trying to ride professionally. So, I got a business degree from a small college close to our home in Tennessee, and the day I finished my degree I entered every qualifier I could find within a three-hundred-mile radius."

"Oh, wow," my mom says before asking, "so you were living in Tennessee before you moved here?"

Colton and Hayes both chuckle as Colton shakes his head. "Nope, I became somewhat of a nomad for a while, living out of a camper and competing as much as I could. My parents divorced when I was a teen, and about ten years ago my mom decided to move off to California with her sister, so I've gotten used to being by myself."

"Oh, bless your heart," Mom says, smiling at him before she takes a sip of her tea. "So how in the world did Hayes convince you to settle down here?"

"It didn't take much. I've heard him talk about this place for years, and since I didn't have anywhere I was tied to, it sounded like the next best move. So I spent the last few months recovering and selling off the camper before moving here. And minus the squirrels, I have no complaints."

While he talks, he catches my eye a few times across the table, and I fight the urge to blush each time.

Come on, Lucy, stop acting like a little schoolgirl with a crush, and get it together. You're a grown woman, I remind myself, but feel my cheeks continue to heat anyway. By the time my mom goes to grab the cake out of the oven, I'm desperate for a moment to collect myself.

"I'll be right back," I say, pushing up from the table and walking to my bedroom. Blowing out a breath and throwing myself on the bed, I rub my eyes. Knox jumps on the bed with me, and I reach out to pat his head.

"God, Knox, how in the world did I get myself into this?" I ask. but he just blinks at me before leaning in to lick my hand.

"Does he ever talk back?" a voice says, accompanied by a knock on my door. I nearly jump out of my skin in surprise at the sight of Colton standing in my doorway.

"What are you doing here?" I ask as Knox gets up and leaves my side to check him out. He sniffs him twice before his tail starts to wag, and he sits at Colton's feet, waiting for pets. *Traitor.*

"So, Drake," I say, putting extra emphasis on the name he gave me. "Some mess we've gotten ourselves into, huh?"

"Okay, first of all, I'm sorry about that. I was planning to tell you tomorrow night when I saw you. But Drake is my middle name. So I swear it isn't a total lie. After spending so long with the rodeo, I got used to the girls only wanting me for my money or to say we'd been together, and I just did it out of habit. Do you actually go by Lulu?"

"No, not really," I admit. "Usually, it's just my mom and Amelia every once in a while. But Amelia convinced me to go out with her last night, and we joked that if we met any out-of-towners we'd give them our nicknames. It sounds dumb now. Obviously, she didn't really hold up her end of the deal, but it just slipped out."

Colton nods before stepping farther into the room and leans down to pet Knox. "Listen, I don't regret what we did last night. I know it probably shouldn't happen again, but I really enjoyed spending time with you. At the same time, Hayes is my closest friend, and I know he wouldn't want an asshole like me anywhere near you. And it's obvious we're going to be spending a good amount of time together over the next few months. So, I'd still like to be friends. What do you say?"

The word "friends" sounds like a dirty word coming out of his mouth, but I have to admit he's right. Nodding, I tell him, "'Friends' sounds good to me," adding air quotes around the word friends.

He smiles, straightening back to his full height, and the sight of him in my bedroom makes me realize just how tall this man is. He's got to be over six foot four, and I have the brief thought that I wonder if he's as big everywhere else before I shake my head to free the thought. *That was not a friendly thought, Lucy,* I remind myself, as Colton steps out of my room.

Clearly, this is off to a great start.

"GOD, AMELIA," I groan out, collapsing onto her sofa the following night and reaching out for the large glass of wine she's holding out for me. "My life is such a disaster.

"I'm gonna need a little more to go off here, babes," she tells me, as we both curl up on our ends of the couch.

I take a long sip of my wine and try to figure out where to

start before blurting out, "I almost had sex with my brother's best friend, and now he's living in my house."

Amelia's blue eyes widen in surprise, and we sit in silence for a minute before she says, "Okayy," dragging out the sound, obviously deep in thought. "I'm gonna come back to the part about him living with you in a second, but first of all, I need details. How did this happen? Is he hot?"

I laugh, knowing Amelia is never going to let me hear the end of this. "Okay, so you know the guy I was with at The Watering Hole on Friday?"

My best friend blinks at me in confusion, and I blow out a sigh of frustration. "Right, of course you don't. You were too wrapped up in that jerk."

Amelia blushes and at least has the decency to look embarrassed. "I'm sorry, Lulu. I was drunk and sad, and it felt so good to be back in his arms for a little bit. I know it was dumb, and I never should have left you the way I did."

"Yeah, I get it," I mumble, not wanting to fight with her. "So are y'all back together?"

"I don't think so. We were having such a fun night, and I thought we were great, but the next morning he texted me and said he still isn't ready to settle down. He wants to stay friends while he works on himself, though," Amelia says.

I feel a stab of frustration at the fact that my best friend continues to let herself be dragged around by this guy who really doesn't give two shits about her.

"Let me guess, he went out again last night, though, huh?" I ask, noticing that Amelia's eyes are red. Clearly, she spent earlier today crying, and I brace myself for what's coming next.

"Worse. Stacey texted me that he was over at Lindsey's house last night. You know, they're neighbors, and she heard he was with me on Friday. So she texted me to make sure I knew."

God, I hate this shit.

I take a breath, trying to figure out what to say.

Instead, Amelia just keeps talking. "I know Stacey's kind of a bitch and she's always in everyone's business, but I drove by after she texted me, and she was right. His truck was there like everyone in town couldn't see it."

She and Mitch started dating almost three years ago, and ever since, it's been a series of makeups, breakups, and the most toxic behavior I've ever seen out of my best friend. At first, I thought they were cute together, but over time, it's become obvious that they bring out the worst in each other. But every time I think they're done for good, he finds a way to reel her back in before he stomps on her heart again.

"I'm sorry, babes. I wish he didn't treat you this way. You already know what I'm going to say."

"Yeah, yeah. I deserve better. He isn't worth my time. Dump him and never look back. Block his number. I feel like I've heard you say something like that before," she says, a touch of sarcasm in her voice. "I know I should, but it's so hard. I just love him so much… you know?"

Instead of arguing, I just nod, knowing pushing the topic won't do us any good.

We're quiet for a minute before she asks, "Sorry, enough about me. Tell me more about this guy. You never have one-night stands!"

"Not for lack of trying," I mumble. "It's just a slim dating pool around here. But anyway, I met a guy at the bar, and we hit it off immediately. Mel, I've never experienced anything like it. We were so in sync, and the chemistry was wild. So after a while, we went outside and made out in the parking lot."

"Lucy, you little wild thing," my best friend teases. "Then what happened?"

"Well, we were just about to take things further when my phone rang."

"Why the hell did you answer it?" she yells, her wine sloshing around in her glass as she shakes her hand at me in frustration.

"I didn't the first few times. Turns out Mama fell and was headed to the hospital," I explain, and Amelia freezes.

"Oh my god, is she okay? Why didn't you call me? I would have gone with you!"

"She's fine," I reassure her. "But anyway, Colton and I were texting, and we had plans for tonight… until he showed up at the house last night as my brother's best friend from the rodeo. And since his house is under construction, my mom and brother offered for him to move in with us."

"Wait. Colton? Like, Colton Harris? One of the most famous bull riders in the world. Colton Harris?"

"Uh, I guess," I answer, cringing at the loud scream Amelia lets out.

"Holy shit, Lucy, I cannot believe you let me sit here and ramble about my boy trouble when you're hooking up with Colton Harris!"

I stare at my best friend like she has three heads. "I did not know you were this into the rodeo, babes."

"Okay, first of all, everyone loves a cowboy, Lucy. And remember, I told you I went with Mitch to see his stepbrother ride last year. He competed in the same circuit as Colton."

"Oh yeah," I say, vaguely remembering her being excited Mitch had asked her to go with them.

"Girl, that man was one of the hottest men I've ever seen. Promise me the next time you see him, you're going to save a horse and ride that mustache!"

I laugh, shaking my head at her, before blushing at the memory of Colton telling me when he likes to take his hat off.

"I need more details, like, yesterday, Lucy Lu. Come on, how was it? When are y'all seeing each other again?"

"Well, I'll pretty much be seeing him every day," I remind her, causing her to roll her eyes at me.

"Not what I meant. I meant, when are you seeing him, seeing him?"

"I'm not. I told you. We agreed to just be friends. He's almost ten years older than me, and he's my brother's best friend. And we both know how overly protective my brother's become since Dad's been gone."

Amelia cringes. "Okay, I didn't think about that. The age thing isn't a big deal. But I can see your brother being an issue, though."

"Yeah, but it's fine. There's not going to be an issue, because, again, we agreed to be just friends," I remind her, and she shakes her head.

"I call bullshit. A man that hot told you how bad he wanted you, and all of a sudden, he's okay with keeping you at arm's length. I hate to tell you, but that man is used to getting what he wants, Lucy. You don't become a six-time world champion bull rider with good looks and a prayer. And something tells me he wants you."

I think about what she's saying, but quickly remind myself not to get my hopes up.

"I don't know," I tell her. "But enough of my drama. We have reality TV to watch."

"Fine," Amelia concedes, reaching for the remote to turn on our favorite dating show. "But when he breaks and decides to give in to what he really wants, I'll be here to tell you I told you so."

CHAPTER 9
COLTON

"Okay, I can do this," I tell myself, staring at the front door. "I rode bulls professionally for the last fifteen years. I will not run from some small wildlife creatures."

Taking a deep breath, I push the door open and step quietly into the house. Immediately, I notice the squirrels seem to have made themselves at home on top of one of the shirts I left out in my haste to get the hell out of here the other day. I've put off coming back here as long as I could, but it's been three days, and I'm tired of wearing Hayes's clothes.

"Just going to get my bag, my guitar case, and a few other things, and then I'm out of here," I whisper to myself, grabbing my phone and taking a quick picture of the animals before heading back to my room.

Once I've silently closed the door to my bedroom, I do a quick check to make sure it's safe before sending the picture to Lucy. I'm not sure if this still falls in the friendship category, but I figure the worst that can happen is she won't respond.

Colton: See, I told you. They're vicious.

Lucy: *laughing emoji*

Lucy: Yeah, they look downright terrifying.

Lucy: Also, I guess this is my reminder to change your name in my phone. ;)

Colton: Just wait until they wake up.

Colton: Haha, yeah I changed yours too this morning.

Lucy: I can't believe you're standing that close to them.

Colton: I'm not too proud to admit that my phone has incredible zoom capabilities…

Colton: But as long as I'm quiet and they stay asleep, I think it's fine.

Lucy: I need an update when you get home about how that goes.

I pause, because, despite the fact that I've been staying at Hayes's for the last few days, I haven't seen Lucy since the night we had dinner with her mom. Deciding to call her on it, I type a quick text and press send before I can think too much about it.

Colton: Does this mean you're done avoiding me?

Lucy: Wow, somebody thinks pretty highly of himself…

Lucy: How do you know I haven't been staying somewhere else, or that I'm just that busy?

Lucy: Not everything revolves around you, Cowboy.

I freeze, worried I've pushed too far. I'm not trying to be an asshole. But the last thing I want is for her to feel like she has to sneak around to stay away from me in her own house.

Lucy: I'm kidding. There may have been a little avoiding. But I promise I'll stop now.

Colton: Deal.

Colton: See you tonight, roomie.

Slipping my phone in my pocket, I make quick work of gathering my things. God, how did I get myself into this situation? It's just my luck that I finally find a woman who I think is attractive and makes me laugh, but every part of me knows I can't have her.

I meant it the other day when I said I've become a bit of a nomad. At first it wasn't on purpose, but since my parents' divorce, I've lost touch with most of my family. Hayes is really the only consistent friend I've had since college, and I know, regardless of how close we are, he'd never be comfortable with me pursuing anything with his sister.

"Colton? You in here?" I hear from outside, and I cringe at the fact that Hayes most definitely just woke up the squirrels. I was clearly so lost in thought, I didn't hear him pull up. Scrambling for my phone, I dial his number and wait for him to pick up.

"Hey, I'm outside. Are you—" he starts, but I interrupt him.

"Quiet, dude. You have to be quiet."

"Uh, what's going on?" he asks, lowering his voice a little. "I knew you were coming to grab your things, so I thought I'd come to—oh, fuck!"

"Yep, that's why I was telling you to be quiet."

I fight to keep my composure as I hear the scrambling in the other room, finally losing it when I hear Hayes let out a squeak of terror loud enough to be heard through the walls.

"Come on now, dude. You ride bulls for a living too. Don't tell me you're scared of them!" I yell with a laugh, making my way over to the window of the bedroom and pushing it open. After throwing my bag out and gently setting my guitar case on the ground, I duck through and step outside, moving quickly so that I'm outside to see Hayes make his frantic exit. Just like I did yesterday, he scrambles outside, letting out another whimper of terror, before slamming the door shut behind him.

"Holy shit, you were right. Those things are fucking terrifying," he yells, bending over and trying to catch his breath.

"Hell if I don't know it," I say, chuckling at his reaction.

"Okay, fine. I take it back," he murmurs.

"Thank you," I tell him. "Now, I've just gotta figure out what to do about them. I've called pest control and haven't had any luck. And I don't want to kill them. I just don't want them in the house."

"That's fair. I'll try to get another number for Andy's pest control business."

"Thanks, man," I say, straightening my hat from where it got tilted on my head in the chaos.

"You got everything you need?" Hayes asks, looking at the items I'm holding in my hands.

"If I don't, are you volunteering to go back in and get it for me?" I tease.

"Hell no," Hayes says with a shiver.

"Yeah, me either. But yes, I've got what I need. Now, let's get out of here. It's hot as hell."

"It's August in Alabama, of course it's fucking hot as hell out here," Hayes points out, and I ignore him.

As we walk to our truck, Hayes asks, "It's been a couple days since we really talked. Have you heard anything about the animals you had your eye on?"

"No, Sam's supposed to call me any day now, though."

"Are you ever going to stop being secretive and tell me what's special about these animals you're wanting? Why can't you just go to the stockyard like everyone else?"

"Because," I tell him, refusing to get into my plan in case it doesn't work out. "I promise once I know something, I'll fill you in."

Hayes mumbles something under his breath that sounds suspiciously like "stubborn asshole," but I ignore him as I open the door to my truck and get in.

"See you at the house."

"HEY, I have good news for you," Sam says the moment I answer my phone later that evening. "I talked to a few of my contacts, and I've got you three bulls and four horses like you asked."

"Hell yeah," I mumble, setting my guitar down on the ground beside me. Music has always been what helps me work through what's coming next, and the two months without being able to play because of my cast were absolute hell. Since then, I've found myself playing even more than usual, trying to work through what the rest of my life should look like. "Is Diesel one of them?"

"Yeah, he is. He's gonna cost you a pretty penny, but I got Mr. Wallace to agree to sell him to you," Sam answers, and instantly, I feel a sense of calm settle over me.

I know it won't make sense to most people why I care so

much about these retired rodeo animals, particularly the bull who ended my career, but I know this is the right decision. A lot of the retired animals go on to live good lives after the rodeo, but that isn't always the case, and after feeling a little thrown away by the sport myself, it just makes me feel like I'm still a small part of the scene where I spent the last fifteen years. Plus, animals were always in the plans for this place anyway.

"You'll have to find some heifers at a stockyard, but other than that, this should get you a pretty good start," Sam continues, and I smile.

"Hell yeah, The Last Lasso is officially a go," I say, letting out a whoop of excitement. I had the idea to create a farm for retired rodeo animals when I was in the hospital, and the name had come to me immediately. I'm hoping to eventually expand it to be a full commercial farm, and it's one of the things that's kept me going after I realized I wouldn't be able to ride anymore. I'm not sure if it's the healthiest coping mechanism, but it's brought me a lot of peace, and now it looks like it'll become a reality.

"Thank you. Do you know how soon I can get them?" I ask, anxious to get everything moving.

"Give them a week or two, and then you should be good to go on the cattle," Sam says before adding, "but the horses will probably be about six months out. I'll talk to them again and let you know."

"Great, that gives me time to fix up the barn later this season. Thank you, Sam," I tell him, and he grunts in acknowledgement on the other end of the line.

"That's not the only reason I'm calling, though. Are you still mentoring that Hayes kid?"

"Yeah, I am. I'm actually at his house right now. What's up?" I ask, curious as to where this is going.

"Well, we had a few last-minute drops for the team

season. I thought about him, and his name's been floated around here a few times as someone who could be a real contender. But I don't know if it's something he'd be interested in or able to make work. He'd have to come out to Louisiana by the end of the week, so it's kind of last-minute. I know it's none of my business, but I just think it would be really good for him, looking from a career standpoint. Are you willing to talk to him?"

I feel a small pang of sadness at his question, the reality of the fact that I'm really done riding, hitting me again. Team riding had always been something I thought I'd get around to eventually, but the timing was never right. I allow myself to feel sad over the fact that this would have probably been my year, but I quickly push it to the side and channel that excitement for my best friend. "Oh, shit. Are you serious?"

"Yeah, because I'm known for my jokes, kid," Sam says sarcastically, and I can't help but laugh.

"You know, you're right. That's my bad," I say with a chuckle. "But I'm almost certain he'd be interested. Give me thirty minutes and I'll call you back."

"Sounds good. Just let me know," Sam says, and I agree before hanging up.

Pushing up from my chair, I walk out to the old barn where Hayes mentioned he was going to train earlier this afternoon. I find him in the middle of the barn, working out.

"Hey, I have some news," I call out over the music that's pumping through the barn. As soon as the words are out of my mouth, one of the pigs runs across the room, charging toward me at full speed. "Holy shit, how do y'all get anything done around here?"

"Denise, let him be," Hayes says, as she looks up at me with her big eyes, waiting for me to pat her head. "So, what's your news?"

"Huh?" I ask, bending down to pet the wiggly pig at my

feet. "Oh, right. I know you were planning on taking the fall off, but Sam just called and wanted to see if you'd be interested in joining the team circuit. Apparently, there's been a bunch of people dropping, and your name's being floated as someone who could really come in and dominate if you decided to compete."

Hayes freezes, his eyes widening. "Wait, are you serious?"

I nod, wanting to chuckle at how similar our responses were. "Yep. But you need to be in Louisiana in two days."

"Wait, but what will I do about the farm? I know Lucy and Amelia think they can run this place all by themselves, but with Mama down too, there's just no way," Hayes says, the disappointment obvious on his face.

"Is that your only hesitation?" I ask, a plan already forming in my head.

"Yeah, pretty much," my best friend confirms.

"Well, what if I offered to help take care of things around here? Then would you go?"

Hayes's eyes widen as Denise bumps her snoot against my nose, reminding me that she still wants attention.

"I mean, yeah. But, Colton, I can't ask you to do that. I promised my dad before he died that I would look after this place along with my mom and my sister."

I shrug. "Isn't making sure that I'm here to help out kinda the same as looking after it too? Everything here will be taken care of, and you get a chance at riding with some of the biggest names in the industry this fall. You've put in the work this year, and you've had really good rides earlier this season already. I know you're ready. You should do it."

Hayes pauses, and I can tell he's considering it. "You'll look after everything? Treat my mom and sister like they're your own?"

I cringe inwardly at that description because the thoughts

I've had about Lucy are far from sisterly, but I push the thought aside. "I've got you, man," I promise.

"Then I guess I need to go get packed," Hayes says, his face breaking into a big smile.

"Hell yeah, you do," I tell him. "I'll call Sam and let him know you're coming."

"Thanks, man," he tells me, walking over and slapping my back in appreciation. "I couldn't do this without you."

"And don't you forget it," I tease as he heads off into the house.

I give Denise one more pat before straightening and rubbing my face with my hands. Now I just have to figure out how I'm going to survive living alone with my best friend's little sister who's now very off-limits.

CHAPTER 10
LUCY

"Okay, I'm really liking this new setup. What do you think, Amelia?" I ask, looking at the small shop beside the pumpkin patch where we sell hand-made goods from local vendors during the season.

"Yeah, I think it's good," she says, without looking up from her phone.

"You didn't even look, babes." I roll my eyes as she finally puts her phone down.

"I'm sorry, okay? Mitch is blowing up my phone, and I can't focus on anything."

"What does he want now?" I ask, preparing myself for her answer. "The last time we talked, he wanted to be friends and was too busy banging Lindsey to have any interest in anything serious."

Amelia shoots me a dirty look, and I hold my hands up in surrender. "I'm sorry. I promise, you won't get any more judgment from me tonight. Pinky swear."

Amelia gives me a skeptical look before admitting, "Apparently, he's decided he wants to try this whole relationship thing again. He claims he's ready to be serious, and he wants to do it with me."

If I bite my tongue any harder, I'm pretty sure it's gonna bleed, I think, trying to figure out how to proceed.

"Okayyy. Is that what you want, though?" I ask slowly, hoping she'll tell him where he can shove it, but knowing that probably won't be the case. *Seriously, how can this man change his mind that drastically in a week?*

"To be honest, I don't know what I want anymore, Lulu. Every time I think I've gotten it figured out, he changes his mind and I'm left reeling."

Unable to stop myself, I ask, "Well, has it ever occurred to you that he does it on purpose? The pulling you in as soon as he thinks you might be ready to move on and then pushing you away as soon as he realizes that he might have to give up hooking up with half the town."

As soon as the words are out of my mouth, I know I've gone too far. But damn it, I'm so sick of seeing my best friend cry over this man.

Amelia looks at me with hurt in her eyes, and I don't miss the tears she's trying to keep from falling.

"Mel, I'm sorry," I say. "I shouldn't have said that. I'm clearly just stressed with the season coming up, and I'm saying stupid shit. Please forgive me."

"It's fine. It'd be different if you weren't right. But I can't even argue with you, and I hate you a little bit for that," she says, and I walk over to wrap her in a hug.

"It's gonna be okay, babes. And I'm here no matter what you decide to do. I just want what's best for you because I love ya," I tell her, rubbing my hand up and down her back as she cries quietly.

"I know. I just need to figure my shit out," Amelia says between her tears. "But I just hate knowing how much you dislike him. And he's not your biggest fan either."

Shocking. Probably because I'm the one who points out how shitty he is to you, but that's just a guess.

Managing to keep my mouth shut, I just nod as she struggles to regain her composure.

"But I love you too, Lulu. And I promise I'm okay, but I think I need to take today to pull myself together. Do you mind if I go ahead and head out?" Amelia asks.

I nod. "Mel, you know you don't need my permission. That's fine. I've gotta train Colton this afternoon anyway."

My best friend's eyebrows shoot up her forehead at that, and she perks up quickly.

"So let me get this straight. The man who you had an almost one night stand with, is not only living in your house, but you're now going to be working with him everyday as well?"

"Sounds about right," I say with a grimace.

"And your brother made roughly how many comments before he left about treating you like his sister in front of you and your mama?"

"Ugh, don't remind me," I groan, remembering how awkward the moment before Hayes left was. "At least five."

"Sorry, babes. I love you, but something tells me you're fucked," she says with a laugh.

"Nope. We've agreed to be friends," I remind her, moving the hand poured pumpkin candles I made last week around until I'm happy with the arrangement.

"Yeah, and how many times have you thought about that night at The Watering Hole?"

I shoot a guilty look in Amelia's direction, causing her to laugh.

"See, it's not as fun when you're the one getting the tough love, is it?" she teases with a giggle.

I don't answer her question, but I'm sure my face gives away my guilt. The truth is, no matter how hard I try not to think about the night with Colton, I can't stop. Every touch, every kiss, every word runs through my mind as I try to sleep at night.

"I thought you were ready to get out of here," I tease, shooing her away playfully.

"That's what I thought," Amelia says with a satisfied smirk on her face. "I'll see you Monday."

"Sounds good. Hey, Mel. It's gonna be okay," I remind her, pulling her in for a quick hug. She nods and makes her way out to her car, leaving me in the shop by myself.

Checking my watch, I realize I have twenty minutes before Colton's supposed to meet me to learn how to run the payment systems and get a general tour of the grounds. I try to busy myself with things around the shop, but time drags, and it feels like forever before I hear him pull up on the Polaris outside.

"Hey," he says, coming in the front door and tapping his knuckles against the doorframe. "Here, and ready for training."

"Hi, great. I promise to make this as quick and painless as possible. To be honest, you're probably the first person we've ever trained out here. Amelia, Hayes, and I all started working out here when we were in middle school, and other than our parents and my aunt, that's been pretty much it around here."

"Well, I'm here to learn. Take as long as you need to. There's no hurry," Colton says, and I nod, trying not to think about the fact that he said something similar when I was all but begging him to fuck me. *God, is this not awkward for him?*

I push the thought aside and gesture for him to step behind the counter next to me. "We'll start in here, since this system is the most self-explanatory. This is the shop, and it has our handmade candles, my aunt's pumpkin-flavored baked goods, and some handmade goods from vendors around town."

"Cool," Colton says, looking around the shop at the embroidered hand towels, the small fall-themed paintings, and the soap from the William's farm across town. "Who makes the candles?"

"I do," I tell him with a smile. "But I promise if you're here long enough, I'll have you in the kitchen pouring wax."

"I don't mind helping. Put me to work wherever. I'm pretty good with my hands."

I smirk, shooting him a knowing look as I pull up the system and quickly show him how to log in. "This is the most sought after position at the farm. So you probably won't be in here much unless you're willing to fight all the women for it."

"Okay, that's fine. Why is it the most popular, though?" he asks, confusion clear on his face.

"It's the only job we have that's in the air conditioning," I explain, causing us both to laugh.

"Yeah, I have to say, before I moved down here, I didn't think the idea of picking pumpkins in ninety-degree weather sounded like a good time, but y'all clearly make it work, huh?" he jokes.

"We do. We're really lucky with the support we get from the locals, and people come from several of the surrounding towns too. Despite the heat, people tend to really start craving all things fall as soon as Labor Day is over. When we open next month, you'll see what I mean."

Colton nods before asking, "So, what do y'all do when it's not pumpkin season?"

"Well, Amelia and I do several markets around the area with my candles. We also host some seasonal events too for big holidays in addition to monthly movie nights during the spring and summer, which helps bring in a profit the rest of the year," I explain. "You actually just missed the one last month, right before you moved in."

'Oh, really? That sounds fun. And I'm sure between the animals and the pumpkins, y'all have more than enough to keep you busy."

"Yeah, that's for sure." I laugh. "Just Denise and Daryl alone are enough to be a full-time job."

"Does it ever freak you out how much they act like dogs?" he asks, looking out across the farm at where Denise and Daryl are chasing a ball across the yard.

"It did at first," I admit. "But now they just keep Knox entertained when he's outside. And they're pretty darn cute, if I do say so myself."

"Yeah, they are," Colton agrees. We spend what feels like the next few minutes going over how to work the online system, taking payments, and talking about the schedule for the fall. I'm shocked when I look down to see that over an hour has passed since we started.

"Gosh, I'm so sorry, I didn't realize how much I was running my mouth, and I've kept you way longer than planned. We haven't even started the actual tour yet, either. Do you need to go? We can always finish this later."

Colton just waves my worry aside before saying, "I told you there's no rush, Lulu. You ready to give that tour?"

"Yep, let's go before it gets dark. And since you brought the Polaris, we'll take it to keep from having to take the big truck," I answer, leading Colton out into the August heat.

I slide into the driver's seat and wait for Colton to wiggle his way in, his large body taking up most of the space in the old ATV.

"Let's go," he says, and I laugh at the sight of his knees crammed into the dash.

We ride for a few minutes, heading out to the back of the property where we keep the majority of our farm animals.

Each time we hit a bump, our legs brush against each other in the tight space, making me squirm as I try to remind myself that we agreed on being just friends.

"We don't need a lot of help out here, but I figured it'd be easiest to show you where everything is at once. We keep a few things for the pumpkins in the horse barn that you may need at some point, too," I explain, smiling at the cows as we pass them.

"Sounds good to me. I don't think I realized this property was quite this big," he says, taking everything in.

"Yeah, most people don't. It's a lot to keep up with, but we love it."

"I can tell. Did you always know you wanted to stay in Mills Corner?"

I laugh at that before answering. "Absolutely not. When I was in high school, I couldn't wait to get out of here. But after a few years away at college, I realized how much I missed it. So I got my degree and moved home. Been here ever since."

"Do you like living at home with your mom?" he asks, and I can hear the curiosity in his voice.

"Actually, I really do. I planned to move out and live with Amelia when I first came back, but the only apartments available were one bedrooms. Mills Corner doesn't exactly have a ton of options for rent. After that, I haven't really thought about it again. I know most twenty-seven-year-olds wouldn't exactly be chomping at the bit to live with their mom, but we stay out of each other's way for the most part. Plus, I don't think any of the apartments in town would have been too excited about having two rambunctious piggies running around."

Colton laughs as I pull up to the barn. "Yeah, that might have been a little hard to accommodate."

I nod, leading us into the barn where we house the horses and keep all of the spare tools. "Alrighty, I want you to meet

Maple, Myrtle, Mack, and Monroe," I tell him, pointing to each of the four horses.

He walks over to the closest stall and sticks out his hand for Myrtle to sniff before petting her mane. "These are some fine animals. Are they all yours?"

"I guess now they are. Maple was my horse growing up, and we used to spend the weekends as a family riding. But I'm the only one who still has time for it."

Colton nods, still petting Myrtle, and I can't stop myself from asking, "I know you're done riding bulls, but can you ride horses?"

"You know, I don't know if it's something my doctor would recommend, but I plan to. I'm willing to give up bull riding because I know the danger. I might not have the reflexes and reaction times I need to still be able to ride, but I refuse to spend the rest of my life living in fear. I think a slow ride on a trained horse would be fine," he says, and I hear the determination in his voice.

I walk over to check that each of the stalls have plenty of hay and water, and stop to pat Myrtle's head as I lean into her stall before saying, "That makes sense. Well, you're welcome to ride any time. All of these cuties are pretty well trained, and they love riding. Are you planning to get horses?"

"Yeah, I've talked to someone about getting a couple retired rodeo horses, but they're finishing out the season first," he explains, and I smile.

"That sounds nice," I say, and for the first time, I realize how close we've moved to each other as we talked. We're both still petting Myrtle, but he's standing just above me, and if I moved my head just a few inches, our mouths would clash.

We stare at each other for a moment before we both lean in, our mouths hovering centimeters away from each other.

We stay that way for a moment, like both of us are afraid to move and ruin the moment between us.

I lean in, deciding to go for it, suddenly desperate to feel his mouth on mine again. Our lips graze, just as Myrtle sneezes beside us, causing each of us to jump away from each other as if we'd been electrocuted.

Blushing, I stammer, "All right, so those are the horses, and right through that door is where we keep all the extra tools I was telling you about. Are you ready to see the pumpkins now?"

Colton stares at me for a long moment, and I can tell he wants to say something about what just almost happened, but after a moment, he just nods.

"Show me your pumpkins, Darlin'."

CHAPTER 11
COLTON

"Here you go, Colton. They're all yours," Logan Wallace says as he gestures to the new farm animals that are being unloaded in front of us. When Sam messaged me last week that he'd organized for someone to bring the cattle to me, I wasn't sure who to expect, but it was a nice surprise to see one of the Wallace brothers coming down my drive along with a caravan of Saddle Ridge Ranch trailers. The Wallace family runs a large ranch in one of the neighboring towns, and the oldest brother, Mason, is a bull rider in the circuit that I spent the last few years competing against.

"Sounds great," I say, reaching out to shake his hand. "Thank you again for agreeing to bring them out here. If you can't tell, I've had my hands full with this property."

Logan looks over at the farmhouse and laughs, taking in its disheveled appearance from here. "Yeah, I'd say so. Have you started working on it yet?"

"The plan is to start today, actually. To be honest, there's a bit of a squirrel infestation that's slowing me down more than I'd like."

Logan laughs, shaking his head at me. "Don't tell me the great Colton Harris is afraid of a few squirrels."

My face turns serious as I tell him, "Man, you laugh, but these things are vicious. I'll take an angry bull in a pen a hundred times over compared to those things."

Logan doubles over as he continues to laugh at me, and I flip him off before walking over to look at the fields where my new cattle are getting unloaded by a few of his employees.

In one field I see Diesel, and I shake my head as the old bull walks out of the trailer and immediately lies down, obviously ready for a nap. Across the fence, there's another bull, whose name I don't remember at the moment, barreling out of the trailer as fast as he can, running circles in his large area of grass.

"Sam mentioned you'd be looking for a few heifers, so we loaded up a handful of them if you want them. I know you've got these bulls pretty divided with the fences, but I don't think it'd be a bad idea to keep them from wanting to fight," Logan suggests.

I nod. "Yeah, that'd be great. How many you got?"

"Ten work for you to start?" Logan asks.

I nod. "Just let me know how much, and I'll write you a check before you leave."

Logan slips away to let his workers know to unload the rest of their trailers, and I take a moment to revel in the feeling of seeing what I've been working toward for the last several months come to fruition.

"Welcome to the Last Lasso," I murmur before heading off to help them unload the rest of my new cattle.

SWIPING the sweat from my brow later that afternoon, I let out a groan.

Isn't early September supposed to be cool? It's fucking ninety degrees out here.

I grab a water out of a cooler on the back of the truck and turn back to take a moment to admire my handiwork on the porch. After the cows were dropped off, I made sure they had plenty of water before starting to replace the old boards on the porch. Thankfully, the foundation is still in great shape, so I managed to replace all the boards before it got too dark. My bad arm is screaming in protest at the strain I've put it under today, but damn, does it feel good to make some progress on this place.

Pulling out my phone, I dial Andy, the local pest control guy again, blowing out a breath of frustration when it goes to voicemail. Again.

"Hey, Andy. It's Colton Harris again. I wanted to see if I could schedule a time for you to come look at the squirrel problem I have. They're really holding up the progress on my new house, so I'd like to get it taken care of as soon as possible. Just give me a call when you get this, please. Thanks!"

Hanging up, I put my phone back in my pocket. I spent yesterday searching for anyone else that might be willing to come take care of relocating these squirrels for me, but came up empty. Damn this small-town life definitely has some cons. I look at the chair I just placed back on the porch and decide to take a few minutes to enjoy the view. I grab my guitar out of the back seat of the truck and make my way back up the stairs to the porch. Sitting down in the chair and looking out at the pasture to see the cattle roaming, I let out a deep breath. For the first time, I can really imagine my life here— eating dinner in the farmhouse, sitting out on the porch, taking care of the cattle, and looking forward to ending each night with Lucy in my bed. *Wait— where the hell did that thought come from?*

I remind myself for the hundredth time that Lucy and I are just friends, and that's the way it has to stay. If my promise to take care of the Phillips wasn't enough to keep me away, Hayes's daily texts checking in on how things are going are enough of a reminder of why I can't push things any further than they've already gone. But, god, that almost-kiss from last night has been on my mind all day. I haven't been able to think of anything else other than her wide brown eyes and her pretty pink lips.

Shaking my head, I take a long sip of my water and strum my guitar, trying to lose myself in the music the way I always do. But unlike every other time I've turned to music to help me clear my head, it doesn't seem to be working the way I want it to. I strum a few chords before immediately thinking of how much nicer this moment would be if Lucy was here.

Damn it, man. Pull your shit together.

I continue to play quietly, looking out at the farm, and I feel a small bit of the peace I've been waiting to come hit me. I can't help the grin that takes over my face. After a few more moments, I'm finally starting to relax when I hear a tapping behind me on the glass. Startled, I turn to see two of the squirrels standing in the windowsill above my head, watching me play through the glass.

Those damn fuckers, I think, shaking my head. I guess it's true that life in Mills Corner will never be boring.

"WHAT ARE YOU DOING OUT HERE?" Lucy asks later that night, coming out to join me on the back porch where I'm strumming my guitar. "And why didn't I know you played guitar?"

I'd given up trying to play at my house after the squirrel fiasco, and I'd wandered out to the porch at Cedar Creek to try to clear my mind.

I shrug, setting my guitar beside my chair and taking a long sip of my beer. "Oh, it's just something I do to clear my head. I'm not going on tour anytime soon or anything like that."

Lucy laughs at that, folding her legs under her as she sits on the other end of the outdoor sofa. "Can I hear you play something?"

I hesitate, trying to decide what to say. No one's ever listened to me play before—not even Hayes. But for some reason, I pick up my guitar and start to strum. As usual, I don't really have a song in mind—just losing myself to the music as my fingers float across the strings.

I don't know how long I play for, but after a while, I stop and fight the urge to look over at Lucy.

"Holy shit, is there anything you aren't good at?" Lucy groans, and I shake my head.

"You're just being nice," I say, taking another sip of my drink.

"I'm serious, Colton. I really enjoyed that. Thank you for playing for me," Lucy says, smiling over at me. She looks so beautiful under the moonlight, and I wish that I could pull her into my lap and kiss her hard the way I did the night we met.

"Sure," I mutter, turning to look at her. "So, since we're learning more about each other, tell me more about yourself, Lucy Phillips."

"Ugh, I never know what to say when people ask me about myself," she groans, causing me to laugh.

"Okay, that's fair. I'll be more specific. What's your favorite color?" I ask.

"My favorite color?" she says, the shock evident on her face.

"Yeah, if you had to choose."

"Um, probably light blue," she answers. "What about yours?"

"Green," I say quickly.

Lucy nods, thinking for a moment before she asks, "Favorite animal?"

"Are cows too obvious of an answer?" I tease.

"I figured that's what you'd say. What about yours?"

Lucy thinks for a moment, shrugging her shoulders. "I don't know. That's a really hard one. Probably a tie between pigs and dogs. I know that's probably not all that surprising either, though."

"Favorite ice cream flavor?" I ask.

"Chocolate," Lucy answers immediately. "Yours?"

"Strawberry," I say.

"Hm, favorite TV show?"

I pause, trying to think. "Not too into television. What's yours?"

"I can see that," she laughs. "And probably *Gilmore Girls*."

"See, that wasn't so hard, was it?" I tease.

"Yeah, you're right. How was your day today?" Lucy asks.

"It was good. My first few animals got delivered over at the farm, and I'm pretty excited about that."

"Oh, that is exciting. I haven't seen that property in years. You'll have to give me a tour soon."

"I'd be happy to," I say truthfully. "What did you do today?"

"I spent most of the day in the pumpkin patch. I also checked in on the horses, mucked their stalls, and poured another batch of candles so that we're ready for opening weekend," she tells me with a yawn.

I nod. "Sounds like a full day."

"It wasn't too bad," she says, moving to stand up. "But to be honest, I'm exhausted. I'll see you in the morning."

"Goodnight, Lucy," I say, picking back up my guitar as she heads inside.

I resume strumming, letting my hands drift across the strings, but the peace I found earlier this evening never comes. Instead, I'm left thinking that I wish Lucy were still here.

CHAPTER 12
LUCY

"One more week," I squeal to Amelia, looking around the shop at Cedar Creek. "I can't believe how fast it's gotten here."

It's been a little over three weeks since Colton started here, and with his help, we've gotten everything almost ready to go. From repainting the sign out by the road to landscaping and organization, I don't know what we would have done without him. But now that the third Saturday in September is close, it's time to put the final touches on opening for next weekend.

"Oh my god, I know, right?" she says, dusting the candle shelf. "I can't wait for everyone to see all the changes we've made since last year. I think the white pumpkins we planted this season are going to be a huge hit too."

"I agree. I'm so glad they came out the way we wanted them to," I say, counting the inventory of new handmade jewelry that Mrs. Frannie made for the shop, so I can add them to the system.

"And since the season is starting next week, you know what that means?" I ask excitedly.

"What's that?" she asks distractedly, looking down at her phone.

"It's time for us to plan for our annual fall bucket list," I say, smiling. Amelia and I made this list together when we were in middle school, and ever since, it's become a tradition for us to check off the tasks each fall. Especially with how busy we stay during the pumpkin season, it's nice to have some fun jobs to look forward to.

"Oh yeah, that thing," she says, still typing away on her phone.

"Do you want to do the hayride Friday before the season starts? We could go to the one in Springside," I tell her, referring to one of the nearby towns that always hosts a hayride through their Christmas tree farm. It's become one of our favorite parts of the list, despite how quirky it is.

"I don't know, Lulu. Aren't we getting to be a little old for that list? Mitch made so much fun of us last year," she says, putting her phone back in her pocket and looking at me. "We're not twelve anymore. I think we need to let that go."

I stare at her in shock before realizing she's serious. "Oh," is all I manage, the frustration and hurt I'm feeling clog my throat.

"Yeah, plus, now that Mitch and I are back together, I just don't think I'll have time."

"Of course," I murmur sarcastically. "If Mitch thinks it's lame, it must be true."

Ever since Amelia came in last week and told me that she'd decided to officially give Mitch another shot, I've been feeling like I'm walking on eggshells around her. I caught her crying two days ago, so I know he's still up to his usual tricks, but I've accepted that there's nothing I can do to make her change her mind. Every once in a while, though, I can't keep from letting her know how I feel about her relationship.

Amelia shoots me a dirty look. "I thought we were done

with this conversation, Lulu. He's different this time, and we're really trying to make this work. And I spend literally all day with you. So we don't need the list."

"Yeah, but we don't actually get to talk at work, Mel. You know how slammed we get," I argue, unable to help myself.

"I just don't want to do it, okay?" Amelia snaps. "Just let it go, Lulu."

She takes out her phone again as I stand there in shock, before she says," I've got to go. Mitch needs me to come home and cook dinner before he meets Bruce for their boys' night. I'll see you next week."

"Fine," I mumble, feeling the tears sting my eyes. "See you then."

Amelia walks out the door, and as soon as I see her car pull out of the driveway, I can't help the tears from falling down my cheeks. Amelia and I never fight, and while I know part of it is still on her, I know she wouldn't be acting like this if it weren't for Mitch. But god, I hate seeing her like this.

"Lucy, what's wrong?" a voice behind me calls, and I jump. Looking over my shoulder, I see that Colton has entered the shop, and I cringe. I was so lost in my thoughts, I didn't hear him come in and now I have to explain the tears.

"Oh, nothing, I'm okay," I promise, hurrying to wipe the tears from my eyes.

"It sure doesn't look like it," Colton says, pulling me into a hug.

My pulse speeds up at the contact, but I remind myself that hugs can be friendly. There's no reason I should read anything into this.

"What happened?" he asks, and I sigh, knowing he won't let it go.

"It's really silly, okay?" I murmur, my cheeks heating. "Just promise not to judge."

"Darlin', nothing that has you this upset could ever be silly. Talk to me," he says, smoothing my hair down.

"Well, every year, Amelia and I have this bucket list we do every fall. It started when we were in middle school, and we've done it every year since. But she just got back with her crappy boyfriend, and he's convinced her it's lame so she'll spend more time with him. We just got into a fight over it."

As I say the words, I continue to cry, knowing I'm overreacting, but unable to stop myself. God, what is wrong with me?

I expect Colton to laugh or make fun of me, but instead he just nods.

"What's on this list of yours?" he asks, continuing to hug me, and I take a second to revel in the feeling of being in his arms and the smell of his woodsy scent.

"Here," I say, reaching into my bag and pulling out the tattered paper we've used for the last thirteen years. "I know it's silly, okay? We've been doing it since we were twelve, but..."

"It's not silly, Lucy," he interrupts, and I look down at the list with him, cringing as I read it to myself.

Amelia and Lucy's Fall Bucket list:
- Paint pumpkins
- Host the hay bale obstacle course
- Drink apple cider and make s'mores
- Go on a hayride
- Watch a movie outside on the projector

After a minute of silence, Colton looks over to me. "What if I did the list with you? I haven't done any of these things in years, and it sounds like fun."

I look up at him, surprised. "Colton, you can't be serious. It's okay. I know it's probably a little ridiculous."

"Lucy, I'm not going to sit here and listen to you put yourself down. This list is something that's important to you, and that's what matters. So, can I do this list with you this fall?"

I blink, trying to decide if he's serious, before nodding. "Okay, if you're sure it's something you want to do," I say hesitantly.

"See! This friendship thing is off to a great start!" he teases, and I resist the urge to laugh. Since our almost-kiss a few weeks ago, we've been nothing but friendly to each other, but, god, do I still want him.

I've tried as hard as I can to fill my time, keeping myself too busy to dwell on thoughts of him, but each night, I fall asleep thinking about the night at The Watering Hole. And the knowledge that he's just a few feet down the hall hasn't exactly helped.

"So, where should we start?" Colton asks, bringing me back to the present.

"Oh, um, well… Normally Amelia and I start off with the hayride the night before the pumpkin patch opens," I say, trying to keep from being embarrassed.

"Sounds fun. I don't think I've ever been on a hayride," Colton admits, and I stare at him in shock.

"Wait, what?" How?" I ask, waiting to see if he's joking.

"Well, there just wasn't one in the small town where I grew up, and then by the time I was an adult, the fall was full of all things rodeo and bull riding, so I never had time. Where's the closest one around here?"

"Uh, Amelia and my favorite is about an hour from here in a little town called Springside. I know it sounds weird, but there's a Christmas tree farm that hosts hayrides each year. After the ride, you can also reserve your Christmas tree, so it's really a great deal," I explain, causing Colton to laugh.

"A fall hayride around a Christmas tree farm?" he says, shaking his head. "That sounds amazing."

"It really is," I continue, trying not to think about the fact that he still has his arms around me. "We've thought about hosting them here at the farm, but honestly, it's a little more of a liability than I'm willing to take on right now. Plus, they're a whole lot of work. We couldn't take them through the patch, and I don't know how scenic a ride through the cow pasture would be."

"Yeah, I've never really thought about the liability aspect, but that definitely makes sense. Plus, I think y'all have your hands full here with the farm and the shop."

"You're right, there's definitely never a dull moment. And don't forget we also have the hay bale obstacle course that we do each October."

Colton laughs. "Oh, that's right. How could I forget? I remember Hayes talking about that last year on the circuit."

I expect him to pull back at the mention of my brother, but he doesn't. "Yeah, it's one of our biggest days of the year. We set up hundreds of hay bales in the pasture on the other side of the house, and the team with the fastest time wins a big prize."

"Sounds like a lot of fun," Colton says, continuing to look down at the list. "I also can't remember the last time I had s'mores. And I've never painted a pumpkin either. Wait, why don't y'all carve them?"

"Ugh, not you too. My dad and brother always gave us the hardest time for that. But painting pumpkins is superior to carving them. There's none of the gross guts involved, and you can make them pretty and pink," I explain. "Did I mention we were twelve when we made this list?"

Chuckling, Colton holds up his hands in a sign of surrender. "Oh, my bad, I didn't mean to upset you."

We both laugh as I look out the window at the sound of a

loud, anguished moooo. Alarmed, I look up at Colton. "The cows are pretty far away. If we're hearing them inside, I'm afraid something might be wrong."

"Well, let's go check," he says, pulling back and making his way towards the door. I take a moment to mourn the loss of his touch before standing and following him to the Polaris. He's already started it up and is waiting for me to slide into the passenger seat. As soon as I'm seated, he takes off up the hill, and I keep my eyes peeled for the sight of anything out of place. After a few minutes of riding, I'm convincing myself that we must have misheard the sound before I spot Clarice, my favorite spotted heifer, lying in the grass by herself in the corner of the field.

"Over there," I yell frantically, and Colton takes off through the pasture, the ATV rattling with every bump and hole on the ground. When we finally make it there, I feel tears stinging my eyes at the sight of a heifer that's obviously in pain. This cow is one my dad bought me when I was a child, and I remember being obsessed with the pretty spots of color on her back.

"What do you think happened?" I ask, jumping off the Polaris to check her.

"Be careful, Lucy. She could still kick you with the way she's lying," Colton cautions me, and I nod, moving to the other side, by her face. As soon as I make it to the side, I let out a gasp, noticing the tiny spotted calf tucked against her stomach.

"Oh my god, Colton, there's a calf!" I whisper, fighting to keep from spooking the heifer, who's struggling to breathe at my feet.

"Lucy, get back. Let me get over there. She's hurting, and I'm sure she's still protective over her calf. I just called the vet, but she's an hour out," Colton says, and I don't miss the concern in his voice. But I ignore him, bending down and running my hand down the cow's face.

"Sweet Clarice, what happened to you?" I ask, looking her up and down.

Her breathing is weak, and she can barely pick her head up. She tries to push herself to stand, but she falls over, letting out another loud anguished moo at the movement. I immediately know this cow doesn't have an hour, and I take a deep breath, trying not to cry. It's silly, but it's another small piece of my dad that I'm about to lose. Grief hits me like a tidal wave, and I feel myself shake with tears as I pet my cow's face. "It's okay, Clarice. It's all gonna be okay. We'll take great care of your girl, okay?"

The cow and I make eye contact for a long moment, and I swear I see her nod before she closes her eyes, and her breathing slows until it stops completely. I pet her the entire time, lost in my tears.

Why does a part of me feel like I'm losing my Daddy all over again?

My mind flashes back to the day he brought home this little calf to my eight-year-old self, and I thought she was the most beautiful thing I'd ever seen. He told me she was all mine, and let me name her by myself. It was the first time I really felt like a "grown-up" around the farm.

I try to breathe through the tears, but I struggle, heaving to catch my breath. After a moment, I feel Colton's arms wrap around me, pulling me back into his chest.

God, this is a disaster.

I try to calm myself down. I've seen plenty of deaths on the farm over the years, but none of them have ever affected me the way this has.

Colton smooths my hair, and I take a deep breath. "I'm so sorry. I know you think I'm overreacting, and I probably am.

But my daddy gave Clarice to me when I turned eight, and it's just hard, you know?"

Understanding fills Colton's eyes, and he tugs me closer to his chest. "Lucy, I don't know who ever made you feel like your feelings were an inconvenience, but they're not. You're entitled to feel however you want. Happy, sad, hurt, scared, whatever. None of those feelings make you immature or too much. They make you who you are, and I happen to really like you."

Hearing his words makes me cry harder, and I cling to him, letting myself feel safe in his arms. After a moment, I pull back and run my finger around the tip of his cowboy hat. "Thank you, Cowboy. I needed that."

He nods, and for a second I think he's going to kiss me again, before he stands from the ground and dusts off his jeans. Holding out his hand for me to take, he lifts me up, and I stand, looking down at the calf in front of us, trying to decide on what to name her. Suddenly, it comes to me, and I smile.

"All right, Carla the calf. It looks like you're coming with us."

CHAPTER 13
COLTON

I take a long sip of my coffee, shaking my head at the vision in front of me. Lucy is sitting with Carla, the calf born earlier this week, practically in her lap, as Daryl and Denise scamper around the two of them in excitement over having a new friend.

After Lucy calmed down, we brought Carla down to the house where the vet from town came to check her over. Thankfully, the calf seems healthy despite the fact that she'll need to be bottle fed for the next couple of months. Lucy made quick work of setting her up in a pen beside the piggies, and Carla has taken an instant liking to Lucy, wanting to be as close to her as possible at all times.

"You know, once she gets a little bigger, that position could be dangerous," I tease, looking at the way Carla has nestled as much of her body as she can into Lucy's lap.

Lucy shoots me an annoyed look as she looks down at the calf in adoration. "He's just a silly boy, Carla. Don't listen to him, you can sit with me as long as you'd like."

"We'll see if you're saying the same thing when she's eight hundred pounds," I remind her.

Lucy ignores me, continuing to pet the calf.

Daryl and Denise run over to me, practically knocking me over with their excitement, so I make my way over to Lucy and sit on the porch beside her. Immediately, the pigs rush us, determined to have every bit of our attention as Carla closes her eyes and immediately falls asleep.

"How in the world can she sleep through all this?" I ask, giving Daryl a run behind his ears. His tail wags in excitement before Denise runs and knocks him in the stomach, hard enough, he falls off the porch.

"Denise, you know you have to share the pets," Lucy scolds them, shaking her head at the pigs.

On the ground, Daryl looks up at us before running off to grab a rubber ball in his mouth, bringing it back to me and dropping it expectantly at my feet.

"Is this pig asking me to play fucking fetch?" I ask, trying not to laugh.

"I had to find some way to burn off all his energy, didn't I?" Lucy says defensively.

"He really thinks he's a dog, doesn't he?" I ask, just as Knox runs out of the door to the house and snatches the ball out from under my chair. He takes off across the porch, and Daryl follows him, letting out a little screech of annoyance.

"This place is fucking nuts," I mumble, as Lucy just shrugs.

"I gave up on organization a long time ago with these three," she says, gesturing to the dog and pigs in front of us. "And something tells me that once she's stronger, Carla's gonna give them all a run for their money, aren't ya, girl?" she coos, petting the sleepy calf's head.

As I watch the animals chase each other around the house, I take another sip of my coffee, trying not to think about how comfortable I feel in this moment. I know I toed the line of friendship yesterday with Lucy, but I couldn't resist the urge to take her into my arms as she cried. The feeling of holding her was just like I remembered. And while I hated seeing her so upset, knowing that she trusted me to comfort her was a feeling I know I could become obsessed with.

But I've got to remember that nothing can happen between us. Even if I didn't promise Hayes to look after his sister, I've got to remember that she's almost ten years younger than me. There's no way she'd be interested in me now that she knows I'm pushing forty.

"So, what's on your list of plans for today?" Lucy asks, bringing me back to the present.

"Oh, uh, I need to go check on the cows at my house, and then I was going to start on the roof over there unless you need me here," I say. As much as I'd love to spend the day with her, I'm smart enough to know that that's probably more temptation than I can stand.

"Yeah, that's fine. I'm gonna go through the pumpkin patch one more time and make sure all the leaves and weeds are cut down for Saturday. Do you think you'd be up for trying your hand at some candle making tonight? A boutique in Crestbrook Cove put in a huge order for a custom scent, and Mama's still not well enough to help me on her crutches."

"Sure," I agree. "I'll be happy to. Around seven tonight work for you?"

"Yep, that's good with me," Lucy agrees.

"How's your mama feeling? The last time or two she came over, I was back at my place," I ask, setting my empty coffee cup down beside me and looking over at Lucy. She's just close enough I could reach down and play with her hair, and the thought of having her dark strands wrapped around my fingers again makes my dick harden in my pants.

Damn it, I am way too old for my dick to be getting hard at the thought of touching some chick's hair. My subconscious reminds me, *She's not just any girl, you asshole.*

"She's fine. Just a few more weeks on the crutches, and then she should be good to go," Lucy answers, and it takes me a moment to remember what we were talking about.

Damn it, am I really arguing with myself? I'm officially losing it.

"Oh, that's good," I murmur, trying not to look too hard at the way the sun's lighting is hitting her pretty face and making her plump pink lips shine.

"Yeah. Speaking of your house–I haven't asked you lately, but how's the house coming along?" she asks, and I blink, determined to focus on the conversation we're having.

"Damn, Andy still won't call me back, so I'm still dealing with the squirrels," I growl, annoyance creeping into my voice.

Lucy laughs quietly, still petting Carla's head as she sleeps in her lap. "Yeah, that doesn't surprise me. He really only works when he feels like it. Have you thought about setting a trap for them? Maybe something in a cage, and then you can let them free outside?"

I let out a humorless chuckle. "Stupid things are too fucking smart. First of all, that would involve me going back in there, which I'm not doing. But even then, I just know they'd find a way to end up with me in the cage. Damn crafty creatures."

"Colton, they're not exactly geniuses. I think you're giving them too much credit. They can't be that bad," Lucy argues.

"It's bad. They taunt me through the windows as I work outside. They try to crawl up my leg when I'm inside. They attacked me as I was trying to get in the fucking shower, remember? I was naked!"

Lucy's shoulders shake with laughter as she tries to keep a serious face, but eventually she breaks into a full fit of giggles.

Carla shifts in her lap and lets out a tiny moo at the disturbance before falling back asleep. "That's right, I kinda forgot about that."

"Well, I sure as fuck didn't," I mumble, causing her to laugh harder.

"Okay, well, I'm sorry," she apologizes just as Daryl comes around the corner of the house and runs up on the porch, ball in his mouth. As soon as he gets beside Lucy, he lies down, letting the ball roll away from him. I watch as Knox's eyes narrow in on the ball and he takes off, jumping over my legs in an effort to get to it first.

Denise follows suit, trying the same maneuver, before slamming into my left leg hard. "Holy shit, Denise," I groan, grabbing my injured leg. "These damn pigs."

"Oh my gosh, are you okay?" Lucy asks, her eyes wide, but I don't miss the smile that's threatening to break through.

"Fine," I mumble, rubbing my sore skin. "I just feel like I've been hit by a truck, it's fine."

"Denise, that wasn't very nice," Lucy chides, leaning over to pet her head. "You need to tell Colton you're sorry. You didn't mean it, did you, sweet girl?"

Denise rolls over, letting Lucy rub her tummy as the pig's tail thwacks against the hardwood floor of the porch.

"Yeah, she looks really damn sorry, doesn't she?" I say before feeling my face break into a grin. "It's a good thing you're fucking cute, isn't it?"

"Yep, and she knows it." Lucy laughs.

"I can see that. Well, now that I've had my entertainment for the day, I'll see you tonight," I say, pushing up from my chair and grabbing my coffee cup.

"See you then." She shoots me a smile before I head inside. Yeah, some distance will be great.

"Alrighty, they're looking good," Lucy says excitedly, looking down at the candles we've spent the last three hours working on.

Like everything else on this farm, the candles ended up being way more work than I realized, and I'm once again impressed by Lucy's determination to make this farm work.

"Yeah, and they smell incredible," I add, leaning down to smell the beachy scent she'd created. "I was kind of worried it would smell like sunscreen, but it doesn't."

"I can't believe you doubted me, Colton Harris," she chastises, pouring the wax into the containers I prepared for her.

"I'm sorry, it won't happen again," I promise, shifting to let her lean across me and grab the last bowl of hot wax we'd prepared.

As she does, I catch the scent of her floral perfume and her peach shampoo and resist the urge to groan. After using her shower for the last few weeks, I'd know the scent anywhere, but, god, the combination is fucking incredible. *Damn, I'm really losing it,* I think briefly before reminding myself that we're just friends.

As much fun as tonight's been, it's also been torture. Having her this close to me as we've chatted and worked together, without being able to pull her into my arms and kiss her, has been one of the hardest things I've ever done. But at the same time, other than our almost kiss a few weeks ago, she hasn't shown any sign of wanting more since we decided to just be friends.

"Can you put those stickers on the lids so they're ready to

go when they finish setting?" she asks, bringing me back to the present.

"Sure," I say, reaching across her to grab the roll of stickers she gestured to with her elbow. As I do, my fingers graze her across her breast, and she lets out a sharp intake of breath at the contact.

"Sorry," I murmur, trying not to think too hard about the sounds she made the last time I touched her.

"No worries," she says, giving me a shy smile.

I struggle to concentrate on placing the stickers on the aluminum tops, but my mind's racing with the desire to be closer to her. After a few moments of working in silence, Lucy leans over and turns up the music playing in the background.

"God, I love this song," she says, singing along and moving her hips to the beat of the country song blasting through the speaker.

"Come on and dance with me, Cowboy. I promise it won't kill you to have a little fun," she teases. I hesitate, not because I don't want to dance with her, but because I don't trust myself not to do something incredibly stupid if I say yes. Finally, my willpower cracks, and I reach out, taking her hand and letting her spin around me. Her body grazes mine, and I feel her everywhere.

It takes every ounce of my restraint not to pull her body into mine and kiss her, but instead, I try to focus on how good she feels in my arms. I soak in the feeling of my hands on her waist and her fingers tangled in my hair underneath my hat. She leans in, letting her forehead rest against my chest as we sway to the music.

After a few minutes, the song ends, and she pulls back, her cheeks pink with excitement, and smiles up at me.

"Thanks, Cowboy, that was fun," she says before pausing and adding, "almost as fun as our first dance."

I freeze at the memory before facing a smile on my face.

"Yeah, almost," I agree, despite the fact that it's not true. I'm pretty sure nothing will ever compare to the first night we spent together.

"Alrighty, well, I think we're done here," she says after a moment, looking down at the kitchen full of candles. "Thank you again for your help. It really helped make this go by faster."

"Of course, I'll see you in the morning," I tell her, wanting to pull her into my arms, but instead, waving awkwardly. "I'm gonna grab a shower and head to bed."

"Sounds good. Are we still on for the hayride tomorrow night?" she asks.

I nod. "Yep, I'm looking forward to it," I say honestly.

"Me too. Good night, Cowboy," she says with a smile as I turn to head upstairs.

As soon as I've locked myself in the bathroom, I let out a deep breath, trying to calm myself down after having Lucy that close to me again. I feel like a man starved, desperate for the smallest taste of her.

We're just friends. We're just friends. We're just fucking friends, I remind myself as I strip my clothes off and step into the shower.

My dick bobs, hard and desperate for relief after the way I've fantasized about my best friend's little sister today. I hoped that the time away working on my farmhouse would be enough to quench the desire I had for her, but clearly that hasn't worked. I'm hornier than ever, and the little brunette vixen downstairs seems to be the only cure.

I don't know how many times I've told myself to take a night at The Watering Hole and find a woman to fill my time with, at least to kill this desperate need I feel. But each time, the thought of touching anyone other than Lucy feels like the ultimate betrayal, despite the fact that we're definitely not together.

Looking down, I see the bottle of Lucy's peach shampoo sitting on the ledge of the tub. Without thinking, I reach down and squirt a dollop of it into my hand and breathe out a sigh of relief at her sweet scent filling the shower.

It's not nearly as good as the real thing, but it'll do, and I reach down to palm my cock.

The second I touch myself surrounded by her scent, I groan, unaccustomed to the feral feeling of need that's currently running through my veins. For the first time since I found out who she was, I allow myself to really fantasize about Lucy, imagining her spread out for me, and begging to take my cock. Letting my tongue lap against her clit as she pulls on my hair, out of her mind with want. Her on her knees, ready to take my cock between those pretty as hell lips of hers.

In less than a minute, I feel my balls draw up and know I'm seconds away from coming. "God, yes. Don't stop, Lucy," I whisper, jerking on my cock and lost in thoughts of what I'd love to do to her. An orgasm tears through me, cum spurting from my dick, covering the side of the shower with proof of how badly I want the girl downstairs.

"Goddamn it. Friends, my ass," I mutter, a wave of shame running through me at what I just did. But that wave of shame isn't enough to make me regret it. The truth is, I want Lucy Phillips, and I don't see that changing, no matter how many times I remind myself I can't have her.

CHAPTER 14
LUCY

"Huh, it really is a hayride at a Christmas tree farm," Colton says, looking at the brightly lit farm in front of us.

"I told you." I laugh. "Did you think I was making it up?"

"No, not making it up. But it's hard to imagine until you see it, you know?" he admits.

I have to agree with him. The Coopers' Tree Farm is nestled in the small town of Springside, and if it weren't for the proximity to Mills Corner, I'd have no idea it existed. But ever since the first time that Amelia and I visited this hayride several years ago, it's been my favorite. Instead of a haunted hayride, they go with a festive approach, lighting the trees with orange lights and lining the path with a series of fall-themed decor made out of Christmas lights.

We make our way up to the ticket counter, and I pull out my wallet, ready to pay for the admission fee for both of us.

"Darlin', why the hell are you pulling out your wallet?" Colton asks, looking down at my small pink wallet with disgust.

"Uh, buying our tickets. You're here because of me, so it's only right for me to cover the cost of everything."

"Absolutely the hell not," Colton growls, and I look at him in surprise.

"Colton, this isn't a date. I don't mind paying."

"I don't care, Lucy. When you're with me, I don't wanna see that damn thing. Let me take care of you."

"Colton, I don't understand why this is such a big deal," I say, trying to piece together why he's so adamant about this.

"Listen, I'm not doubting your ability to take care of yourself. But even though I'm not riding anymore, I have more than enough money to take care of you. I like spending time with you. This isn't an inconvenience, and you take care of everyone else. So just let me fucking take care of you for once," he begs, and I nod.

"Oh, uh, okay. Well, thank you," I say, trying not to smile at his compliment. "And I like spending time with you too."

He smiles down at me as we step up to the ticket counter. It's surprisingly chilly for the mid September evening, and I feel a shiver run through me despite the fact that I'm wearing jeans and a T-shirt. After purchasing our tickets, he wraps his arm around me and leads me into the inside of the tree farm.

"Are you cold?" Colton asks, and I nod, letting myself nestle into him a little, telling myself it's just to shield me from the wind.

"Just a little bit," I admit. "Usually I'm sweating my ass off on this thing, but this year it's chillier than I expected."

Colton wraps his arm tighter around me, pulling me into him as we make our way to the concessions line.

"What do you want?" Colton asks, looking up at the menu.

"Their apple cider is to die for. So that and a hot cinnamon pretzel, please. But I promise I don't mind getting my own," I say, trying not to laugh at the look he shoots my way at that statement. "Fine, fine. Thank you."

After a few minutes, he hands me my cider and pretzel, and I lead us to the line for the ride. "So, how excited are you for your first hayride?"

"I cannot contain myself, can't you tell?" Colton teases, causing us both to laugh. "I'm kidding, I'm really actually looking forward to it."

"Good, I hope it's not a disappointment. I've gotta admit that it's kind of one of those things that's better in theory, riding on a bumpy tractor with hay sticking up your ass, but what can I say? It's a tradition."

"Wow, you're really selling this, aren't ya?" Colton says sarcastically.

"Well, I just figured you'd want to go into it with realistic expectations," I tell him. "Now that you're here, and it's too late to back out."

"I appreciate the honesty," he admits, as the employee waves for us to climb the ladder up to the large trailer in front of us.

"Uh, I'm not a hundred percent sure this is safe," Colton points out, watching as the ladder shakes with each step the person in front of us takes.

"Yeah, I don't think there's any safety clearance here, Cowboy," I laugh.

"I'd say so," he agrees, holding the ladder for me to climb up. It's tough to manage with my hot cider, and when I get to the top, I lose my balance, certain I'm about to fall to the ground. But Colton's right behind me, and he reaches out to steady me, grabbing my waist and holding me tight.

"Thanks," I say with an embarrassed laugh as he lets go of me. Instantly, I miss the feeling of his hands on me, and I try not to pout.

"No problem," he says, gesturing for me to pick a place to sit. I lead the way to the left side of the trailer and sit on the empty haybale, patting the area beside me for him to come join me. He obliges, wrapping his arm around me and letting me nestle into his side, protecting me from the wind.

"Oh, honey, aren't y'all just the cutest couple, the elderly lady beside me says, gesturing at us. *How in the hell did she even manage to get up here?* I think, looking at how frail she looks.

I open my mouth to remind him that we're just friends, but Colton surprises me by saying, "Oh, thank you. It's all her, though. I'm just lucky she gives an ugly bastard like me the time of day."

The old lady laughs, shaking her head. "Trust me, honey. If my husband and I looked like you two, we'd never leave the bedroom," she teases, shooting us a wink.

"It's tough," Colton agrees. "She's pretty much all I think about."

My breath catches at the admission before I remind myself that he's just playing along with the lady's assumption.

"With good reason, I'd say," the lady says, wrapping her blanket tighter around her frail body.

Turning back to Colton, we share a secret smile as he leans in to whisper, "I already know you were right about the whole hay up your ass part."

I laugh, leaning into him and nodding. "Yep, it's not really the most pleasant feeling, is it? I always say that I'm going to bring a blanket thick enough that I won't be able to feel it, but I always forget. So I've just accepted that this is a part of the experience."

"Fucking fantastic," he mumbles, taking a sip of his cider. "Damn, this stuff really is delicious."

Just as he says it, the tractor pulling the trailer starts up, and we start moving at a crawl through the tree farm.

"Yeah, it's usually pretty incredible," I agree, taking a sip of mine and groaning when the taste hits my tongue.

Colton shoots me a look, and I smile at him, briefly thinking how sexy he looks in the glow of the orange lights. His worn cowboy hat sits slightly crooked on his head, and I reach up to straighten it. As I lean in, I notice a small bit of sugar from his pretzel stuck in his beard. Without thinking, I lean in and rub his lip with my finger. Immediately, his eyes dart to mine, and I don't miss the desire in his expression.

"You're playing with fire, Darlin'," he drawls, and the tone of his voice is anything but friendly. And I know he's right, but I can't find it in myself to care. But just as I'm about to throw myself at him, a woman from across the aisle calls out, "Lucy Phillips, is that you?"

Looking up, I'm surprised to see Caroline Tyler sitting across from me. Caroline and I were both selected for a leadership conference when we were in high school, and we spent the week together, becoming friends, until the conference ended. I keep up with her through social media, but I haven't seen her in person in over ten years.

"Oh my god, what are you doing here?" I squeal, pushing away my earlier frustration at being interrupted with whatever was just happening with Colton.

"Babes, I live here! What are you doing here?" she says with a laugh, leaning into the man beside her. "Oh, I'm sorry, this is my fiancé, Theo Johnson."

The man beside her doesn't say anything, but he tips his head in acknowledgement.

"Oh my gosh, I saw your post. Girl, that ring is gorgeous!" I tell her truthfully, remembering the vintage engagement ring she posted with their engagement pictures.

"Thanks," Caroline says, sending her fiancé a small smile. "And who's this with you?"

"So sorry. Where are my manners? This is my boyfriend, Colton Harris," I say without thinking.

Caroline looks between us, and she must be able to tell that there's something going on because she just smiles.

"Sounds like we have a lot to catch up on," she says, and I can't help but giggle at that.

"Yeah, for sure. You know, this is our busy season with the pumpkin patch, but y'all should drop by sometime."

"That would be fun! I've been telling Theo we needed some pumpkins to decorate the house with. We'll see if I can convince him to venture into Mills Corner territory," she teases.

"Hell no," her fiancé grumbles beside her, and my eyes widen in surprise.

Caroline grimaces and shoots her fiancé a look of disapproval. "Sorry, he's a bit of a grump when he wants to be. He's a coach for the high school team here, and they had a not so great experience when they played y'all earlier this year."

"Oh no! The first fight," I gasp, remembering the way the town gossip had gone crazy over the players starting a major brawl with one of their rivals. But I hadn't paid enough attention to remember which team it was.

"Yeah. It wasn't pretty. But if you can promise no fist fights, I promise we'll try to swing by," Caroline says.

"I think we can promise that," I tease, and Caroline nods.

"Sounds like a plan. So good to see you," she says, turning back to look out at the light displays happening around us.

I turn to do the same, nestling back into Colton for warmth, as he leans forward to whisper, "Boyfriend, huh?"

"Hey, you said it first," I defend myself, causing him to laugh.

"You're right," he admits, wrapping his arms around me. "Might as well go with it for the night then, right?" he teases. "Unless you don't want to."

"I'm good with it," I confess, my heart racing. Does this mean he's finally going to kiss me again?

He leans in and my breath catches, confident I'm finally going to feel his lips on mine again. But instead, he presses a kiss to my temple and shoots me a wink.

"Let's enjoy the ride then."

CHAPTER 15
COLTON

"All right, everyone, we'd like to welcome you all to the forty-third season of Cedar Creek Farms," Lucy says into the microphone, causing the crowd to cheer.

I couldn't believe it when I looked outside the kitchen window this morning at the crowd already forming at the gate leading into the farm.

"Please watch your step as you make your way through the patch, and have fun. Our store is open over to your right, and there are several local musicians who will be here playing music throughout the morning. There's also a photographer set up by the check out counter so you can grab pictures with your family."

At the end of Lucy's announcement, Amelia swings open the gate, and the crowd cheers again as they pour into the pumpkin patch and the shop.

Walking over to Lucy's side, I wrap her in a side hug that seems friendly enough and squeeze her to me. "Congrats, Lulu. Are you ready for all this?"

"Ready or not, right?" she says, gesturing to the crowd that's continuing to pour into the pumpkin patch.

"I guess so. So I've been thinking about that list of yours, and I want to see if you're ready to knock off the next one tonight?"

Her eyes widen in surprise before she laughs. "You mean I didn't scare you off last night by forcing you to be my pretend boyfriend?"

Hell no. I'm still kicking myself for not using the pretend boyfriend card as an excuse to kiss her. But I've promised myself I'd behave, and even if I decide to break that promise, I want her to know how much I care about her. How I actually feel about her.

"Nope, not even a little bit, Darlin'," I tease. "So what if we went with the movie night tonight? I have a feeling we'll both be dead on our feet after all this, so I thought we could order pizza and watch a movie. I'll even let you choose."

Lucy nods before agreeing. "Yeah, I think that sounds like fun."

I feel a rush of relief at her words, relief that I didn't push her too far last night. Having her in my arms felt so right, but after we agreed to just be friends, I can't figure out where the line is between us anymore. I can't imagine my time in Mills Corner without her friendship, and I genuinely enjoy spending time with her.

"Great, I'll meet you out back around eight," I say just as Mrs. Phillips sticks her head out from the shop.

"Are you two gonna stand there yapping all day, or are you gonna get to work?" she calls out, hobbling out to the porch and nearly losing her balance in the process, causing Lucy and me to laugh.

"We're going, we're going," Lucy yells. "I need you to take yourself back inside, though, before you wind up breaking something else."

"Yeah, yeah," Charleen yells, turning and making her way back in the shop.

Lucy turns back to me, pointing toward the exit. "Are you still good being on loading duty today? A couple of the older ladies who come through here need help getting things in their cars."

"Feeding me to the wolves, huh?" I tease, and Lucy laughs.

"I'm sorry, okay? But it's usually my brother's job, and I didn't spend enough time at the gym this summer to be ready to take it on."

"No worries. I'm just giving you a hard time. I'm happy to help out wherever you need me."

"We'll see if you change your tune by the end of the day," she says hesitantly.

"They can't be that bad. They're just some little old ladies."

Lucy grimaces. "Okay, I want you to remember this conversation tonight, though."

"Sure thing," I tell her, heading out toward the exit.

Surely, she has to be exaggerating. This should be the easiest job I've ever had.

THIS IS, in fact, the worst fucking job I've ever had.

I've just loaded what has to be the hundredth pumpkin of the day. But the job itself isn't what's really making me want to throw my hat at the ground. It's that every single older lady who comes through this line has tried to set me up with various women in town.

One of the first ladies who came through the line this

morning said her name was Miss Audrey, and she asked if I had a girlfriend. After telling her no, it must have triggered some sort of alert system to the rest of the whole damn town because within a few minutes, everyone was trying to push me into dating their neighbor's best friend's cousin's sister in law.

"Hey, Sugar, can I get your help loading these things?" another older lady says, making her way over with one of the wagons from the farm.

"Sure," I tell her, pasting on a smile and following her out to her car.

"So, you must be Mr. Colton Harris. I've heard so much about you. I'm Miss Bernice," she says, holding out her hand for me to shake.

"Nice to meet you," I tell her, offering her a small smile.

"Yes, dear. So, I heard you're single. I have a cousin whose stepdaughter would be just perfect for you. I think you two would be just darling together. She has a great job working as the head of marketing down at the Mini-Mart downtown.

"Oh, as nice as that sounds," I tell her, trying not to cringe as we make it to her old sedan. "I'm not really looking to date right now. I'm still working on getting settled."

"Hmm, well, if you change your mind, her name's Susan Smith," she says, and I nod, making quick work of depositing the two small pumpkins in her truck."

"Alrighty, well, Miss Bernice, you're good to go. Nice to meet you."

"Nice to meet you too, dear. And don't wait too long, I bet she's a hot commodity around here," she says seriously, waving her wooden cane at me.

"I'm sure," I say, smiling as long as I can, before scowling at her car driving away.

Pulling out my phone, I send a quick text to Lucy.

> Colton: Are you trying to kill me?

> Lucy: *laughing emoji*

> Lucy: I tried to warn you.

> Lucy: What happened?

> Colton: A woman named Miss Audrey came through here first thing this morning,

> Lucy: SHIT

> Lucy: Let me ask Mama if she's checked her book club group chat.

I look down at my phone, confused at what her mom's book club has to do with the weird day I've had, just as it pings again with another text.

> Lucy: Oh Colton I'm so sorry.

> Lucy: Miss Audrey is the town busybody. Once she talked to you, she sent out a message to their bookclub that the man helping load the pumpkins was new to town, single, and handsome.

> Lucy: I thought I noticed more elderly ladies than we usually have around here today, but I figured it was just my imagination.

Shaking my head, I let out a small laugh as I type out a reply.

> Colton: Definitely not your imagination.

> Lucy: Now that you say that, I'm definitely looking at a minimum of ten ladies who are over seventy coming your way.

Colton: Great.

Lucy: I'll ask Mom to remind everyone about our delivery option.

Colton: Delivery?

Lucy: Yeah, usually one of us just drops their order off at their house. They don't actually come here to pick anything out.

Colton: So you mean they don't come out here to torture Hayes like this?

Lucy: Nope.

Lucy: He may load seven or eight cars all day.

Lucy: I think that's why this job is his favorite.

Colton: Lucy...

Colton: I've loaded at least a hundred cars today.

Colton: And I've turned down fourteen potential blind dates.

Lucy: Oh my gosh.

Lucy: I'm sorry, but I'm dying

Lucy: I can't stop laughing.

Colton: Glad I could entertain you.

Lucy: I'd offer to switch with you, but I'm pretty sure that they'll find you no matter where you are.

> Lucy: These ladies may be old, but they're pretty determined.

> Colton: Great.

> Lucy: Sorry! I'll make it up to you tonight.

> Colton: I'm counting on it...

Tucking my phone away, I grimace as I see the group of elderly ladies heading my way.

"Hi, dear. You must be Colton. I'm Miss Louise. We've heard so much about you!" the one in the front yells, just as she steps in a small hole in front of her, and crumples to the ground with a loud thump.

I run over, eyes wide as she waves her cane around in the air.

"Damn, cane ain't good for nothing," she complains, gesturing for me to help her up.

"Are you okay, Miss Louise?" I ask, genuinely concerned about the frail elderly lady at my feet.

"I'll be a lot better when you get me off the damn ground," she mumbles.

I hesitate. "Are you sure you're not hurt?" I ask, trying to check her over for injuries.

"Ain't nothing hurt but my pride, Sugar. Now get me off the damn ground. I'm getting sand in all my crevices."

Grimacing at that mental image, I lean down, gently helping her rise back to her feet. She stands and moves around, adding a little bounce to her step to prove that she's not hurt. I start to smile, just as she hobbles over to me, wrapping her arm around me.

"Oh, dear. Thank you for your help. Anyway, I need to tell you all about my granddaughter's best friend's sister. I think she'd be just perfect for you."

Yeah, Lucy, you fucking owe me one.

CHAPTER 16
LUCY

"I can't believe you set me up today," Colton teases, looking at me with a look of betrayal. "Just when I was starting to think I trusted you."

"Wait, you can't put this all on me. You know, none of this would have happened if you hadn't told Miss Audrey you were single," I argue.

"How the hell was I supposed to know?" he says, crossing his arms over his chest.

"Well, everyone knows that Miss Audrey is the biggest busybody around."

"Nope, not everyone, because I was pretty damn clueless," he reminds me, and I grimace.

"Okay, maybe that's fair. But in my defense, I thought I was giving you the slowest job to ease you into the season."

"Yeah, sure. We see how well that worked out," he teases.

"How many dates were you offered today?" I ask, interested to see what he'll say.

"At least thirty," he admits with a cringe, and I can't contain my laughter anymore.

"I'm sorry, it's not funny," I wheeze out, trying to catch

my breath. "But I was expecting you to say like five or ten. Not thirty."

Colton shoots me a withering look, and I hold my hands up in surrender. "You're thinking too small. Not only that, but Miss Louise also took a spill right in front of me, and I had to help her up. Shit was fucking scary."

"Oh no. Was she okay?" I ask, concern evident in my voice.

"She was fine. So fine, in fact, that when I stood her up, she tried to set me up with not one, but three different women."

"Look, I'm sorry. But at least you got some potential dates out of it," I tease, and he flips me off in response.

"Yeah, sure. I asked Miss Louise how old one of the women was that she was trying to set me up with after she kept mentioning how 'young and fun' she was, and she was in her seventies. Don't get me wrong, I could be down with an age gap, but I think that's a bit much for me," he confesses, shaking his head at the thought.

"Well, you never know. Maybe you should take her up on it. Options are pretty slim here in Mills Corner, you know," I tease.

He pauses, and his throat bobs as we stare at each other. "I'm pretty happy where I am right now," he whispers, looking me up and down. In typical Alabama fashion, the weather turned hot again today, and it's over eighty degrees, despite the fact that it's almost eight in the evening.

I blush, trying to decide what to say, just as the doorbell rings. We both jump apart as if we'd been electrocuted.

"That must be the pizza," Colton says, moving quickly to open the door.

Shaking my head at his retreating form, I take a moment to compose myself while I'm alone. God, this man has my head in a mess. No matter how many times I remind myself that nothing can happen between us, every time his hands graze mine or he wraps his arms around me, I fight the urge to beg him to kiss me. But the truth is, I want to do a whole lot more than just kiss.

I've lost track of how many times I've touched myself in the darkness of my bedroom, thinking about our night at The Watering Hole. But even that isn't enough to satisfy me because I know that nothing I can do with my own fingers would compare to how fucking good it'd feel to have his hands all over me.

"I got the pizza," Colton says, coming back into the kitchen.

I jump and take a moment to compose myself, sure that my face is flushed from the turn my thoughts just took.

"Oh, great. You ready to go outside? The projector's all set up, and I pulled some blankets out of the cabinet for us," I babble, trying to get my thoughts back on track.

"Let's do it, Lulu," he agrees, grabbing the drinks out of my hand.

Before we head outside, I take a moment to admire the way he looks in the faded black gym shorts and white T-shirt. It hits me for the first time that he's not wearing his hat, and my stomach flutters at the reminder of why he usually takes it off.

Well, that might not be happening tonight, but a girl can dream, right?

Taking a steadying breath, I shake the inappropriate thoughts from my head and follow him outside.

"This is really some setup," Colton tells me, gesturing to the large screen we have set up on the other side of the house. The blankets I set up while Colton was in the shower are spread out in the middle of the wide open field, looking like the perfect oasis to relax and watch the movie.

"Thank you. I can't claim too much credit, but I really love it," I admit, sinking down on the large soft blankets I set up. "It's one of my favorite places on the farm."

"Honestly, I can see why," Colton agrees. "So, what movie should we watch? Or are there any rules associated with this part of the list that I should know about?"

"You can pick," I say, leaning over to open the pizza box and taking out a large slice of bacon pizza. Groaning at the taste of the greasy bread, I smile at Colton. "Damn, I don't know if I'm that hungry or if it's that good. But either way, I think that might be the best pizza I've ever tasted."

"Maybe it's a little bit of both. I don't know about you, but I definitely haven't had anything of any substance since breakfast this morning, thanks to the crowds we were dealing with today."

"Yeah, you're right. Now that you say that, I'm just realizing I never got lunch either. No wonder I feel like I could eat just about anything," I say with a laugh before taking another large bite.

Colton reaches for the box between us, selecting his own slice and taking a large bite. "God, you're right. That's fucking delicious."

"Told you so," I murmur before taking another bite. "Damn, so back to what we should watch."

"Are you feeling something scary or something more fun?" Colton asks, using one hand to flip through the options on the screen and the other to eat his pizza.

"Something more fun," I say immediately. "I'm usually a fan of scary movies, but I'm permanently scarred from the time Amelia and I tried to watch a scary movie out here."

"What happened?" Colton asks, pausing his scrolling as he waits for me to explain.

"Well, we were watching something about these girls who get taken. And just as the girls were about to be attacked, Knox chased a field mouse our way, and it slipped in between the blankets we were using. It kept running across our feet, and we couldn't get out of the blankets. I've never heard Amelia scream so loud in my life. My brother came running out with a baseball bat, convinced we were the ones being attacked. Once he realized what happened, he tried to help us take out the mouse, but he missed. And in the process, he accidentally ended up hitting me in the face with the bat just before my senior prom. I had a huge black eye in all my pictures. Honestly, the whole experience scarred me for life."

Colton chuckles at my description until I get to the part about my brother accidentally hitting me, pausing his job of flipping through the options on the screen.

"I can't believe he hit you," he seethes. "What an asshole."

"Usually I'd agree with you, but it really was an accident. He felt so bad about it that he offered to let me hit him back *and* he did my laundry for a solid month."

Colton continues to scowl, and I nudge him with my shoulder. "Let's turn that frown upside down, Mr. Grouchy Pants."

He rolls his eyes at me, but begrudgingly smiles as he continues flipping through the movies.

"Oh, what about that one?" I say excitedly, pointing to one of the new releases.

"Isn't that a musical?" Colton asks, wrinkling his nose. "That's not usually my thing."

"*Wicked* is more than just a musical. It's one of the best theatrical experiences I've ever been a part of," I argue, causing Colton to roll his eyes.

"All right, fine. Whatever you want, Darlin'," he drawls, and I resist the urge to smile.

"Thanks, Cowboy. I promise you'll love it."

CHAPTER 17
COLTON

As soon as we sit down to watch the movie, I'm, once again, reminded that I'm absolutely fucked.

Why? Because every time I'm this close to her, my brain forgets all the reasons why I need to keep my distance.

We finished eating a little while ago, and after putting the trash inside, washing up, and grabbing the small cartons of ice cream out of the freezer for dessert, we made our way back outside to start the movie.

That was over an hour ago, and I couldn't tell you the first thing that's happened in this damn movie. Each time I try to focus, Lucy shifts closer to me, or I smell that damn peach shampoo and loose track of everything that's happening again.

I know Lucy and I agreed to just be friends, but the more time I spend with her, the more I'm convinced that that was a mistake. She's nothing like anyone I've ever met before, and for the first time, I can really picture myself settling down with a woman. The promise I made to Hayes to treat her like family plays on repeat in my mind, but the more time that passes, the less I seem to care about it.

I try to focus on what's happening on the screen, promising myself that I'm going to behave myself, as Knox runs over, a happy smile on his face.

"You want to come watch the movie with us, sweet boy?" Lucy asks, patting the space between us. Instead, the dog jumps on the blanket and wiggles himself until he's moved my legs, pushing me closer to Lucy, before collapsing with a big sigh at our feet.

"It's tough being a puppy, isn't it?" Lucy coos with a laugh, leaning across me to pet Knox. In the process, she ends up with her face right at my semi-hard cock. I freeze, trying not to move and wait for her to move back to her position on the blanket.

Instead, she smiles up at me through her lashes and grazes her mouth across my still clothed cock before sitting up and placing a surprised look on her face. "Oh, whoops," she gasps, and I don't miss the mischief in her eyes.

I take a deep breath, trying to keep my composure. I try to focus on anything else to keep myself from snatching her into my lap and taking her mouth the way I desperately want to. "I told you last night—you're playing with fire, Lucy," I whisper, unable to take my eyes off of her.

"What if I've decided I don't care if we get burned?" she whispers.

Holy. Fucking. Shit. This girl is going to be the death of me.

I grasp desperately to the last strand of my control, murmuring, "You're trouble, Darlin'."

She leans closer, and I soak in her scent as I feel the last bit of my restraint snap. "God, Lucy, I don't know if I can keep doing this," I mumble as she presses her body into mine.

She pulls back to look up at me, and I don't miss the hurt

on her face. Fuck, she definitely thinks I'm shutting her down.

"No, no, no. I meant I don't know if I can have you this close to me without wanting to kiss you," I admit, and Lucy's eyes spark with excitement.

"I'm not stopping you," she whispers. "I've decided that I think this whole 'friendship' thing is overrated."

I stare at her for a moment, trying to decide if she's serious, before whispering, "Fuck it," and pulling her mouth to mine.

Just like the night at the bar, the moment our lips touch I'm completely lost in her.

I pull her to me as close as I can, desperate to feel her everywhere.

A small part of my brain tries to remind me of all the reasons I shouldn't be doing this with her. She's my best friend's little sister. I promised him I'd take care of her while he's gone. She's a good bit younger than me.

But honestly, when she wraps her leg around me and moves to straddle me, letting out a moan of contentment as our mouths continue to tangle, I decide to tell that part of my brain to fuck all the way off.

"God, I haven't been able to stop thinking about this," she admits between kisses. "So damn good."

"That makes two of us," I admit truthfully. "I've been losing my damn mind thinking about you like this."

We continue to kiss, and after a moment, she trails her finger down my chest. "Are you going to tell me to stop, Cowboy?"

I breathe, trying to make myself force out the words I know that I should say, but I can't do it. Instead, I grab her hand, pausing its descent down to my shorts, and look at her seriously.

"I'm not gonna tell you to stop, baby. But before we go

any further, I need you to know that if you're looking for a one-night stand, you need to look somewhere else. Because once I have a taste of you, I don't know if I'll ever get enough."

"What about Hayes?" she murmurs, and I shrug.

"We'll keep it between us until after the season's over, and then we can talk to him. But after that, I'm not hiding this. Hayes is my best friend, but I'm not willing to sacrifice my happiness for him. And right now, you're making me really damn happy," I confess, and I feel the truth of the words settle through me. "So, if you're not interested in giving this thing between us a real shot, then we should stop."

Lucy stares at me for a moment before pouncing on me and attacking my mouth with a new determination.

"I take it that we're on the same page?" I ask her between kisses, needing to hear her say it before I give myself fully over to her.

"Yeah, Cowboy. Same fucking page," she groans. "Now, please, touch me."

Her words are the only encouragement I need, and I feel the desire I've tried to keep at bay flood my veins at her words.

"Yes, ma'am," I murmur, flipping us so she's under me. I take my time kissing her, running my hands up and down her soft curves, determined to memorize every inch of her.

"Colton, please," she whimpers, rolling her hips against mine in an effort to try to convince me to go faster.

"Darlin', I've driven myself crazy over the last month thinking about your sweet cunt, and I plan to take my sweet time with you tonight, do you understand?"

She moans at my words, and I smile at the sight of her under me. I lightly trail my fingers under her shirt, letting the feeling of her hot, soft skin against my fingers make me crazy.

Finally, I slide my hands up, pulling her shirt over her head and groaning when I realize she isn't wearing a bra. "Damn, these tits are fucking perfect."

She grins at my compliment, arching her back into my touch. Leaning in, I drop slow, lazy kisses on her chest, trailing down until I can pop her rosy nipple in my mouth.

"Fuck, your tits taste like heaven," I groan, using my other hand to palm her breast.

"More," she begs, and I pull back, smiling at her.

"I thought I was supposed to be the one to beg, Lulu," I tease, lightly letting my fingers wander down her bare stomach to play with the waistband of her shorts.

"So, tell me, how many times have you touched this pretty pussy thinking about the night we met, huh?"

Even through the dark shadows, I can tell she's blushing at my words. Leaning in, I drop a soft kiss to her mouth before whispering, "Because I'm pretty sure I've lost count of the number of times I made myself come, picturing your sweet mouth wrapped around my cock."

My admission must give her the courage she needs, because she reaches up and palms my painfully hard dick through my gym shorts. I let out a low whimper, momentarily startling us both at the low, needy sound.

"Looks like I'm not the only one who's needy, Cowboy," she whispers, gripping me harder and drawing a low moan from my lips. I've never in my life made a sound during sex, but god, she feels good.

"I heard you, you know?" she whispers, and I stare at her with wide eyes, trying to piece together what she's talking about. "The other night, when we finished making candles, I walked past the bathroom while you were in the shower. I heard you moan my name. Hottest damn thing I've ever heard."

Filled with a new wave of desire, I reach down and yank

off her pants, drawing in a breath when I see the tiny white pair of panties she's wearing under them.

"So damn gorgeous," I mumble, running my finger down her hot slit and resisting the urge to groan when I feel how wet she is for me.

"Is my sweet girl's pussy wet for me?" I tease her seam through the thin fabric.

"Yes," she moans, writhing her hips against my hand. "Please, please, touch me, Colton."

"Since you asked so nicely," I murmur, pulling her panties to the side and teasing her clit with my finger before pushing slowly into her tight pussy.

"Damn, Darlin', you feel so fucking good," I whisper, groaning as I feel her clench around me.

I speed up, sliding my finger in and out faster as she grinds against me.

Pulling out, I grin as she whimpers at the loss, as I lean down to drop a soft kiss on her lips. "I've got you, Lucy," I whisper, adding another finger and pumping my fingers in and out faster. "Now, are you gonna be a good girl and soak my hand?"

"Oh my god," she whispers, looking up at me with wide eyes full of desire. I try to memorize the desperate look on her face, confident that it's just become one of my new favorite sights. "I'm close," she mumbles, grinding her clit harder against my palm as I plunge my fingers in and out of her tight heat.

"That's my girl," I murmur, feeling her clamp down around my fingers as her climax tears through her.

"God, Colton," she screams, bucking against me, riding out the wave of her orgasm.

"That's right," I whisper. "Such a good fucking girl."

I continue pumping my fingers in and out of her until she stills, gasping for breath.

"Holy shit," she whispers, looking at me with a dazed expression. "I've never come that hard in my life."

Pulling out of her, I make sure she's watching as I bring the fingers that are dripping with her arousal to my mouth and suck.

She stares at me in shock as I lick them clean, before winking at her. "I knew you'd taste like fucking sugar, but god, I didn't know you'd taste that sweet."

Even in the low lighting from the movie screen, I see her cheeks growing pink at my words. Smiling, I reach out and pull her to me as I say, "Now come here and let me hold you."

She leans in, curling her body into mine, and I reach down to brush her hair out of her face.

We lie like that for a while, and I'm almost certain she's fallen asleep before she jerks into a sitting position and looks up at me in concern. "Wait, but what about you?"

"What about me?" I ask.

"I need to make you come now, don't I?" she whispers, her eyes wide.

"This isn't a competition, Lulu," I say, pulling her body back into mine and ignoring the way my cock pulses, desperate for her. "Tonight was about you, and you just made me one of the happiest men in the world. Plus, when I finally come for you, it's gonna be buried in that tight cunt of yours."

"You and that mouth," she mumbles sleepily.

"Don't even try to pretend like you don't like it." I laugh. "Your body already gave you away on that one."

She blushes again, curling around me before she whispers, "Okay, you're right. It's really fucking hot, okay? Happy now?"

"Delirious," I whisper, and despite the long day I've had, and the fact that there's a whole lot of shit that we're gonna have to figure out, I realize it's the truth.

CHAPTER 18
LUCY

Beep, beep, beep. beep.

I groan as the alarm clock rings, wrenching me out of my peaceful sleep. Covering my eyes, I reach for my phone to silence the blaring noise. I run my fingers up and down the bedside table, across the spot where I always leave my phone to charge at night, but come up empty.

"Damn it," I mumble, cracking open my eyes to search for the stupid thing through my still dark bedroom, determined to shut the thing up and go back to sleep for another hour or two.

Why in the hell is my alarm going off this early? It should be illegal to be up before the sun. I'm looking for my phone and it takes a moment, but eventually I realize it's not there, and I sit up, confused.

After looking around the room, I spot my phone sitting on my dresser, far enough away that I have to get up to turn the alarm off. Suddenly, the events of last night come rushing back— the mind-numbing orgasm Colton gave me, falling asleep outside in his arms, and the vague recollection of him carrying me inside and placing me in my bed.

"Real fucking funny," I moan, throwing the covers off and walking over to pick my phone up off the dresser with a huff. Tapping the screen, I turn the alarm off and see a text from Colton on my screen.

> Colton: Good morning Darlin'.

> Colton: I'm running over to my place to check on the cows before things get too crazy around here. I made sure your alarm was set. And when I get home, I've got breakfast for you.

My annoyance is immediately squashed as I read his text, and I can't help the smile that takes over my face at the knowledge that last night really happened. My phone buzzes with another incoming text, and I look down to see what else he said.

> Colton: And I know you're gonna want to, but don't go back to bed. When I get back there's something I want to show you before we have to open for the day. Get dressed, and I'll be home soon.

Damn him for knowing me well enough to know I fully intended to lie back down.

> Lucy: Not sure how I feel about you at the current moment.

> Lucy: I'm all for surprises, but it's fucking early.

> Lucy: I'm not sure if you're aware, but I don't really do early.

> Colton: I know, but I promise it'll be worth it.

Colton: Coffee is waiting on you in the kitchen though.

Colton: And I bought you more of that pumpkin creamer you like. It's in the fridge.

Damn it, this man is impossible to stay mad at.

Lucy: I guess you're forgiven.

Lucy: But you're on thin ice with me, Cowboy.

Colton: Noted. I'll see you in a few.

Setting my phone back on the dresser, I go to the bathroom to wash my face and pull my hair into a messy bun before throwing on a pair of jean shorts and a T-shirt and head to the kitchen in search of coffee. Sure enough, the pot is full of steaming hot coffee, and I grab the biggest mug I can find in the cabinet and fill it almost to the brim. The scent fills the room, making me smile as I move to the refrigerator to grab the creamer.

Pouring it into my mug, I lose myself in thoughts of last night. I knew I was pushing him with the way I teased him, but a large part of me never thought he'd actually give in to what we obviously both wanted. But now that he has? I'm pretty damn happy with how the evening ended.

I bring the cup to my lips, take a large sip, and sigh as the taste of the liquid hits my tongue just as the back door opens. I turn as Colton enters the kitchen, sliding up behind me and wrapping his arms around me.

"Morning, Lulu. You almost ready to go?" he asks, dropping a kiss to my temple as I take another sip of my coffee. "If you're good with it, I'll wait to cook breakfast when we get back."

"As soon as I finish this," I say, holding up my coffee.

"There's no way I'm going anywhere this early without at least one full cup."

"Fair enough," Colton says with a laugh. "But hurry. I don't want us to miss it."

I give him a dirty look before taking a couple more sips and setting my mug down on the counter. "Fine. But whatever this is better be pretty damn good."

"I really think you'll enjoy it, okay? Come on, we'll take the farm truck," he says, grabbing the keys to the orange pickup from their spot by the door and threading his fingers through mine.

I follow him outside into the dark morning to the beat-up Ford and slide across the broken leather to sit next to him. He smiles and leans over to plant a soft kiss on my lips. "So damn pretty," he murmurs. "Now, for that surprise."

He takes off down the long dusty drive, and I lean my head against his shoulder, waiting to see where he's taking me. We ride for a few minutes in silence before he pulls into his driveway next door.

"Did you really wake me up at the ass crack of dawn to go see your house?" I growl, looking at him accusingly.

"No, Darlin', not the house. Just trust me, okay?" he asks, passing his house and pulling down a small dirt road trail off to the side of his house.

We ride for a few more minutes through a heavily wooded area until he finally stops at a small opening in the trees.

"You woke me up to look at trees then?" I ask, still trying to figure out what's going on.

"Nope. We just have to walk the rest of the way. But don't worry, it's not far," he says, opening his door and jumping out of the car. He comes around the front of the truck, waiting for me to get out, and holds out his hand for me to take.

The sun is starting to rise, giving us just enough light to see the small path in front of us. After walking for a couple minutes, I see a large meadow in between the trees, covered with small orange and yellow wildflowers. There's a small pond across from us, and the sun is rising in the distance, casting the entire field in a pink and orange glow.

I freeze, the sight taking my breath away as I stare at the land that looks like it's never been touched.

"Oh my god, Colton. This is the most beautiful sight I've ever seen," I breathe out. "I had no idea this was even back here."

"I didn't either until I was exploring earlier this week. I've been wanting to share it with you ever since, but you only get the full effect at sunrise," he explains, before leaning in to kiss me. "It's nowhere close to as beautiful as you are, though."

I blush, knocking his shoulder. "Aww, who knew that Colton Harris could be such a softie?"

"Only for you," he says, pulling me into his arms.

My stomach growls loudly, causing both of us to laugh.

"Okay, so about that breakfast," he mumbles, turning to grab the backpack he brought with him.

"I brought us breakfast sandwiches and coffee. Oh, and a blanket to sit on."

He spreads out the blanket and hands me a breakfast sandwich wrapped in tin foil, along with a thermos of coffee made just the way I like it.

"Is there anything you didn't think of? And when the hell did you make these?" I ask, tearing into the sandwich wrapper.

"I fixed them before I checked the cows," he says. "I knew we'd be pressed for time when I got back."

"What time did you get up?" I ask, my eyes wide.

"Around four this morning," he says nonchalantly, and I stare at him in shock.

"Oh my gosh, that sounds terrible," I groan, taking a long sip of coffee from the thermos.

"It was worth it," Colton says, looking over at me.

I smile, waving him off. "Well, either way, I love this place. Thank you for sharing it with me."

"Of course. I thought you might like it. Was it worth the early morning?"

I pretend to think about it before answering. "I guess. But only because you brought coffee," I tease.

"Glad to hear it," Colton says, taking another bite of his sandwich.

We eat in comfortable silence, and after we finish, Colton wraps his arm around me.

"You know, everything's much brighter with you around," he murmurs, leaning in. And when he kisses me, I'm convinced this is the happiest I've ever been.

CHAPTER 19
COLTON

Taking a long sip of water, I step back to admire my handiwork. I've spent all day working on the house to replace the rotten boards on the one side of the exterior, and I'm pretty impressed with how much better the farmhouse looks already.

My arm aches with the strain I've put it under today, but the satisfaction of seeing this place come together is more than worth it. Plus, it's nothing some ibuprofen and a hot shower won't fix.

"All right, now to get these old boards to the burn pile, and I'm done for the day," I mutter, picking up the first rotten board by my foot. It takes me almost two hours and six trips to the back of the property where I've started a small burn pile, and once it's done, I collapse into the chair on the front porch in exhaustion.

Pulling out my phone, I type out a quick text to Lucy. She's been on my mind all day as I worked, and all I've been able to think about is getting home to her this evening. The rational part of my brain knows that I shouldn't be this obsessed with her, but what can I say?

This girl has gotten under my skin, and I don't see that changing anytime soon.

Colton: Do you have plans tonight?

Lucy: I've got to draw up the plans for the obstacle course this weekend.

Colton: Do you need any help?

Colton: Or I can cook dinner for you while you work.

Lucy: Oh you don't have to do that.

Lucy: I wouldn't mind the company, but I'm warning you now that it's pretty boring.

Colton: Sounds like a plan.

I set my phone down on the arm of the chair and lean back, looking out at the pasture. The smaller calves continue to chase each other around, and next to them, Diesel grazes on a patch of grass. With the addition of the white picket fence I added around the perimeter of my yard last week, this view is exactly what I always dreamed of in a house.

But it still feels like something is missing. My mind immediately flashes to Lucy, and I imagine how much more perfect this moment would be if she were sitting beside me.

I never expected to fall this hard and this fast for a woman, but the more time I spend with her, the more I'm convinced she's everything I've been missing. I know she's worried this attraction between us is only because we're living together, but the truth is, I've been obsessed with her since the moment I laid eyes on her. She's everything I wasn't expecting, but now that she's here, I don't know what my life in Mills Corner would look like without her.

I've always been independent and sure that I don't need

anyone but myself. But the days that we spend apart seem empty, and every moment I steal with her seems more fun and full of life.

My phone buzzes, and I grab it immediately, expecting to see a text from Lucy. But instead, Hayes's name appears on my phone, and I sigh.

> Hayes: Hey, man. Just checking in on everything. Is Lucy okay?

I freeze, wondering how I'm supposed to reply to that. I hesitate before typing a response.

> Colton: Hey. Everything here is good. The opening weekend last weekend went great. And Lucy is fine as far as I know. Why?

> Hayes: I talked to Mama last night and she said Amelia's gone MIA for the most part.

> Hayes: Do me a favor and just check on her please. I know I can trust you to take care of her when I'm not there.

I cringe as I read the words, trying to squash the guilt I feel. I meant it when I told Lucy I cared about her too much to let my friendship with Hayes stand in the way of pursuing her, but it doesn't make me feel like less of an asshole. At the same time, if I've learned anything about Lucy since I met her, it's that she doesn't need anyone to take care of her. She's one of the most incredibly independent women I've ever met, and I can understand why she gets frustrated with the way her family treats her like a child at times, despite the fact that she's almost thirty.

Sighing, I just send Hayes a thumbs-up emoji and stand from my chair. I can sit here all night and worry about how he's going to react when we tell him, or I can go spend time with my woman. Easiest fucking decision I've made all day.

"Dinner's ready!" I call as I take the chicken out of the oven.

Lucy pads out of her bedroom, her hair wet from the shower she just took. Her scent fills the room, and I can't resist pulling her into my arms and dropping a kiss on her lips.

She kisses me back, threading her fingers through my hair at the base of my neck. I deepen the kiss, pulling her bottom lip into my mouth and sucking it lightly, causing her to moan beneath me.

Pulling back, I drop a kiss on her forehead and grab her hand, pulling her to the counter.

"I'm sorry, Darlin', but if I let that go any further, we'll be eating cold chicken. And I'm starving,"

"Okay, fine. You're right," Lucy says with a laugh, leaning over the counter to grab plates from the top cabinet. "I told you that you didn't have to cook for me, but this looks incredible."

I look down at the grilled chicken, salad, and baked potatoes I'd pulled together.

"Well, it's not anything special, but I hope it tastes okay."

"I'm sure it's perfect. Thank you," she says, leaning up and dropping a kiss to my cheek.

We sit down at the table together with our plates, and Knox immediately jumps from his spot on the couch, running over and dropping to sit at our feet, looking at Lucy expectantly.

"Gosh, you're a spoiled little pup, aren't you?" she asks

with a laugh, pinching off a small piece of her roll and feeding it to him.

The dog lies down at her feet, content, as Lucy and I start eating.

"So, this obstacle course. What do you need help with?"

"Ugh," Lucy says with a sigh. "I've been trying to revamp the plans for it this year, and I just can't figure out what I want to do. This is usually the part where I let Hayes and Amelia help, but apparently I'm on my own this year."

"No, you're not. I'm happy to help. And where's Amelia?"

"She's not responding to my texts," Lucy admits, and I don't miss the sadness in her voice.

I reach over to grab her hand across the table and squeeze it reassuringly.

"It's her loss," I say honestly. "So, back to this maze. What are you working on?"

"I need to draw up some rough plans so the volunteers who are coming to help set up tomorrow night know where everything goes. But I don't know how to change up the course."

"Okay, wait, this sounds like fun. What do you have so far?" I ask, pausing to take a bite of my chicken.

"Well, I thought we could set up the big round bales at the beginning and have them leap from one to the other. And then a sack race through some smaller square bales set up in a zigzag pattern. And then we always have them climb over a wall of the big round bales we stack up so that it's about fifteen feet tall. But I'm stuck with how to end it."

I nod, thinking about it for a moment before suggesting, "What if you make the end a maze? You could create one with all the hay bales that are left so they have to race through to get to the finish line."

Lucy looks at me, nodding in excitement. "Wait, that's

actually a great idea. We have more than enough hay bales to make this work. Do you have a pen?"

I hand her the black pen I always keep tucked into my shirt pocket, and she draws out a quick sketch on the napkin and holds it up. "You think something like that would work?"

"Yeah, I do. You could even let the contestants look at the plans before the race starts so they have an idea of how to get out."

"Oh, that's smart," Lucy says, still sketching on the napkin in front of her, her food completely forgotten. She continues to draw for several moments, and I watch her as I finish eating.

After a few more minutes, she looks up and glances from me to my empty plate and blushes.

"Sorry. My family hates it when I zone out like that. I just wanted to get everything out while it was fresh in my mind. Sometimes, when I have an idea everything goes out the window. But I know it can be super annoying to everyone else."

"You don't have to apologize for being who you are, Lucy. Your beautiful brain is part of what I like about you," I tell her. "I'll heat your food up and then after you eat, we'll finish up these plans."

CHAPTER 20
LUCY

"Here you go, sweet girl," I coo, holding out the bottle for Carla. She runs over to me, from where she was chasing Daryl, wobbling clumsily on her hooves in excitement, and almost knocks me over as she skids to a stop in front of me.

"Whoa, take it easy, wild thing," I tease, holding up the bottle for her to take. She immediately starts sucking the bottle and bouncing from side to side as she eats.

"Silly girl, you can't even be still for a minute, can you?" I ask, shaking my head at her antics.

As she feeds, I find myself thinking about last night. Colton and I have spent a lot of time together over the last few weeks, but each time we're together, it shocks me how easy everything feels. When I'm alone, it's easy to convince myself that he's only spending time with me because we're living together. That the kisses and touches are just because I'm convenient for him in this little town. But the more time we spend together outside of sex makes me wonder if that's really true. I've never felt so seen by anyone in my life.

A tap on my leg lets me know that Carla has finished

eating, bringing me back to the moment. She looks up at me expectantly, rubbing her side against my calf.

"It's all gone, sweet girl, but you'll get some more later," I promise, reaching down to pat her head. As soon as I do, Knox, Denise, and Daryl all rush toward us, jealous of the attention.

"Whoa, whoa, whoa," I say with a chuckle. "There's enough pets to go around for everyone."

I sit in the grass, trying to give each of the animals their own attention as they all fight to sit in my lap. Denise tries to head butt her brother out of the way, and Knox uses his thick tail to try to move Carla farther away. I watch them push each other around for a few moments before finally throwing up my hands.

"Guys, I love you, but this is getting out of hand." I giggle, patting their heads again and standing back up.

"Y'all go play," I tell them, and they immediately run off to chase each other around the back of the house.

Heading inside, I rinse out Carla's bottle in the sink so it's ready to go for later and grab myself a bottle of water out of the fridge. I know I need to get ready for all the volunteers that will be coming tonight to help set up the obstacle course, but instead, I grab my phone and collapse on the couch.

Realizing I haven't heard from Amelia in a few days, I tap out a quick text.

> Lucy: Hey, are you coming to set up tonight? If so, I thought we could get dinner after or something. I miss you, Mel.

I wait for the bubble to pop up, indicating she's typing, but they never come. After waiting over fifteen minutes, I sigh and stand to go get ready.

All right. Looks like I'm doing this one by myself.

CHAPTER 21
COLTON

"All right, everyone, thank you so much for coming," Lucy yells into a bullhorn from the middle of the pasture. "I really appreciate your help getting set up for this year's annual hay bale obstacle course. As y'all know, this event is one of the farm's biggest fundraisers, and we couldn't do it without your help."

The small crowd around us cheers, and Lucy pauses to smile at them. "As you can see, we have a record number of hay bales this year, and I can't wait to see everything come together."

"I'm gonna divide you into sections and come around to give you the plans," she continues, holding up pages of plans we worked together to create. "I'm really proud of what we have in store for this year, and I think it'll be our best one yet."

"Okay, here's those plans. Other than that, just let me or one of the other Cedar Creek employees know if you need anything."

The crowd disperses as Lucy walks around, handing out the plans and sending everyone in their respective directions.

Looking around, I shake my head at the number of volunteers who brought their tractors and other farm equipment to help make this event a reality. I'm starting to recognize a few faces, and it makes me feel like I belong in this quirky little town. I watch Lucy interact with the crowd, and it becomes clear that everyone here loves her.

"You know, she's something special," Miss Louise says, hobbling over to me with her cane.

"Yes, she is," I agree under my breath before staring at the elderly lady in surprise. "Now, Miss Louise, I've gotta ask, what in the world are you doing here? Don't tell me you're going to lift any hay bales today?"

"No, but that doesn't mean I'm gonna stop participating in town events. I'm not dead yet, dear," she declares, and I resist the urge to laugh at her tone, "I'm just here for moral support," she continues, shaking her cane in my direction. "I'm sure it's no surprise to you that people tend to do what I say."

"I have no doubt." I laugh, as Miss Louise leans in closer.

"Now, you don't need to say anything, because unlike most of the nosy old bitches in this town, I don't usually feel like I need to make everyone's business my own. But I just want you to know that if the look on your face is any indication, you're a goner for that girl. And let me just tell you, you better not fuck it up. Women like that don't come around more than once in a lifetime, do you understand me?"

I stare at her in shock for a moment, completely caught off guard by the turn that this conversation has taken, before just nodding silently.

"Good, now that that's taken care of, I'm off to go do my directing duties. Have a good day, dear," she says, patting my face and heading off to a small ATV.

I stand there for a moment, shaking my head. The people in this town are so damn full of surprises.

Eventually the crowd thins, until it's just Lucy and me standing in the middle of the field. "All right, I think that went well, right?" she asks, walking over to stand beside me.

"I think so too," I tell her honestly. "This town really comes together to help each other out, doesn't it? I can't believe how many people came out to help."

"Yeah, it has its perks sometimes," she says with a laugh. "Before my dad died, we used to do a smaller version that he set up all by himself. It was still a tradition, but it was nothing compared to what it's turned into. The year after he died, we said we were going to stop doing it. It was just too much for us... you know? But instead, the town came together and made it even bigger than any of us could've imagined."

"I know he'd be really proud," I tell her, pushing a stray piece of hair back behind her ear.

"Yeah, I think so too. This event was one of his favorite traditions, and despite how hard it was at first, it makes me feel closer to him. And now that we've grown so much, we're able to donate a portion of the proceeds to charity in his name."

"That's incredible," I say honestly. "So, where do you need me today?"

"Hmm, if you don't mind checking on the groups around the perimeter, that would be great. I'm sorry it's just us today. Mama wasn't going to be any help on her crutches, and Amelia called her mom and cancelled at the last minute."

"I'm sorry, Darlin'," I tell her, dropping a quick kiss to her forehead since we're alone. "She'll come to her senses soon, and then everything will be fine."

Lucy nods, not looking convinced as she forces a smile on her face. "Yeah, you're right. Enough about her. Let's get going. Once we get everything set up tonight, I'm totally gonna kick your ass on the course."

"Oh, you're totally going down, Cowboy," Lucy gloats as soon as the last car pulls out, leaving us alone with the newly assembled maze.

"Baby, I know you haven't seen my competitive side, but I didn't become a six-time world champion bull rider with a hope and a prayer."

"Yeah, yeah," she says, rolling her eyes. "Now I know during the real thing everyone competes one at a time, but I suggest you and I go head to head. What do you say? Or are you scared?"

"Fine by me," I agree, shrugging my shoulders. "It doesn't matter. Either way, you're going down."

"We'll see about that," Lucy gloats, lining up to start the course. "Are you ready?"

I nod, and Lucy takes a deep breath. "Okay then. On your mark. Get set. Go!"

We both take off, running as fast as we can to the first hay bale. I'm faster than she is, but I know that she can make up the time at the obstacles. As soon as I'm close enough, I jump, struggling to push myself on top of the first hay bale.

"See ya, babe," Lucy teases, easily scrambling up the bale and leaving me behind as she starts to leap from bale to bale.

I curse and ignore the pain in my bad arm as I finally make it to the top. I watch Lucy ahead of me, gaining on her as she jumps down and slips into the sack for the sack race. She starts jumping, losing her balance, and falling over onto the bales beside her.

"You okay?" I call out, stepping into the burlap sack and passing her while she's down.

"I'm fine," she grumbles, pushing herself up and struggling to straighten herself from where she got twisted around.

I cross the sack race finish line first, but she's not far behind me. Ditching the sack, I run as fast as I can to the wall, groaning as I struggle to push myself on top of the hay bales with my arms.

Damn it, this is really annoying.

Lucy catches up to me, easily pushing her small frame up and over the bales like she's done it a thousand times. Which, knowing her, she probably has.

"Told you you were going down," she yells over her shoulder. Her words push me, and I finally make it to the top of the wall, carefully lowering myself back to the ground.

As soon as my feet hit the ground, I take off toward the maze. Lucy's right in front of me, and I push myself to pass her as we race through the maze we designed.

"Come on," I mutter to myself, pushing my legs to run faster. Lucy's right beside me as we come to the end of the maze, but she crosses the finish line we painted on the ground seconds before me.

"Hell yeah," she screams, panting for breath.

"Damn it," I mutter, knowing she's never going to let me hear the end of this.

She holds out her hand for me to shake, her smile wide. "Good job. That was a great effort for such an old man," she teases, causing me to laugh.

"Congrats," I tell her. "That was a lot of fun."

"Yeah, it was," she agrees, leaning over to drop a kiss on my lips. "Sorry, we can't all be winners."

I laugh, shaking my head at her. "At least you're not letting it go to your head."

"Come on," I yell, rattling the feed bucket and pouring it into the weathered trough. "Dinner time! Come on!"

Standing back behind the gate, I smile, watching the cattle pour into the enclosure, as two of the older calves chase each other around in the open pasture.

Diesel walks up to me, sticking his large head through the gate to get my attention. I reach out, rubbing the snout of his nose. He lets out a contented sigh, and I shake my head at him. "You aren't anything but a big baby, are you?"

He blows out a breath of hot air onto my hand as I continue to pet him.

"You know, most bulls aren't known for wanting pets, buddy," I say, and he shoots me a look of judgment.

"I didn't say there was anything wrong with it." I laugh, continuing to run my hand across his head.

I know I sound crazy standing out here talking to my animals, but I feel more at peace out here than I have in a long time. "You know, old bud, you and I aren't all that different, are we?"

The bull looks at me, like he's waiting for me to continue. "Well, the way I see it, we're both figuring out what life looks like after the rodeo, you know? I didn't think I'd know who I was without riding, but I'm realizing that, while it was a major part of my life for years, it doesn't mean it's all of who I am."

"I don't know if you know this, but I had a rough time after the accident," I admit, saying the words out loud for the first time. "I didn't want anyone to know because all I kept hearing was how lucky I was to have survived. And I'm grateful, don't get me wrong. But no one prepares you for what it feels like when everything you've worked for goes away."

Diesel moves closer, rubbing the gate with his shoulder. I continue to pet him as I say, "I held it together pretty well in the hospital. But when I got out, I had this moment of, 'holy shit, everything about your life has just changed.' I know you probably know what that feels like."

The bull blows out another quiet snort, and I take that as confirmation. "Yeah, I figured you would. But as much as it sucked, I think we both ended up right where we're supposed to be. What do you think?"

He blinks back at me, and I laugh. "Yeah, I know you can't respond, but I'm pretty sure we're on the same page. And just so you know, I don't blame you for how it all ended. You gave me one hell of a last ride. Oh, and thanks for the whole not killing me part."

Diesel blows out one last snort and ducks his head in a gesture that looks pretty damn close to a nod before turning and making his way over to the full trough.

Damn, I'm officially spending too much time alone. The thought rolls through my mind as I watch the cows continue to eat. Since last weekend with Lucy, I've been desperate to have more time alone with her, but with the craziness of opening weekend and all the planning that's gone into the obstacle course, it's been impossible to steal more than a quick kiss from her.

The desire to slide into her bed each night has been almost impossible to ignore, but I meant it when I told her that I wanted to give this thing between us a real shot. Despite the fact that we're living together, I'm determined to keep her from feeling like I only want her because she's convenient.

The truth is, I don't remember if I've ever been this obsessed with a woman. I've never craved slow mornings, sipping coffee in the kitchen the way I do with her. I've never looked forward to planning date nights or enjoyed the anticipation that's been building between Lucy and me, the longer we're forced to keep our distance.

But I'm tired of waiting, and I don't know how much longer I can keep my hands to myself. My cock is desperate to finally slip inside her, and I've become obsessed with thoughts of all the different things I want to do with her. Pulling out my phone, I type out a quick text.

Colton: I'm pretty sure we're falling behind on our official list duties.

Lucy: Colton, we have all month to knock the other things off.

Colton: Right, but what if something comes up? I think it's better to be prepared.

Lucy: You think so?

Colton: Yep. So I was thinking. We should knock off the pumpkins task this weekend after the obstacle course.

Colton: Think of it as our first official date.

Lucy: Hmm, I don't know. I'll have to check my schedule.

Colton: What if I told you that I'm a little desperate to have some more time with you?

Lucy: You do realize that we live together right?

Colton: Come on, Darlin', don't make me beg.

Lucy: Well, you know how much I love it when you beg, Cowboy.

Lucy: But I'm kidding. Sunday night would be great.

Colton: Sounds good. I'll take care of everything. Just meet me outside at seven.

Lucy: Sounds like a plan.

CHAPTER 22
LUCY

"Go, go, go! You're so close," I yell, cheering as Jack Williams climbs over the stack of hay bales before racing into the maze that'll end the race.

"I can't believe he's won this thing for three years in a row," Colton murmurs beside me. "That man has gotta be pushing seventy."

"He says this keeps him young," I explain, not taking my eyes off the race. "And it looks like he's on track for year four. He's already got the fastest time so far."

"We'll see. It won't matter if he gets turned around in the maze like Zach did," Colton points out.

"Yeah, I think we really surprised everyone with that part of the course this year," I laugh. "That was a great suggestion."

"Thanks. I still can't believe how packed this place is. There's gotta be over a thousand people here today."

"It's definitely a new record," I agree, looking out over the crowd. "A few of the people who signed up to participate are from the surrounding towns, so I guess they brought their own fan clubs."

"Probably," Colton agrees, pausing when Mr. Jack crosses the finish line.

"I'm telling you right now, that's our winner," I say, before grabbing the microphone beside me.

"All right, everyone. With that, Jack slides into first place with a time of two minutes and fifty-four seconds. Samantha Sorrels, you're up next, and Bruce Flowers, you're on deck," I announce to the crowd as Colton walks over to update the small leaderboard behind us. "While they're getting set up, I'd like to thank everyone for coming. Cedar Creek Farms wouldn't be what it is without your support. And don't forget to grab your pumpkins and other handmade goods from our store on the way out."

Putting the microphone down, I send a quick text to my mom to make sure that everything is going smoothly at the shop. She replies after a moment, and I blow out a sigh of relief when she sends me a thumbs up and a picture of the store packed with people shopping around.

"Mama just sent me a picture of the shop, and it's just as packed as it is down here. If this keeps up, we're gonna have to look at bringing in some extra help. Although, it would probably help if Amelia hadn't called out again this morning," I murmur, trying to keep the frustration out of my voice.

"Yeah, I heard you mention that earlier. Is she okay?" Colton asks.

I shrug. "I guess so. I didn't talk to her. She told her mom that Mitch wasn't feeling well and needed her to stay home. Which would be fine if this wasn't our busiest day of the year."

"Well, maybe he's really sick," Colton says skeptically.

"Maybe. But I'm pretty sure it's his version of a temper tantrum because he didn't win the race last year."

"Oh." Colton grimaces. "That guy sounds like a piece of work."

"A little bit," I agree. "I'm not trying to be a jerk. He really could be sick, but I'm just saying nothing would surprise me about him at this point."

"Well, it's okay. We've made it work. Your Aunt Martha has the pumpkin patch under control, and clearly, your mama has everything covered up at the store. Do you need me to do anything else?"

"Nope. I just need to announce these last two contestants, and we'll have a winner," I say, picking up the microphone.

"Okay, Samantha Sorrels, you're up. On your mark, get set, go," I yell, as the crowd erupts with cheers. The teenager sprints, making quick work of launching herself on the top of the first large round hay bale and jumping from one to another.

"Please tell me y'all have a really strong liability waiver," Colton murmurs as the girl wobbles, almost losing her balance on the top of the hay bale.

"Yeah, all the contestants sign one," I tell him. "Plus, we have several medical staff on site just in case, even though I really hope we don't need them."

"Me either."

We watch in silence as Samantha jumps down from the last hay bale and immediately leans down to pull the burlap sack up her legs for the sack race portion. Jumping along, she weaves between the hay bales, and the crowd erupts again, realizing she's on track to beat Jack's record.

"Wow, she's really fast…" I muse, watching as she struggles to climb the wall of hay bales. "But I'm afraid this is gonna knock her out of the running."

Colton nods. "Hey, that wall is tough. My bad arm wasn't too happy with me for trying that one the other day."

"Yeah, you're right," I agree, and we watch in silence as Samantha struggles to finish the race. As soon as she crosses the finish line, I grab the microphone again to announce the results.

"Okay, great job, Samantha. With a time of three minutes and twenty-seven seconds, she slides into the fourth-place spot. For our next contestant, we have Mr. Bruce Flowers. He's our last contestant of the day, so y'all get ready to cheer him on."

The crowd below us makes a lot of noise, and after giving him a moment to get set, I announce, "All right, Bruce. Close it down for us. On your mark, get set, go."

Bruce races out, and as he hoists himself onto the hay bale, Colton reaches out and grabs my hand under the announcer's table. It's a subtle gesture, but it lights my body on fire. I've been desperate for him to take things further since the night we shared last week, but with how crazy this week has been preparing for the race, there just hasn't been time.

All I've been able to think about is the feeling of his weight pressed against me, writhing against him as I come harder than I ever have in my life on his fingers. How good he felt teasing my clit with the palm of his rough hand. How fucking sexy he looks sitting across me with that damn mustache, begging me to take a ride.

"Lucy, the race is over," Colton murmurs, leaning over to tap his shoulder against mine. "Looks like Mr. Jack pulled out another win."

I blink, struggling to bring myself back to the present. I'm sure my face is the same shade as the burgundy sweater I'm wearing, and Colton gives me a look of suspicion.

"What were you thinking about, Darlin'?" he asks, and it's obvious from the shade of my face and the tone of his voice that he has a pretty good idea.

"Nothing," I mumble, looking around for where I set the microphone. God, this man has completely scrambled my brain, and all he did was grab my hand.

"Hmm, sure. Well, if that 'nothing' is anything like the thoughts I've been having about you all week, I'd say it explains the pretty blush on your face right now," he whispers. "And trust me, I'm going just as crazy as you are."

I blink at him in surprise as he reaches over and places the microphone in my hand. "You can finish fantasizing about me later," he says with a wink. "But for now, you have some winners to announce."

"So, honey, how's everything going with the pumpkin patch?" Aunt Martha asks later that night, setting a large pot roast on the table in front of us. "Your mama and I were so impressed with how well the obstacle course went this year!"

"It's going pretty well," I tell her as Amelia nods beside me.

"Yeah, Lucy really went above and beyond this year," Amelia says, bringing over the salad from the bar as my mom follows behind her on her crutches. I give her a look, grateful for the compliment but knowing I would have much rather had her help.

"Well, you really should have been there to help her," her mom says, shooting her a look of disapproval.

"I told you that Mitch was sick. He had a cold, so I was tied up with that. But Lucy did just fine without me," she says, checking her phone.

"I still missed having you there," I say honestly, and she just gives me an apologetic look.

"I missed being there," she admits, and I don't miss the sadness in her voice.

"I feel like I've barely seen you since the season started," I add, and Amelia shrugs.

"We've both been busy, Lulu," she says.

I wait for her to say more, but she doesn't, so we sit in silence for a moment while my mom and Aunt Martha compare pot roast recipes.

"So, thank you both for coming, girls," my mom says as the four of us reach to fix our plates. "We just figured it would be a good time to check in on how the season's going. We also need to decide which causes we want to donate to with the proceeds we made from the course."

"Yes, thank you for making time in your schedules to come eat with your mamas," my aunt adds.

Amelia and I both nod, and Amelia reaches back to grab her phone to respond to a text.

"Honey, do you think you could put that away while we eat?" my aunt asks as Amelia types away on her phone.

"Sorry. I'm trying to figure out where Mitch is. He told me he was staying in tonight, but he's not answering my texts, and his location is turned off for some reason," Amelia sighs.

My mom, aunt, and I all share a look, trying to decide how to respond to that before Amelia adds. "Can we just eat? I want to get home before it's too dark."

My aunt sighs, and for a moment, I think she's going to say what we're all thinking, but instead, she just nods.

"So, girls, I know y'all have been taking on more responsibility for the last few years, and your aunt and I just wanted to make sure it's still what you want. I know it can be overwhelming this time of year, and we just wanted to make sure you're not regretting that decision."

I shake my head quickly. "No, not at all. The farm's always been our dream, right, Amelia?"

I look over at my best friend, waiting for her to agree with me, but she's back to typing frantically on her phone.

Deciding that she's not going to be any help in this conversation, I continue. "I think that we're really hitting our stride—and business is better than ever. I was telling Colton that it might be time next year to bring in a little bit more help, though."

"I think that's a great idea," my aunt says enthusiastically. "That's actually part of what we were wanting to talk about. Your mama and I are happy to stick around and help out as long as you'd like, but the truth is, we're getting old. And we think having some extra trustworthy help would be great."

I nod, looking over to Amelia. "Mel, what do you think?"

"Oh, uh, whatever you want," she says, looking up from her phone for a moment. "It doesn't matter to me."

"Honey," her mom starts, her tone kind but firm.

"I can't do this right now, Mom," Amelia interrupts, and I don't miss the tears that are pooling in her eyes. "I'm sorry, but I've got to go. Thank you for dinner," she says, rising from her seat and leaving her untouched plate behind as she exits the room.

The three of us sit in silence as the front door slams, followed by the sound of Amelia's car pulling out of the driveway.

"Well, this is fun," I murmur in frustration, trying to remind myself it's not my responsibility to fix the mess my cousin has made.

"I just don't know what to do with her anymore," my aunt says, looking toward the door. "I know she's grown and she's gotta figure it out on her own, but god, it hurts my heart to see her like this."

"Me too," I agree, moving my fork around my plate. "My bet is someone texted her to tell her Mitch was misbehaving at The Watering Hole again."

My mom winces, taking a bite of her food. "Yeah, she

looked pretty upset. One of these days I'm gonna give that boy a piece of my mind."

I nod in agreement as my mom turns to me. "Enough about that. How's everything at home? Is Colton living there still working out okay?"

"Oh, yeah, we actually don't see each other that often," I say, wishing I wasn't telling the truth. "He's really nice, and everything seems to be going well."

Mama narrows her eyes at me, and I brace myself for her to meddle. Instead, she just nods. "Glad to hear it. I should be able to move back home in a couple weeks."

I freeze, trying to decide how I feel about that. I've always loved living at home with her, and for the most part, we stay out of each other's way. But I've gotten used to Colton's stolen kisses as he heads out the door in the morning, and I don't want the bubble we've built around ourselves to pop.

"Sounds good," I lie, adding it to the list of things Colton and I will have to figure out.

CHAPTER 23
COLTON

"Hello?" I say, setting my guitar down to answer my phone.

"Hey, man," Hayes answers. "How's everything going at home?"

"Oh, everything's good," I reassure him, leaning down to pet Denise's head from her spot at my feet. After we closed the patch for the day, Lucy decided to run to the next town over to knock out some grocery shopping for the week, and I've been enjoying the quiet as I wait for her to get home to start our date.

"How'd the maze go yesterday?" Hayes asks, bringing my attention back to the present.

"It was actually a lot of fun. Did you get the picture of the obstacle course I sent?"

"Yeah, I gotta say, it looked pretty fucking epic. Was the maze at the end your idea?"

"Lucy and I came up with it together," I admit. "How's the season going? I know it's been a few days since we talked, but Sam sent me a text last night that you had a hell of a ride."

"I've never felt like that before in my life," my best friend responds excitedly. "I feel like everything's finally clicking for me, you know?"

I nod before realizing he can't see me, awkwardly adding, "That's awesome, Hayes."

"Thanks, man. You know I couldn't do all of this without you," he says. "I feel so much better knowing Mama and Lucy are in good hands while I'm out here."

"It's no problem," I tell him truthfully, trying to ignore the stab of guilt I feel at the words. I meant it when I told Lucy I was serious about her, and I know I'm gonna have to figure out how to tell him the truth. But all that can wait until he's home.

I hear a crash from behind the house, and I look up in alarm, trying to figure out where it came from.

"Hey, sorry man, but I've gotta go. Congrats again on your ride last night, and good luck at this afternoon's competition."

"Thanks, I'll talk to you later," Hayes says, and I hang up. Standing, I look around the porch, searching for the source of the crash.

Denise follows me as I head down the steps, making my way to the back of the house. Turning the corner, I freeze at the sight in front of me. Carla is frozen in mid-air, half her body on the ground and the other half dangling from the railing on the side of the stairs. Below her, Daryl and Knox stand beside her on the ground, looking guilty.

"What in the world have you gotten yourself into, girl?" I ask, moving closer to examine the predicament. "Did you try to squeeze in through these posts?"

The calf looks up at me, her hooves tapping the stairs as she tries to free herself.

"It's okay," I tell her, running my hand down her snout and sitting down on the stairs to get a closer look at how she's stuck. Thankfully, she doesn't seem to have cut herself in the process, so I try to wiggle her gently out of the tight space. She lets out a loud moo in protest, and Knox and the piggies move up the stairs to stand next to me at the sound.

"How in the world did you manage this?" I mutter, continuing in the effort to free her from the posts. "Were y'all playing chase or something? And how did you all manage to get out of your pens in the first place?"

The animals all blink back at me innocently, and I shake my head. "Y'all are something else."

I stand and walk around to the other side of the stairs, looking at Carla's hind legs barely touching the ground as she tries to back herself out from the space.

"Let's try it this way," I say, gently grabbing her middle and wiggling her again to try to get her free. But she doesn't budge as she lets out another loud moo.

All four of the animals look up at me, waiting for me to figure out a way to solve the current predicament. "Oh, so you all can get yourself into this mess, but it's my job to get you out, huh?"

Knox's tail thumps the ground in response. "All right, I guess I'm going to find a saw. Looks like we're gonna have to cut you out."

OVER AN HOUR LATER, I'm wiping the sweat from my brow and shaking my head at the sight in front of me. After tracking down a hand saw from the horse barn, I managed to cut the posts, finally freeing Carla from her spot on the stairs. She immediately licked my hand in thanks before turning to Knox and the pigs and starting another game of chase. They almost took me down, hitting my knees in their haste to play and leaving me to figure out how to fix the spot in the stairs.

No more than five minutes after I've finished replacing the post, I'm admiring my handiwork when I hear another loud noise. "I swear to God, y'all are gonna be the death of me," I groan, pushing myself up from the ground. My bad arm screams in protest, but I ignore it, hustling around the house.

"Y'all have got to be fucking kidding me," I murmur. This time, Daryl is stuck under the post of a chair on the front porch, and my guitar lies beside him, knocked over from where I left it when Hayes called. Thankfully, there doesn't seem to be any damage, but every time he moves, Daryl's short tail strums the strings, adding an extra layer of chaos to the predicament.

"Damn it, Daryl," I whisper, hurrying up the stairs and moving my guitar to safety before looking down at the pig in front of me. "Now I understand why Hayes can't stand y'all."

Daryl looks up at me, giving the most pitiful look I've ever seen through the wooden slats of the chair, and I sigh. "Okay, I'm sorry. That was a little harsh, but damn do y'all know how to get yourself in a bind."

I move the chair, freeing Daryl, thankful this seems to be an easier fix than the earlier situation with Carla.

The pig takes a moment to shake, making sure he's really free, before he runs at me at full force, knocking me in the knees. "Damn, Daryl," I mutter, bending down to pet him.

"All right, now that that's over, I'm gonna set up for my date with Lucy, and y'all are gonna go in your pens. Not that I think it'll do any good, but I've been looking forward to tonight for far too long to let your antics mess them up."

I lead the pigs and the calf into their pens, as Knox whines from his spot on the porch. "I know, buddy, but y'all can play tomorrow," I promise, petting the lab on his head.

Once the animals are securely tucked away, I pull out my phone to send Lucy a quick text.

> Colton: Just so you know, these animals of yours are fucking nuts.

> Lucy: Tell me something I don't know.

> Lucy: Sorry, I got held up in town, but I'll be home soon.

> Colton: Sounds good. You still down for a date night?

> Lucy: I wouldn't miss it.

> Colton: Good I'll see you soon. I'm jumping in the shower. Hopefully we can avoid any animal fiascos in the ten minutes they'll be unsupervised.

> Lucy: Not a chance in hell. :)

Tucking my phone back in my pocket, I walk around the house, stopping by where I set up for the date earlier this afternoon. After double-checking that everything is ready to go, I head inside, trying to hide the smile on my face. I never expected to be this excited to paint pumpkins as a thirty-six-year-old man, but what can I say? Lucy has a way of making everything more fun.

CHAPTER 24
LUCY

"Okay, I've got to admit, I think you might be right about the whole painting pumpkins argument," Colton admits, looking down to admire his work. "This is much more fun than carving them."

"I told you." I laugh, dipping my brush in the pink paint and putting the finishing touches on my own pumpkin.

"Are you ready to show them off?" I ask. "My curiosity is killing me."

"I don't know if you're ready for the pure masterpiece I just created," Colton gloats, and I roll my eyes.

"I'm sure I can handle it," I assure him as Knox perks his head up from his spot beside me. "See, even the dog is ready to see what sort of artistry you've come up with."

"Well, I'd hate to disappoint Knox," Colton says. "But you both have to promise not to laugh."

I look down at my dog and try not to laugh at the skeptical expression on his face. "Well, I'll do what I can, but Knox said he can't make that promise."

"Good enough," Colton says, picking up his pumpkin and

turning it around for us to see. "I now present to you, Mr. Jack."

I stare at the pumpkin with a crudely painted green jack-o'-lantern face on top of a light blue background.

"I can tell I've stunned you speechless," Colton says confidently, and I nod in silence. "Let me see yours."

"I'm not sure I can compete with your raw talent," I say hesitantly.

"Come on, show me," Colton encourages, and I turn the pumpkin to show him what I've been working on.

He stares for a second before he starts laughing.

"Lucy, did you forget to tell me that you were fucking Picasso or some shit?"

"What do you mean?" I ask, looking down at the pumpkin. I painted the background to look like the castle in *The Wizard of Oz*, but instead of the movie characters, I painted Daryl, Denise, Carla, and Knox. Around the outside I wrote "There's no place like Cedar Creek."

"Lucy, that's the most incredible painting I've ever seen. How in the world did you do that?"

I shrug, feeling embarrassed. "It's not that big of a deal. I've always liked art, but there's never been that many opportunities to take classes around here."

"Darlin', when are you going to realize how fucking talented you are?" he asks seriously.

"You're just being sweet," I tell him, not sure of what to say.

He shakes his head and looks down at his own pumpkin. "I can't believe I just showed you this when yours looks like that."

"I think it looks great," I promise, trying to keep a straight face.

"Lucy, the eyes aren't even the same shape. And it took me thirty minutes to try to get his mouth the right size."

"Well, I love it," I tell him, standing from my spot on the ground. "I can't wait to display both of them on the porch."

Colton groans. "Great, I can't wait for everyone to see how pitiful mine is."

I pick them both up and stagger them on the front porch before heading back to the side of the house to help Colton clean up.

I'm just bending down to grab the glass of water we used to clean our brushes, just as something cold hits me in the chest.

"Oh my god! Did you actually just do that?" I ask, looking down at the large blue glob of paint on my old shirt.

"Yep, I sure did. What are you gonna do about it, Darlin'?" Colton drawls, and I don't miss the glimmer of mischief in his eyes.

Without breaking eye contact, I reach across the table and grab a bottle of paint.

Grinning, I flip the top and squeeze a long stream of pink paint across his chest.

His eyes widen in surprise before he lets out a loud chuckle. "Pretty sure you just started something you won't be able to finish, Lulu."

He takes his hat off and sets it out of the way before reaching down and using both hands to grab a couple bottles of paint.

"You're on, Cowboy," I say with a laugh, running away from him as fast as I can.

In the excitement, Knox runs out from his spot under the porch and chases after me, his tail wagging happily. Colton chases us both, sending a constant spray of green and blue paint in our direction.

I laugh, turning to face him and send my own stream of pink and purple paint back at him. I expect the paint to slow him down, but instead he rushes me, grabbing me and picking me up.

Knox barks at our feet, completely covered in paint. Colton gestures for him to go back to the porch, and my mouth drops open as my dog does as he asks without complaint. But there isn't time to think about that, as Colton captures my mouth with a brutal kiss. Just like the last two times we've kissed, my body immediately ignites with desperate desire the minute his lips touch mine. We're a tangle of arms and legs as I rush to take my paint-covered shirt off, and I somehow end up with just as much paint covering my bare skin as I had on my shirt.

Colton pulls back long enough for me to yank his shirt over his head, and I groan in admiration as I look down at his muscular, bare chest.

Dipping my finger in the paint on his cheek, I slowly trail my finger down his chest, tracing the lines of his abs as low as I can while he continues to hold me in the air against him.

"Damn it, Lucy, you're driving me fucking crazy," he murmurs, leaning in to claim my mouth again.

"Back at ya," I mumble as he walks us back to the picnic blanket and gently sits me down before covering my body with his.

His cock rubs against my clit in this position, and I'm pretty sure I'm already ready to combust at the feeling.

"Are you finally going to fuck me?" I whisper.

"I thought I was supposed to be the one to beg tonight, Darlin'," he murmurs, smiling as he leans back in to kiss me.

We kiss for another moment as he slides his hand under my shorts and eventually yanks them down, leaving me in just my panties in the cool October air.

"You're so fucking beautiful," he murmurs, trailing his hands down my side, covering more of my bare skin with paint before pulling down his own pants, freeing his massive cock. "Please, I need you to tell me you want this as bad as I do."

"Yes," I moan, writhing my hips between us. "Please, yes."

He leans in, kissing me again hard before pulling back and kissing down my body. My breath catches as he stops, hovering directly above my pussy. He doesn't break eye contact as he leans in and runs his tongue across my slit, nipping me with his teeth as he sucks the damp fabric of my panties into his mouth.

"Oh my god, yes," I moan, lost in the feeling of him.

When his hands trail up, finally yanking my panties down my legs, I resist the urge to let out a sigh of relief. He blows a breath of hot air against my pussy, and I moan as he kisses my slit. I'm convinced he's finally going to taste me, and I buck my hips, desperate for contact. But instead, he sits back and rolls me over, pulling me into his lap.

"I'm sorry, baby, but if I start eating this pussy, I'm never gonna last," he groans, positioning me on top of him.

His tip is teasing my entrance in this new position, and when I wiggle my hips against him, he lets out a low whimper.

"Lucy Phillips, you're gonna be the death of me. Your cunt is already fucking dripping for me," he mutters before freezing. "Condom. We need a condom."

I buck my hips against him again, groaning at the way his cock grazes my clit. "No, we don't," I whisper, causing him to freeze.

He stares at me for a moment, and I start to second guess what I said. "I mean, if you're comfortable with it... I'm on birth control and all my tests have come back clear. But if you'd rather..." I ramble, before Colton slams his mouth onto mine.

"Darlin', I'd love nothing more than to slide into you bare. I just didn't want to make you uncomfortable. All my tests are clear too. Are you sure?"

"Yes," I moan, grinding myself against him.

With my confirmation, Colton pumps his hips, pushing into me hard. I scream, my eyes widening at the intrusion.

"Big," I murmur. "You're so fucking big."

He grabs my hips and lifts me until his cock teases my entrance as he looks at me with wide eyes. "I'm so sorry, Lucy. Did I hurt you? Are you okay?"

"I will be once you start fucking me," I rasp out, repositioning myself on top of him and dropping myself back down on his cock.

"Fuck," he groans, letting me take control. I fuck myself on his cock, sliding up and down as my pussy clamps down around him. "So fucking good, baby."

I moan in agreement, speeding up as his cock hits a spot inside me that makes me see stars. Speeding up, I swirl my hips on top of him, as he reaches down and teases my clit with his fingers. The combination of sensations is more than I can stand, and I whisper, "I'm about to come."

My words seem to encourage him, and he pistons his hips harder, driving into me from below as he continues to tease my clit with his fingers. My body tightens until it feels like it's going to break, just before my orgasm slams into me.

"Oh my god," I cry out, continuing to ride him. I feel my release rush through me, and freeze, my eyes widening in shock as I feel it coat the inside of my thighs.

"Darlin', did you just soak my lap?" he asks, looking up at me in surprise.

"Uhh. I—I'm sorry," I stammer, my cheeks heating from embarrassment. "That's never happened to me before and I—"

"That was the hottest fucking thing I've ever seen," Colton

says, interrupting me. He moans as he continues working his hips into me, chasing his own release. I bob on his cock, both of us desperate again as he works his way inside me. "You're gonna give me another one, aren't you, sweet girl?" he asks, and I moan.

I've never been able to come again so quickly, so I'm shocked when I feel another orgasm building. After a few more flicks of my clit, I feel myself tighten again, bringing me to a smaller orgasm, just as I feel him come inside me. I groan at the feeling of his cum filling me, as he lets out a low growl.

"So fucking perfect," he murmurs, pulling out of me and laying me gently on the blanket beside him. Rolling over, he watches as his cum starts leaking out of me, before reaching up to push it back inside me.

"Holy shit, Cowboy, you're gonna be the death of me."

I GROAN as my alarm goes off the following morning, reaching for my phone to silence the most annoying sound in the world.

"Fuck early mornings," I growl, tapping the button to turn the alarm off.

I look over, hoping to find Colton still in bed next to me, but I'm not surprised to see he's already up, probably checking on The Last Lasso before we start the day. Usually, Mondays are my day to sleep in, but one of the local schools is bringing their students for a field trip today, so I need to be dressed and overly caffeinated by the time they get here at eight.

Field trips are some of our most chaotic days, and having over a hundred elementary students spread across the pastures always makes me a little on edge. But watching their excitement as they see the pumpkins makes it worth it.

Forcing myself out of bed, I head to the kitchen in search of coffee. The smell of it hits me as soon as I step into the kitchen, and I smile. Walking over to the machine, I pick up the note Colton left for me.

Good morning,
I needed to run next door to make sure everything
was under control before we start the day. You
looked so peaceful that I didn't want to wake you.
The coffee's ready for you. I'll be home soon.
Colton
P.S. Last night was incredible. Pretty sure I'll never
look at a bottle of paint the same way again.
P.P.S. Knox is outside because he's still covered in
paint. I'll help you bathe him when I get home before
the school group gets there.

Smiling down at the note, I pour myself a cup of coffee and head to the front porch. Sitting in the chair that looks out over the property, I take a long, slow sip.

"Hey, Miss Louise asked me to tell you she'd like four more pumpkins delivered tomorrow morning," I say, turning to Colton as he comes into the store the following weekend.

"I'll make sure she's taken care of," Colton promises,

walking behind the counter to grab a water out of the small cooler we keep there.

"Thank you," I say, smiling as he trails his hand up my leg behind the counter before standing and taking a long sip of his water.

We share a look, and I know both of us are thinking about our night in the pasture last weekend before he says, "Hey, what do you think about coming to take a look at the house tomorrow? The furniture I've ordered is finally here, and I've decided I can't let the squirrels run wild forever."

"Oh my goodness, I didn't think this day would ever come," I tease. "But I'd love to. Did you ever get a hold of Andy?"

"Nope. And now that I'm done with fixing the outside, I can't put it off any longer."

"I'm proud of you, Cowboy," I say with a laugh. "How's Diesel and the rest of the cows doing?"

"They're good. I think they've finally gotten all settled."

"That's good." I nod. "He's really a big ol' softie, isn't he?"

"Yeah, he is," Colton agrees, bumping his shoulder against mine.

I lean in, momentarily forgetting where we are, and I'm just about to pull him down for a kiss when the door blows open. We jump apart, and I look up, surprised to see Caroline Tyler standing in front of us.

"Well, I'll be," she teases. "Am I interrupting something?"

Colton offers her a small smile before grabbing his water from the counter. "Nope. I was just on a water break, but I've gotta get back to work. I'll see you in a while, Lucy."

Caroline and I both stare at him as he leaves, before Caroline runs over with a squeal. "Okay, well, I just came by to grab some pumpkins and say hi, but it looks like I'm getting a show too. That man is really something, isn't he?" she asks excitedly.

I smile, trying to decide what to say. "I think that's a bit of an understatement."

She laughs, waving her arm at me. "Oh, girl. Trust me, I get it. When Theo came into my life, I didn't even know what way was up. And you look pretty dazed and confused yourself right now."

"So I'm not losing it?" I tease, and Caroline shakes her head.

"Nope, not at all. But I promise it's worth it. Theo and I had a lot to work through, but I never thought I'd end up this happy."

"Really?" I ask, curiosity clear in my voice.

"Oh my gosh, yes. But that's a story for another time. Right now, I want to know about you and the cowboy."

I hesitate, trying to figure out what to say, before deciding to tell the truth. "Well, it's complicated," I start. "He's my brother's best friend, and he's a good bit older than me, but I really like him. I guess you could say we're still figuring things out."

Caroline nods as I talk, reaching out to pat my hand. "Oh, girl. I've been there. Well, not the brother's best friend part, but the figuring it out part. And I know it sounds cliché, but it really will work out. And for now, all you can do is enjoy the ride. If you can make it out to the other side, it's pretty damn incredible. And if not, you just have to believe that something better is out there."

As she talks, I realize she's right. I can't control how everyone around us is going to react to Colton and I being together, but I need to decide if it's worth it. Immediately, I know the answer, and I feel a bit of peace rush over me.

Over the last week, I've driven myself crazy wondering about all the possible ways this relationship could end. Real- istically, I know that there's no way the path we're on won't come without some resistance, and no matter how many times Colton reminds me that he's serious about this, I can't help but feel like I'm going to wake up one day and find that he's changed his mind about everything.

I look up at Caroline and pull her into a hug. "Thank you. You're right. Now, let's find you some pumpkins while you tell me more about that grumpy fiancé of yours."

CHAPTER 25
COLTON

"Okay, but remember, no matter how cute they look, they're dangerous creatures. They'll lull you into complacency, and as soon as your guard is down, that's when they attack," I say, looking over at Lucy.

I can tell she's trying to hold back her laughter, but she just nods at me. "I promise I'll be careful."

"Maybe this was a silly idea," I say hesitantly. "We could always come back another time."

"Nope, Cowboy, you've put this off long enough," she says, leading the way up the stairs and placing her hand on the door. I follow behind her reluctantly, wincing as she pushes the door open and steps inside.

"Be careful, baby," I warn, searching around for the squirrels.

"I will, I promise," she says, moving easily around the room as if she doesn't have a care in the world.

She peeks around the corner of the room, looking into my bedroom. "Oh, hey there, little guys," she says, her voice bright and cheerful. I hear a small amount of scampering in the adjoining room, and I wince, preparing to see an army of wildlife all rushing towards me.

But after a moment of nothing happening, I blow out a breath and follow the sound of Lucy's calm voice as she talks away to the animals.

"I know you all have made yourself right at home here, and I don't blame you. But the big man who lives here is really scared of y'all, so he needs y'all to leave," Lucy continues to explain. "But...I have a really cool compromise I promise y'all will really love."

I look at her in confusion as she pulls out a bag of sunflower seeds and sprinkles them on the floor for them. The squirrels pounce on them, devouring them as if they haven't eaten in days, before looking back up at her for more.

Lucy takes a couple of steps back and drops another small handful closer to the hallway. She repeats the process until all ten squirrels are outside on the back porch, and I'm left staring at her in shock.

"And since I promised y'all a compromise, I also have this," she says, bending down and dragging a large children's outdoor playhouse out from the side of the house.

My eyebrows shoot up as I look at her in confusion. "Wait, where the hell did that thing come from?" I ask, unable to stay quiet any longer.

Lucy turns to me as she sprinkles the rest of the bag of seed inside the house in the yard, and we both watch as the squirrels race into their new home.

"I found it on Marketplace. Mr. Nichols was getting rid of it now that his grandkids are too old to enjoy it, and he offered to bring it by this morning. I wasn't sure if it would work, but they look really happy, don't you think?"

I turn to look through the small window at the squirrels, who admittedly look a lot less menacing than they did when they were in my house.

"You're fucking something, Lucy Phillips," I say, shaking my head.

"Oh, it's nothing," she says, waving her hand at me. "But I do think we should patch all the holes they were using to get in just to be safe."

Nodding, I grab her hand and lead her through the house. I look around the wide space and shake my head. "It's crazy how much lighter and more open this place feels already."

"Yeah, are you excited that you're reclaiming your house?"

"I've gotta be honest and say I'm having pretty mixed emotions about it," I murmur, and she looks up at me in surprise.

"Wait. Why? I thought you'd be over the moon," she says, and I shrug.

"I'm excited to get to work on the inside of this place. I've really fallen in love with the property over the last two months, and it's exactly what I want—minus the squirrels."

"So, what's the problem?" Lucy asks.

"I've gotten pretty used to being close to you," I whisper, and Lucy's eyes widen.

"Oh," she says simply.

"Yeah, oh," I agree. "I meant it when I said I'm serious about this thing between us, Lulu. But, until we get this out in the open, we both know there's a storm heading our way, and I can't help but feel like finishing this house is moving me further away from you. I know it's not rational, because the setup we're in now was never meant to be permanent, but..." I trail off, realizing I'm rambling.

Lucy wraps her arms around me, and I feel some of my anxiety melt away at her touch.

"Listen, Colton. I really like you," she confesses, and I feel my heart race at her words. "I know that you and Hayes are going to have some things to work out, but I'm an adult. My brother doesn't get to decide who I date. So if you're willing to stand up to him and choose me, then I'm all in. I agree it's not something we should do over the phone, so I'm fine with waiting until he's home next month. But I know how important he is to you, so if that's asking too much, I need to know now. I can't keep developing feelings for you if that's where this is headed. And as much as I'll miss having you in the house, it's not like I can't stay here from time to time... You know. If you wanted me to."

Staring at her, I pull her into my arms and kiss her hard. "I told you, Darlin', I'm serious about this. You've got me so turned around, I don't know which way's up. But I don't care. And you know you're welcome here any time."

I drop another kiss onto her lips, and she smiles up at me. "But first, we have a house to squirrel-proof."

"Such a good girl, Maple," Lucy praises, running her fingers through her horse's mane as we ride through the pasture, checking on the cows.

After working on the house today, I mentioned wanting to ride, and Lucy quickly agreed. I wasn't sure how I would feel getting back on the back of an animal, but as soon as I settled onto Myrtle, I knew it was the right decision.

"So, how does it feel to be back on the saddle?" Lucy asks, shooting me a smile as she looks over to check on me.

"Pretty damn good, I'm not gonna lie," I laugh, patting Myrtle's head. "Thank you for agreeing to let me come out with you."

"Anytime," she says, pausing to check the fence line at the

edge of the pasture. "This is the last field, so are you done for the day, or do you want to keep riding?"

"I'm good. The sun will be setting soon, so we'd better head in."

Lucy nods and clicks her tongue, directing her horse back toward the barn. Myrtle and I follow behind her until we're back at the big open doors.

Dismounting, I grab the reins and lead the horse back inside, gently taking off her saddle and grooming her before leading her into her stall.

"Thanks, sweet girl," I tell her, running my fingers through her stall and passing her the apple I brought for her.

She makes a happy sound, and I watch her chomp away as Lucy slides behind me, running her hands up my chest to hug me.

"Thanks for riding with me," she says, and I wink at her.

"Don't worry, I'll take you for another ride tonight," I tease, causing her to roll her eyes at me.

"Bet you've used that line before, Cowboy," she quips sarcastically.

"Nope, just with you," I tell her honestly, dropping a quick kiss to her lips.

"I don't know about you, but I'm pretty desperate for a shower," she says, grabbing my hand and leading me outside to the Polaris.

"Same," I murmur, my mind immediately imagining her naked and wet in front of me.

"If you're good, I might let you join me," she says, clearly reading my mind.

"Oh, is that right?" I quip. "Whatever it takes."

She smiles up at me and leans in to kiss my cheek as I drive down to the house, and I wrap my arm around her, pulling her closer to me.

Her mouth trails against my throat, dropping kisses on my bare skin and making me feel a little crazed.

I let my hand float down her body as we approach the house, and I kill the engine.

As soon as we're stopped, I pull her into my lap, claiming her mouth with mine.

"You make me crazy, you know that?" I tell her, dropping a trail of kisses down her neck before pulling back to nip at her throat.

She yelps at the move, as I continue to kiss down her lips before pulling back and stepping off the Polaris. She looks up at me, confused, until I lean down and lift her into my arms, carrying her inside the house.

My mouth stays on hers as I carry her through the living room, and she reaches up, taking my hat and throwing it on the sofa. As she threads her fingers through my hair, I carry her into the bathroom and sit her on the counter.

I'm certain that the desperate look she's giving me mirrors my own, as I trail my hands up her side, pulling her top over her head. I suck in a sharp breath at the sight before me, her rosy nipples peeking through the lacy red bra she's wearing.

"Damn it, Lulu," I mutter, dropping my mouth down to suck her nipple through the thin material as I reach around to unhook the clasp.

She moans quietly as I nip and suck at her sweet skin, pulling back to pull her bra off and baring her perfect tits.

"I wish you knew how fucking pretty you look," I whisper, continuing to tease her as she arches her back into me.

Her hands grasp frantically for my shirt, yanking it over my head.

"I need you," she says, undoing my belt and shoving my jeans down my hips until I'm left standing naked in front of her.

I lift her into my arms, keeping my mouth on hers as I

push her jeans down. I feel the now familiar wave of desire rush through me at the sight of her bare for me, and I fight to keep from rushing this moment as I carry her to the shower and turn the water on. Steam quickly fills the small room, and I groan as she wiggles her hips against me, making my already hard cock ache to be inside her.

I step inside the shower with her, carefully pressing her against the tile wall as the hot water cascades around us and letting one leg fall to the floor so she's open for me. My fingers trail up her leg, teasing her before grazing her clit. She sucks in a breath at the contact, rolling her hips to move me closer.

"Hmm, is my girl feeling needy?" I tease, slowly letting my finger lightly rub against her clit.

She moans in agreement, continuing to grind against me.

Deciding I've teased her enough, I slide my finger into her, groaning when I feel how wet she is.

"Pretty sure this will never get old," I rasp out, letting her fuck herself on my fingers.

Before long, I feel her tighten around me, and I soak in the sounds of her moans as she rides out her orgasm.

Pulling my fingers free of her, I suck them into my mouth, cleaning her taste off them and groaning at the taste.

"So damn sweet," I say. "The next time you come, it's gonna be with these perfect thighs wrapped around my face and my tongue buried in your sweet pussy."

She looks at me with wide eyes as I grab the peach shampoo that drives me mad and pour a dollop into my hand. She stares at me as I lather her hair, soaking in the feeling of her soft curls.

"Are you really going to wash my hair?" she asks, and I don't miss the surprise in her voice.

"I've told you, this isn't all about sex for me, Lucy. Let me take care of you."

CHAPTER 26
LUCY

"*Let me take care of you.*"

Those words have floated through my head on a loop as Colton washes my hair and runs the washcloth over my wet curves.

After he turns off the water, I stare at him in a lust-filled daze, alternating between wanting him to fuck me and hug me.

"Come on, baby," he says, stepping out and lifting me out of the tub before sitting me down on my feet as he goes to the cabinet to grab two towels. I shiver as the cold air hits my wet skin.

"I'm coming, just give me a second," Colton says, noticing how cold I am. He dries himself off quickly before holding out the other towel and pulling me into his arms, drying the water from my skin.

Once he's satisfied I'm dry, he picks me up again and carries me into the bedroom. Dropping me softly on the bed, he crawls into bed beside me, covering me with the blanket from the foot of my bed and wrapping me in his arms.

I lean into his touch, closing my eyes and letting out a

happy sigh. We sit like that for several minutes until I stop shivering, and I look up at him. "You know, I can take care of myself. I love all these things you do for me, but I don't want you to think I'm not capable of doing things on my own. Despite what the rest of my family thinks, I'm not some hurt little girl who doesn't know how to fend for herself."

"You think I don't know that, Lulu? I think you're fucking incredible. I've watched you run this whole farm basically by yourself while keeping your whole candle business going, too. You work your ass off around here, and I'm so impressed by the way you manage everything. But just because you can do it alone, doesn't mean you should. I don't do things for you because I think you're incapable—I do them because I want to."

The sincerity of his words takes my breath away, and I struggle to understand what he's saying. But as it hits me, I lean in, desperate to have Colton everywhere. This man is like no other I've ever met, and the feeling of safety his words are making me feel is the hottest thing I've ever experienced.

Smiling up at him, I pull him closer to me and feel his hard cock press between us. I reach down, running my fingers across the tip of his cock, as he lets out one of the low whimpers I've grown to love.

"Tease me all you want to baby," he whispers, pulling back from my touch. "But nothing's happening until after I've eaten that sweet pussy."

I stare at him, waiting to see if he's serious, until he leans up and starts to move me until my pussy is hovering over his face.

"You really don't have to do this," I promise, suddenly feeling self-conscious.

"I know I don't, Darlin', but I'm desperate to taste you. All I've been able to think about since the night we met is having my face buried inside you. So, are you gonna sit that pretty cunt down on my face and give me what I want?"

I stare at him another moment before slowly lowering myself down for him to taste me. I yelp the first time his tongue touches my clit, hovering awkwardly above him.

"Lucy, relax. Stop holding yourself back, and ride my face."

"I don't want to hurt you," I admit. "How are you going to breathe?"

"To be honest, I'm not the least bit worried about that," Colton murmurs, wrapping his arms around my thighs and pulling me down onto his mouth. His tongue traces my slit before he leans up and sucks my clit hard.

I let out a loud moan as one of his hands slides up to finger me, his tongue and hand working in tandem to bring me to the brink of an orgasm. The feeling of his mustache rubbing against my sensitive skin adds another layer of sensation to the moment, driving me wild.

"God, you feel so good," I mumble, giving into the desire running through me as I begin to grind down on his face.

I feel my walls tightening around Colton's finger as he continues to tease my clit, and I roll my hips frantically, desperate for him to reach the spot inside me that drives me wild. He adds a second finger inside me, and the addition is enough to cause me to detonate.

"Colton," I scream as the orgasm tears through me, completely lost to the sensation of his mouth on my clit and his fingers in my pussy. His free hand clamps down around my hips, pulling me closer to his mouth as I come on his tongue. I ride out my orgasm, panting for breath and struggling to lift myself off him.

As I try to pull back, Colton grabs my hips, pulling my pussy back to his face to slide his tongue through my slit one last time. I look down at him with an expression that I'm sure is a mix of wonder and embarrassment.

He smiles up at me, dropping a quick kiss to the top of my pussy before letting me collapse beside him on the bed.

"God, I'm pretty sure you're the sweetest thing I've ever tasted," he groans, reaching down to adjust his extremely hard cock.

I slide over, struck with the urge to make him feel as good as he just made me feel. Reaching out, I slowly let my fingers drift over his hard length, teasing him with my touch.

His hips buck into my hand, searching for contact as I pull back my hand and let it drift up and down the inside of his leg.

"Playing with fire again, baby," he groans, and I can't help but laugh.

Deciding to give him a little more, I lean down and suck just the tip of his dick into my mouth. My hands continue to tease his length, and Colton moans quietly above me.

"Please, baby. You're driving me wild. Give me more."

Popping him out of my mouth, I whisper, "Well, you know how I feel about a man who begs."

I lean in and suck him back into my mouth. Starting at the tip, I continue to tease him, taking a little bit more of him into my mouth each time. Colton continues to groan above me, and I feel a surge of power run through me at having him at my mercy this way.

"Please, Lucy," he mumbles. "Please make me come."

Deciding I've tortured him enough, I wrap my hand around the base of his cock, working it in tandem with my mouth as I take more of him down my throat. He continues making sounds of approval as I speed up, bobbing my mouth up and down on his cock until I feel his body tighten beneath me.

"I'm coming," he warns, but I ignore him, continuing to

work him with my mouth and hand until the first hot burst of cum hits my tongue. Swallowing around him, I continue to take him, savoring the feeling of his cum coating my throat as he loses himself in his orgasm.

Sucking him clean, I pull back, smiling up at him. He looks down at me, lust still coating his expression as he reaches down and pulls me up to him. He tucks me against his arm and holds me, pulling the blanket around us.

"Fucking perfect," he mumbles, dropping a kiss to my forehead first before kissing my lips.

We lie in silence for a few minutes, and I'm almost certain he's fallen asleep before he mumbles, "I don't think I wanna fall asleep without you in my arms anymore."

I smile at his words, burrowing further into his arms. "Me either, Cowboy."

Colton: You ready to finish up that list?

Colton: All we have left is s'mores and apple cider, so I was thinking I'd build a fire tonight and we could knock it out.

Lucy: That sounds perfect. I need something to look forward to after this field trip group leaves.

Colton: Are you sure you don't need my help?

Lucy: No, I promise I'm good. Amelia actually made it in today so I left her in charge of the shop and the register while I help out in the patch.

Lucy: Trust me, you don't want any part of this chaos. Even Carla and the piggies went to hide on the other side of the house when they heard all the screaming.

Colton: Yeah, the group last month did me in, but I'd suck it up if you need me. This is the last one of these for this year, right?

Lucy: Yep. We're done after this one.

Colton: Okay then it's almost over. Just make it through the next hour. After that, I'll cook you dinner and we'll celebrate.

Lucy: You've got yourself a deal.

TUCKING my phone back into my pocket, I turn back, watching as the group of third graders runs around the pumpkin patch, arguing over whose pumpkin is bigger.

"Thank you so much for letting us come," Miss Hadley says, walking up to pull me into a hug. "My class looks forward to this every year, and they have so much fun."

"Of course, we're glad you're here," I tell her. "Let me go grab you a couple wagons for their pumpkins."

Leaving her standing there with a couple of the chaperones, I run over to the side of the shop to pull out a few of the orange wagons from the storage closet where we keep them during the week.

As I'm headed back down to the pasture, I hear Amelia's voice from behind me. "Hey, Lucy, wait up," she yells, running behind me to catch up.

I smile at the sight of my best friend, trying not to think about all the times she's cancelled plans with me or how many texts she's left unanswered over the last few weeks.

"Hey, Mel," I say. "What's up?"

"Oh, nothing, just wanted to say hi. It's been a while since we talked, and I miss you," my cousin says, and I stop walking, looking over at her in shock.

"I know I've, like, majorly suckled lately, but there's just a lot going on," she continues, looking around at the farm. "But you and Colton have done a great job keeping everything going."

"Thanks," I say, my mind still trying to make sense of her words. "And I love you, but that's a bit of an understatement, Mel."

"I know, you're right. I'm sorry. Y'all are really cute together, though," Amelia says quietly.

"I don't know what you're talking about. We're just friends," I say, trying to keep a straight face.

"Uh, yeah, sure. That line might work on everyone else, but I know you, Lulu. And right now you're full of shit." She smiles at me knowingly, and I can't help the giggle that escapes me. My chest fills with warmth, and I let myself enjoy the moment of feeling like I have my best friend back.

"Well, either way, you look good, and I'm happy for you."

"Thank you," I say before eyeing her. "What about you? You're never around anymore, Mel."

"I know," she says with a wince. "I'll explain, but—"

The sound of her phone ringing interrupts me, and I stop talking as Amelia pulls out her phone.

"Hey, baby," she answers, her face falling in disappointment. "I told you I had to work this morning… Okay… Are you serious?"

I watch as her previously cheerful expression falls as my best friend seems to shrink in on herself. "Mitch, I really can't… Okay, fine, give me twenty minutes."

Hanging up, she gives me an apologetic look. "Sorry, Lulu, but I've gotta run. Mitch ran out of gas on his way to work, and he needs me to pick him up."

"Of course," I murmur, reaching out to grab her hand. "Hey, Mel, are sure you're okay? I'm worried about you."

She hugs me quickly, tugging me hard into her chest. "I'm fine, I promise. I just have to go."

I watch as she pulls back and heads back toward the shop, leaving me alone in the field with the wagons.

Pasting on a smile, I pull them along behind me, making my way back over to Miss Hadley's side.

"All right, kids, who wants to see the biggest pumpkin in the patch?"

"God, what a day," I groan, curling up in Colton's lap on the small wooden sofa outside by the fire. After wrapping up the school group, I came inside and took a hot bath with a gigantic glass of wine before coming down to find Colton, just as he finished cooking dinner. After his admission the other night, we've spent every night together, taking turns cooking dinner before cuddling up in my bed and falling asleep.

We devoured the tacos he'd prepared. eating in comfortable silence, other than when he listened to me recount the situation with Amelia.

His arms wrap around me, and he drops a soft kiss to my mouth.

"Darlin', I don't know what to say, but I'm sorry. It sounds like you're both hurting," he says, pushing a piece of hair back from my eyes. "But obviously, I agree that she's been acting really strange, and it sounds like there may be more to the situation than we know. But I don't think it removes her from the responsibility she's been ditching out on."

"Yeah, you're right," I agree, curling further into his lap, as he leans down and kisses me gently. We kiss for a moment before I pull back to ask.

"So, about this cider and s'more situation?"

Colton nods, lifting me as he stands from the sofa and putting me back down while he walks inside and comes back with a bag of stuff to make s'mores, along with two mugs of cider.

He holds out one of the mugs for me to take. I reach out to take the coffee cup from his hand and take a large sip. My eyes widen at the taste, and I look up at him in surprise.

"What kind of cider is that?" I ask, taking another sip.

"Blackberry apple cider," he says. "It's all they had at the Mini Mart."

I laugh, setting the mug down beside me as Colton straightens an old coat hanger. "I don't hate it," I muse. "It just isn't what I was expecting."

"Well, I figured it was better to grab that than risk not finishing the list," he says, holding out the hanger and gesturing for me to start roasting my marshmallow.

"Oh, yes, that would have been tragic," I agree, sliding my marshmallow on the thin piece of wire and holding it over the small fire Colton built while I was in the bath.

"So, do you spend forever trying to get the perfect golden consistency, or do you just light the whole thing on fire?"

"I don't really care too much about the marshmallow, as long as there's extra chocolate," I say, and Colton laughs.

"That's fair."

We both sit in silence, watching the fire burn away at our marshmallows until mine nearly falls off the hanger. Pulling it back from the flames, I reach for the graham crackers and chocolate, holding them up in triumph.

I look over to see Colton finishing his as well, and I hold out my finished s'more in his direction. "To finishing the list."

Colton bumps his against mine, and I take a bite, groaning as the sugar hits my tongue.

Colton's eyes flash to mine, and I don't miss the flare of desire in his eyes. Leaning over, he kisses me, pulling my bottom lip into his mouth and sucking it gently.

After a moment, he pulls back and winks at me. "Delicious. Now, finish your dessert so we can go to bed, and I can have mine."

CHAPTER 27
COLTON

"How's everything going at home? Are you still taking care of my favorite girls?" Hayes asks. over the phone.

"Oh, we're good here," I answer, ignoring the guilt that creeps in every time I talk to my best friend. It's been over a month since Lucy and I started spending each night together, and since then, I've become somewhat immune to answering his questions. Despite the secrecy, my time with Lucy has been the best of my life, and I've settled into the comfortable routine that comes with spending my days working at The Last Lasso and my nights in bed with my girl.

"How's the riding going?" I ask, interested to hear what he'll say. The last few times we've talked, he told me about how well he's been doing, and it sounds like his team is really making a name for themselves this season.

"It's great, man. I really can't believe how much I've improved in the last few months with Sam's help. Listen, I know you might not be ready, but our last ride of the season is next week. It's only an hour from Mills Corner. Do you think you and Lucy would be able to come watch?"

I pause, trying to decide how to respond. The idea of going doesn't fill me with the dread I expected to feel, and I pause, trying to make sure I'm really okay with it.

"I think that could be fun," I say hesitantly. "But let me talk to Lucy and make sure it works for her."

"That'd be awesome. I've really missed having you here, man," Hayes admits. "But I'm really grateful you're holding everything down at home."

"No problem," I say, trying not to think too hard about his words. "We wrapped up the season at Cedar Creek, and Lucy said it's the best season yet."

"Awesome. I know she's been so glad to have your help over the last few months," Hayes says enthusiastically before I hear someone calling for him in the background. "Listen, man, I've gotta go, but I'd really love to see you next week."

"Sure, I'll let you know," I promise, hanging up the phone.

I sit in silence, trying to sort through how I feel about that conversation, until I hear Lucy moving around in her room.

"Good morning," I say, smiling as Lucy makes her way out of bed a couple minutes later.

I can't believe how fast time seems to be flying, and I feel a little panicked at the reminder that it's almost Thanksgiving. We wrapped up the season with the pumpkin patch last week, and to be honest, it didn't help my stress. It just feels like, no matter how I try, I can't help but feel like we're running out of time.

"Morning," she mumbles, bringing me back from my thoughts as she heads directly to the coffee pot.

We sit in silence as she pours her massive cup of coffee and tops it off with her favorite pumpkin creamer before I ask, "How'd you sleep?"

"Pretty good. You wore me out last night," she confesses.

I smile at the memory of pinning her against the shower wall and fucking her hard.

"Yeah, but it was pretty fucking incredible, right?" I ask, walking over and wrapping my arms around her.

"It was," she agrees, bringing her cup to her lips and taking a long sip. I smile at the contented sigh she lets out, dropping a kiss to her forehead.

"You and your coffee," I tease. "I gotta be honest, those sighs and moans sound a lot better when they're coming from your lips wrapped around my cock, though." Lucy blushes and rolls her eyes as she takes another sip.

"Don't flatter yourself now," she taunts, shooting me a wink. "If you make me choose which one I like better, you might not like the answer."

I chuckle, pulling her in for a quick kiss. "So, what do you have planned for the day?"

"I just need to make sure the floors are good to go at the house so I can start painting later this week. What about you?"

"I got another large candle order this week, so I'll be here working away," she says.

"That's great. What did they end up ordering?" I ask.

"There's a hotel in Crestbrook Cove that wants thirty of the new Christmas scent I showed you last week for some holiday gift baskets they're making. I'm really excited they seemed to like the new scent as much as I do."

"That's great, Darlin'. Is Amelia coming over to help?"

Lucy rolls her eyes over the rim of her coffee cup. "What do you think?"

"Busy with Mitch?" I guess, and Lucy shrugs.

"I guess. I texted her, but she didn't respond to me.".

"I'm sorry, baby," I say sincerely.

I know how much she misses her cousin and best friend, despite the fact that she's been completely MIA over the last few weeks. Between calling out of work and ignoring Lucy's texts, she's done everything she can to avoid spending time away from Mitch, and each time, I fight to do what I can to cheer Lucy up.

"It's fine. I'll get the majority of the candles done during the day, and you can help me with whatever's left when you get home."

I smile, dropping another kiss to her lips.

"That sounds like a plan," I tell her, surprised by how much I'm looking forward to it.

"Oh, and while I'm thinking about it, Hayes called this morning," I say, and Lucy freezes, the concern evident on her face.

"Nothing's wrong," I reassure her quickly. "But he wants to know if we'll come watch him ride next Saturday."

My girl's eyes widen, and she scoffs in annoyance. "I love my brother, but he has some nerve, doesn't he? First, he leaves you here to 'take care' of his family because, obviously, we're incapable of taking care of ourselves. Then, he calls you and asks you to come back to the rodeo? I mean, have you even been back since the accident?"

"No, I haven't. But I think it'll be fine," I answer, hoping that's the truth. "Do you want to go?"

"I'm down, but only if you're sure. If not, I'll tell my brother where to shove it," she murmurs, and I shake my head.

"I have no doubt, Darlin'." I laugh, kissing her softly.

"Damn it," I mutter as another drop of white paint hits the dark wood floor of the living room. When I first decided to paint over the brown paint on the interior walls, I didn't think it would be too difficult… but as it turns out, I'm a terrible painter. I consider myself pretty handy, but obviously, this is where my skills run out. I guess the pumpkins the other night should have been a clue that this wouldn't go well, but here we are.

"It can't be that hard, Colton," I mutter. "You just roll the roller up and down the walls."

Determined, I stick the roller back in the paint tray and roll it quickly up the wall. Apparently, a little too quickly because paint droplets spin off from the roller, spraying in every direction and covering my face with paint.

"Shit." I set the brush down and grab a shop towel to wipe my face and neck. It does more to smear the paint than anything, and I groan in frustration.

"Fuck, this whole painting thing was much more fun with Lucy," I mutter, thinking back to how incredible she felt wrapped around my cock after our paint fight.

I think back over the last few months we've spent together and sigh, remembering that our time of keeping this to ourselves is slowly coming to an end. Hayes's call earlier this week was like starting the timer on a ticking time bomb, and I've got to figure out how to tell him I'm obsessed with his sister.

As soon as the thought crosses my mind, my phone pings in my pocket with a text.

> Hayes: Hey, did you and Lucy talk about coming to the rodeo next week?

> Colton: Yeah, we're gonna try to make it.

> Hayes: Hell yeah! I'll send y'all the tickets.

Hayes: I don't know if I'll actually get to see you, but I'll be home for Thanksgiving the week after. I forgot to ask the other day on the phone, but how's the house coming?

I take a picture of my face covered in paint and send it to him.

Colton: Fucking fantastic.

Hayes: Damn man, did you have a fight with the paint can?

Colton: I hate painting.

Hayes: Same. Lucy gives me a hard time because I can build anything in the world, but when it comes to painting I'm out.

Hayes: Wait, Lucy's a great painter. Ask her to help you.

Hayes: I've gotta go, but I'm looking forward to seeing you soon. Thanks again for taking care of everything while I'm gone.

I pause and decide to say screw it and accept defeat. Sitting down on the cooler I brought in, I call Lucy.

"Hey there, Cowboy," she says. "What's up?"

"Are you busy? I know you mentioned that you have a candle order to take care of," I say, not wanting to interrupt her if she's working.

"Nope, I finished it up this morning. You must miss me or something," she teases.

"Always, Darlin'. Can I talk you into coming and helping me paint this house? I'm trying, but it turns out I paint walls about as well as I paint pumpkins."

"Hmm, what's in it for me?" she teases.

"Anything you want. I'll be honest and tell you I'm desperate and covered in paint."

"Well, since this sounds like an emergency, I'll see what I can do. Give me fifteen and I'll be there."

"Have I told you lately how much I like you?" I ask, and Lucy just laughs.

"Yeah, yeah. See you soon," she says, hanging up the phone.

As I wait, I continue trying to fix the place I painted on the wall, but I'm pretty sure I'm making it worse. After a few minutes, I hear Lucy pull into the driveway, and I cringe at the wall, knowing I've set myself up for some merciless teasing when she sees the mess I've made.

"Hey, so just in case you were wondering, you majorly owe—" she starts, freezing when she looks between the blotchy wall and my paint-covered face. "What on earth did you do?"

"I tried to paint the damn wall," I growl, and Lucy dissolves into a fit of giggles.

"Oh my god." She laughs. "I know you said you needed my help, but you *really* need my help."

"Yeah, that's why I called you," I tell her. "So, will you help me?"

"Sure, I will, Cowboy. You know it's a good thing you took your hat off for once before you started."

"Yeah, something told me this might not go the way I wanted it to."

"Well, come on then. Let's see if we can't get this knocked out."

CHAPTER 28
LUCY

"I have a surprise for you," Colton says. We're sitting on the couch later that night watching TV, and I look over at him in surprise.

"For me?" I ask, looking around the room. "What is it?"

"Well, if I tell you, it wouldn't be a surprise, now would it?" he teases, and I roll my eyes.

"Okay, then why'd you tell me?" I laugh.

"Because I'm too excited to give it to you to wait any longer. Hold on, I'll be right back."

He stands, walking to his bedroom and coming back with a large laundry basket.

"Uh, you washed my clothes for me?" I guess, trying to figure out what's going on.

"Nope," he says simply, setting the basket down in front of me.

My mouth drops open as I stare at the contents, feeling tears spring to my eyes. Inside, there's a new sketchbook, pastels, markers, paints, and colored pencils, along with a couple of drawing books and an iPad.

"Colton, what the hell is this?" I yell, sinking down on the floor to look at everything in front of me.

"I've seen how much you enjoy painting and drawing, so I went to the art store in Smith's Valley and asked the salesperson to help me make you a starter kit. I also found you some online art classes, and the iPad is loaded with some drawing apps as well," he says, looking a little nervous. "I've seen those sketches you do on every piece of scrap paper you can find. That pumpkin you painted. The drawings you did for the hay bale maze. You're incredibly talented. I've watched you these last few months, and I know you'd never take the time for yourself to really pursue this. I just wanted to do something to show you I believe you should."

Tears continue to fill my eyes as he talks, and Colton looks at me hesitantly.

"So… do you hate it? Is it too much? I'm sorry, I just wanted to do something for you."

"This is the nicest thing anyone's ever done for me," I cry, leaning up to kiss him. "But it's too much. I can't accept all this."

"Sure, you can," he says, shrugging his shoulders. "Just promise me you'll use it. Take it from me, you shouldn't wait to chase your dreams because you never know when it can all come crashing down."

I pause, realizing the truth in his words. "You're right. I know we haven't talked much about the accident, but you know I'm always here to listen."

"Yeah," Colton says. "I think I've finally come to terms with everything that happened. When you ride bulls, you know that there aren't guarantees about the future. All it takes is one bad ride to end a career. And I don't know how many times I watched guys come and go over the last fifteen years. But I never really thought about what happened once they were done. I spent so many years completely focused on riding. Every decision I made was with the goal to win another buckle. And it was gone in under eight seconds."

I reach out my hand and thread my fingers through his as he continues. "If I'm honest, I knew my years of riding were coming to an end. I just hate that I didn't get to end it on my own terms."

"There's nothing wrong with feeling that way," I tell him.

"Yeah, you're right. Anyway, while I was in the hospital, I thought I had accepted everything. Sam kept asking if I was okay, and I thought I was. But I wasn't prepared for what came after I got out. I've never felt so lost in my life. No one prepared me for how it feels when there's nothing left to work for."

I nod before asking, "Do you still feel that way?"

"Nah, I don't. But that's where The Last Lasso came in. The thought of taking in animals who were in the same boat as I was just really brought me some peace. I know it probably sounds silly, but—"

"It's not silly at all," I interrupt. "Colton, you went through something really traumatic. There's no handbook for how to handle that. And I think it's really special. Do you have plans for more animals?"

"Yeah, I do. Now that I'm finishing up with the house, I'm gonna start working on the barn so that I can take in some horses. Eventually, I'd like to be able to expand into injured animals too and keep a vet on staff full time. I just want it to be a place for anyone who needs a fresh start, the same way I did."

I smile, leaning up to kiss his cheek. "I think that's beautiful. What made you decide on Mills Corner, though?"

"Well, Hayes mentioned the farm next door to his house was for sale. At first, it started out as a joke, but once I looked into it, it just felt right."

"Did you even see pictures or anything?" I ask, and Colton shakes his head.

"Nope. Just sold off the camper I was living in and drove down. But, I'd say it worked out okay," he says, dropping a kiss to my lips. "It's not how I saw my life going, but I wouldn't want to be anywhere else."

God, this man.

"Are you sure you're ready to go back next week? I know you told my brother we would come, but we really don't have to."

"No, I promise I'm good. I want to go, as long as you'll be by my side," he says. "I think it's time."

"Okay. Now, if you'll excuse me, I have some art supplies to go through." I tease, leaning down and grabbing the sketchbook and the colored pencils.

"I like the sound of that." Colton laughs, watching me as I open the book.

I start sketching the view from the meadow the other morning, getting lost in my own world as I draw. Colton wraps his arm around me and turns his attention back to the TV.

"Oh, and Cowboy?" I say, looking up from my sketchbook. "There's nowhere I'd rather be, either."

CHAPTER 29
COLTON

"Are you sure you want to do this?" Lucy asks hesitantly.

I nod as I pull into the parking spot outside the arena where tonight's rodeo is being held. Reaching over to grab her hand, I press a kiss to her fingers.

"Yeah, I'm ready," I reassure her as she looks over at me in concern. "I promise. I want to do this. Are you ready to go?"

She nods, straightening her cowgirl hat before she turns to open her door. I do the same and meet her at the front of the truck, admiring how perfect she looks in her boots, jeans, and brown sweater. Her long hair falls in waves down her back, and the extra hat I usually keep in my truck looks ten times better on her than it ever has on me.

"What? Is something wrong?" she asks, looking down at her clothes. "I knew this outfit wasn't quite right. You should have told me to change."

"Baby, you'd look perfect no matter what you wore. I was just thinking that I can't believe you're wasting your time on an old, ugly bastard like me."

She rolls her eyes and presses a quick kiss to my lips. "First of all, I know I like to give you shit, but you're not old. And don't act like you won't have girls crawling all over you tonight, Mr. Rodeo King."

"The only person I want all over me is you," I tell her truthfully. "If you haven't figured it out yet, I'm not interested in anyone else but you."

Lucy blushes at the compliment, and I take her hand, leading her towards the entrance to the arena. She frowns down at our hands, leaning in to whisper, "Are we allowed to hold hands here?"

"I don't think anyone's going to stop us." I laugh. She continues to look up at me, the hesitation clear on her face, so I continue. "Listen, Hayes sure isn't gonna be wandering around out here to see us. Your mama decided not to come after her doctor appointment earlier today wore her out. So, unless you aren't comfortable being seen with me, I don't see a problem with it."

She nods, and I try not to cringe at the reminder that our time of keeping this thing between us is quickly coming to an end. Hayes will be coming home this week for Thanksgiving, and between now and then, we'll have to figure out how to break the news to him.

Pushing the thought from my mind, I focus on leading her through security and into the crowded arena. Lucy follows me through the tight corridors, passing the vendors selling cowboy hats, stuffed animals, and popcorn. "Are you hungry?" I ask, pulling her into the line as we reach the concessions stand.

"I'd love a pretzel and a Diet Coke, but I can get it," she offers, laughing as I shoot her my usual look of disdain at that statement. "Fine, fine," she says, holding up her hand in surrender. "Thank you."

"Sure thing," I say, dropping a quick kiss to her forehead.

"Hey man, aren't you Colton Harris?"

I turn to see a boy who looks to be in his teens standing in front of us, watching me. His cowboy hat is slightly too big on him, sitting crooked on his head and partially covering his eyes.

"Uh, yeah, that's me," I say awkwardly, preparing myself for whatever he's going to say.

"Wait, that's so cool," he says, his face bright with excitement. "I've followed your career since I was a little kid. You were always my favorite rider."

"Oh, thank you. That means a lot to me," I say truthfully. "What's your name?"

"Billy. And I just want you to know, I hate how it ended for you, but I hope that you've found something else that makes you happy," the kid says.

I look down at Lucy before shooting him a smile. "Yeah, Billy. It's all worked out all right."

He nods, reaching out to shake my hand. "It's really nice to meet you, Mr. Harris."

"Nice to meet you, too," I say before he walks off and the concession line moves forward.

"Wow, that was really sweet," Lucy murmurs, her eyes wide.

"Yeah, it was," I agree, as we step forward and grab our food. After making sure we have everything, I lead the way to our seats just as the music for the opening ceremony starts to blare through the speakers.

We're just getting settled into our seats as the lights go out, and the spotlight hits the riders making their way out onto the dirt floor.

Through the darkness, Lucy reaches out and squeezes my hand in comfort as I try to decide how I feel. This is the first time since I was a teenager that I've been on this side of an opening ceremony, and a sharp pang of longing hits me. Part of me would give anything to still be part of this world, but as I think back over the last few months, it hits me that the part of me that longs to be on the back of a bull tonight is much smaller than it used to be.

"Look, there's Hayes," Lucy points out, pointing to her brother riding a beautiful white horse slowly around the arena floor.

My earlier wave of longing fades, and I smile as more riders I recognize fill the competition floor. I watch as they make the circle, until a voice comes through the loudspeaker announcing the end of the opening ceremony. Lucy's hand squeezes mine in reassurance as the lights flicker back on.

"You okay?" she whispers, leaning in so I can hear her over the noise of the crowd.

"Yeah, I'm just fine," I tell her, stealing a quick kiss from her lips. And as I wrap my arm around her and settle in to watch the events, I know it's the truth.

"FIRST UP, *riding on behalf of the Bama Bulls this evening, we have Hayes Phillips.*" The announcer's voice booms over the loudspeaker, and I lean over to grab Lucy's hand.

I drop a kiss to her knuckles, both of us watching as Sam leans over to pull Hayes's rope tight. They exchange a few words before Hayes nods, and the gate swings open.

The bull charges out of the chute, turning and bucking hard, but Hayes is ready, keeping his body ahead of the bull's motions.

Lucy cheers along with the crowd as I watch, quietly cataloging every shift of his hips to dissect with him later. Just before the time ends, the bull turns hard to the right, his whole body seemingly frozen in mid-air. But Hayes manages to stay ahead of him, keeping his balance just as the buzzer rings, signaling the end of his ride. Hayes jumps off, letting out a yell of triumph as soon as his feet hit the ground.

"It's been forever since I watched him ride. That was good, right?" Lucy asks, leaning over so I can hear her over the roar of the crowd.

"Yeah, it was a good ride. The bull bucked hard enough to get him the points he needs, and he stayed in control of the ride the entire time. If I had to guess, he's looking at something between an eighty-seven to a ninety."

Lucy nods, turning her attention to the Jumbotron above us as we wait for his score. After a moment, a large red eighty-nine point four lights up the screen, and the arena erupts in cheers. Hayes throws both arms up in excitement, and Sam leans over to clap him on the back.

"*Up next for the Louisiana Lightning team, we have Arthur Coleman,*" the announcer says, and we turn our attention to the other team's chute. The rider nods, and the gate swings open as the bull charges into the open area of the arena.

As soon as he's no longer confined in the chute, the bull goes wild, turning frantic circles as he bucks. The rider manages to keep his balance at first, but after another hard turn to the left, he flies through the air, hitting the side of the arena before crumpling to the ground. I wince as the arena sucks in a collective gasp of shock, followed by a moment of silence as everyone looks to see if he's okay. My heart feels like it's in my throat as I watch, trying not to think too hard about the fact that the last time I rode ended in a pretty similar fashion. I can't count the number of times I've been bucked off a bull, never mind watching someone else take the fall.

After the accident, it feels a little harder to watch. I take a deep breath, trying to calm my nerves as the rider pushes to his feet, waving his hands to let everyone know he's okay.

Lucy lays her head against my shoulder, letting out a sigh of relief. "You okay, babe?" she whispers, gripping my hand hard.

I squeeze hers back, before I admit, "I'm fine. That just hit a little harder than I expected."

The announcer's voice crackles through the speakers, interrupting my admission. *"All right, folks. Right now, the Bama Bull team is in the lead, but we've got a lot of riding to get to tonight. So, without further ado, next up is Mason Wallace, riding for the Bulls."*

I lean into Lucy, grateful for the distraction after the way the last ride ended. "His family owns the big ranch in Saddle Ridge. His brother is actually who I bought most of my cattle from."

Her eyes widen in surprise. "Wait, that's cool. Are you and Mason friends?"

I shrug. "He keeps to himself for the most part, but we've ridden in the same circles for years."

Lucy nods, watching as the gate opens again, the crowd going wild. Clearly, he's become a bit of a crowd favorite this season, and after watching him ride, I can see why. His movements are confident, keeping his control over the bull, while still making sure the bull bucks hard enough to give him the score he wants.

After the buzzer rings out, signaling the end of the ride as half the people in the arena jump to their feet, screaming his name.

"Wow, that was really something," Lucy mutters.

"Yeah, I wouldn't be surprised if he scores in the mid-nineties," I agree.

A moment later, a large ninety-three pops up on the screen. The Jumbotron pans to him, Hayes, and the rest of his teammates throw up their hands in excitement. I expect him to celebrate, but Mason just nods once and walks over to sit in an empty chair behind the chute.

"He doesn't seem to get too excited, huh?" Lucy asks.

I shrug. "Yeah, some guys aren't into all the showy celebrations. They're just here to ride."

Lucy nods, and we watch a few more mediocre rides. I'm about to ask her if she's ready to go when her eyes widen and she points at the rider who's up next for the Bulls.

"Wait, oh my gosh. That's Mitch's stepbrother," she says, and I look at her in surprise.

"Wait. Really? Like Amelia's Mitch?"

She nods before saying, "Yeah, his name's Luke, right?"

"Yeah, Luke Ashford."

"Is he as big of an asshole as Mitch is?" Lucy asks, looking down at the chute curiously as Luke gets set for his ride.

"No, he's a good guy. He actually only started riding professionally a few years ago, but he moved through the ranks pretty fast. We've done a lot of the same events, and he's a hell of a rider."

We fall silent as the gate of the chute swings open again. The bull barely makes it out of the gate before he starts bucking, but Luke manages to keep his balance, holding tight to his rope and shifting his hips as he digs in his spurs.

The bull puts on another good show, but Luke stays on until the buzzer. He throws himself off and raises his hand, acknowledging the cheering crowd before walking back behind the chute to join his team.

When the Jumbotron screen fills with his score of eighty-eight, I realize there's only a few more riders left. I know Hayes probably wants us to come see him after this is over, but I don't think I'm ready to see him and pretend like what Lucy and I have isn't real until we can tell him the truth. I just want to go home and fall asleep with her in my arms.

"You about ready, Darlin'?" I ask, leaning over to whisper in her ear.

She looks at me and nods quickly. "Let's go home, Cowboy."

And as I stand, I can't help but think that sounds like the best plan I've heard all night.

CHAPTER 30
LUCY

"How are you holding up?" I ask as we drive home. Since we left the arena, Colton has been incredibly quiet, and I'm worried he's struggling to process everything we just watched. But at the same time, I don't want to push him if he isn't ready to talk.

"I promise, I'm fine. It's just... I don't know how many times I've watched other riders get bucked off. Hell, I've been thrown on my ass more times than I can count. But watching it tonight was different. Not because I'm sad it wasn't me out there, but because I've realized how damn fast it can all come to an end, you know?"

I nod, understanding what he means.

"I think that's completely fair," I say, running my fingers across his weathered knuckles, and encouraging him to continue.

When he falls silent, I ask quietly, "Do you still miss it?"

He sighs, rubbing his hands over his eyes. "I never thought that would be such a hard question. To be honest, I think a small part of me will always miss it. The feeling you get when they open that gate is like nothing else in the world, and I'd be lying if I said I didn't miss the rush. Outside of that, the sense of community it builds is unlike anything else I've ever experienced. We may compete against each other every weekend, but those guys were the closest thing I had to a family."

I nod even though he can't see me as we drive through the dark country roads of Mills Corner.

"I think that makes a lot of sense," I tell him, trying to understand what that would be like.

"But, at the same time, I'm really fucking happy with my life now, Lucy. These last few months have been incredible, and I'm so obsessed with you. I—" he starts as we pull into the driveway of Cedar Creek.

My breath catches as I wait to see what he's going to say, hoping he's going to confess to feeling as crazy about me as I am about him. But when I follow his gaze back to the house, I see my mama's car sitting out front.

I freeze, trying to remind myself that I should be happy that she's finally feeling well enough to come home. But instead I'm hit with a tidal wave of disappointment that I can't spend tonight—or any other night in the near future—wrapped in Colton's arms.

Our time is officially up, and now we've got to figure out how to come clean about how we've been spending the last few months.

Colton narrows his eyes, looking into the distance before he asks, "Wait, isn't that Amelia's car too?"

I squint, trying to see through the darkness, but as we get closer, I realize that he's right.

"Uh, yeah, it actually is. Do you think something's wrong?"

"Probably not," Colton says calmly as he pulls up in front of the house. "But whatever it is, we'll figure it out."

I nod, nerves running through me as we get out of the car.

Colton walks around and drops a quick kiss on my lips, squeezing my hand in reassurance. "Let's see what's going on."

He drops my hand, gesturing for me to lead us inside the house, and I miss his contact instantly. Straightening my shoulders, I force myself to walk up the walkway of the house, stopping to lean down and pet Daryl and Denise as they run to me.

I pat their heads, and their short tails wag in excitement before I stand and tell them, "I'll come back for more pets in the morning, okay?"

The pigs blink back at me, making themselves look as pitiful as possible. Shaking my head at them, I walk up the steps and prepare myself for whatever might be inside.

As soon as I step into the living room, I know something's wrong. Amelia is curled up on the couch crying, while my mom and Aunt Martha sit on either side of her, trying to comfort her.

But she seems inconsolable, big sobs wracking her body, and I look at Colton in alarm.

As I step farther into the room, my mama sees me, and I don't miss the relief that flashes across her face when she sees me.

"Hey, y'all. What's going on?" I ask, hurrying over to sit on the floor beside the couch.

Amelia looks down at me, noticing me for the first time, only to start crying harder as she reaches for me.

"Mitch… had… a a fiancée… in… S—S-Saddle—Ridge," she cries out.

I freeze, positive I've heard wrong. But as I look between my cousin and my mama, I know I didn't.

"What the flying fuck?" I mutter, rage filling my body as I piece together what this means.

My mom gives me a disapproving look, but for once, she

doesn't comment on my word choice, highlighting the severity of this situation.

"How did this happen?" I ask, looking over to see Colton standing beside us, looking as confused as I feel.

Amelia cries harder at my question, and my Aunt Martha pipes in. "To be honest, we're not really sure. All we know is the poor girl showed up at Mitch's apartment to surprise him, and she found Amelia there with him. Obviously, neither of the girls had a clue the other existed. The fiancée called off the wedding with Amelia sitting there. And then when Amelia said she was leaving him, Mitch lost it. He started going on and on about how much better he could do. Called her a bunch of names and told her she needed to get out."

"How in the world did this even happen?" I ask, trying to piece together what she's saying, but struggling to make it make sense. "I thought he was basically attached to your side."

Amelia wipes her tears, hiccuping as she tries to talk. "He was w—w—when he needed s—something, but h—he had a lot of boys' nights."

Rage fills me as Amelia continues to cry, and I gesture for my mama to move so I can sit beside my best friend. Colton, Mama, and Aunt Martha all head into the kitchen, leaving us alone as Amelia continues to cry in my arms.

"I'm s-so so-sorry, Lulu," she sobs. "I know I—I've been the w—worst friend ever. M—Mitch told me I—wasn't allowed to t—talk to you. I should have never listened to him, b—but I was trying to keep us from fighting."

I stare, stunned. I didn't make it a secret how I felt about the asshole, but hearing that I was right about him hating me that much.

"I—I tried to ignore it. But e—every time I came home from seeing you, he'd start a fight with me. And I just wanted to be happy," she admits miserably.

"That's not what's important right now," I tell her, rubbing my hand up and down her back to calm her down.

"You can say I told you so now," Amelia says with a miserable smile. "You were right about Mitch all along, and I was just too stupid to listen to you."

"You're not stupid, Mel," I say, hating how she's putting herself down. "Now you listen to me, and you listen good. You may have made some choices I don't agree with, and obviously, I was hurt when you basically ghosted me, but we'll work that out later. For now, I want you to know that nothing that man did is your fault, do you hear me? The sneaking around, the cheating, the manipulation? That's all that's on him. Nothing you did would make you deserve to be treated that way, and it says way more about him and his character than it does about you."

Amelia cries as I soothe her, hugging me hard. "Oh, and let me just say, if you ever pull that shit again, I'm coming for you," I add, causing her to laugh.

"I wouldn't expect anything less," she says. "Now, can I stay here with you tonight? I don't want to be alone right now, and something tells me we have a lot to catch up on."

CHAPTER 31
COLTON

can't fucking believe I'm doing this, I think as I grab the bag of sunflower seeds off the kitchen counter.

Walking outside to the back porch, I shake the bag and look at the playhouse where the squirrels have made themselves at home over the last few weeks.

"Come on, my scary little fuckers," I mutter, cringing as the animals run out of the house and start to try to crowd around me. "It's a good thing my woman likes you, or I'd never be doing this. But you little assholes better not get too close."

The squirrels look at me expectantly, waiting for me to drop the seeds. Turning the bag over, I dump half the contents on the ground, watching as they pounce on the seeds.

Shaking my head at them, I cautiously back away and start to make my way to the cattle pasture. After grabbing their food, I head over to their troughs.

"Good morning, y'all. Time for breakfast," I yell, rattling the bucket as loudly as I can.

Dumping it into the trough, I look down to see some of

the feed starting to fall through the cracks of the weathered wood. I groan, making a mental note to build a new one as the cows come running from across their pastures. As always, the smallest calves lead the way, trotting happily over to the trough, eager to get their breakfast. The heifers follow closely behind them, and Diesel brings up the rear, walking slowly through the green pasture.

As soon as he's close enough to the gate, he bypasses the food and sticks his large head through the iron bars, looking at me expectantly.

"You know, Diesel, you're definitely not what I was expecting," I laugh, leaning over and running behind his ears. "You know you're a mess, don't you?"

He looks up at me, chewing a piece of hay lazily as I continue to pet him.

"All right, it's time for you to go eat," I say, giving him one last pat and shaking my head as he lumbers off. Satisfied that the cows are taken care of, I turn back to look at the house. It's hard to believe that this is the same place I pulled up to three months ago, and I shake my head at the memory of my first few encounters with my new place. But between the new siding, the updated floors, the new tin roof I had put on, and the fresh paint inside, it's finally resembling what I pictured in my mind before I moved here.

Walking back up the drive, I realize it's probably time I moved in here for good. Other than putting together the few pieces of furniture that I've ordered over the last few months, all of the renovations I planned to do are done, and there's nothing keeping me from moving in for good. I try to decide how I feel about that and decide that, as much as I've loved living at the Phillips, it's time. Now that Lucy's mom is back, our days of cuddling and slow, quiet mornings are over.

The thought crosses my mind that once everything is out in the open, I could finally ask Lucy to move in with me. My mind immediately flashes through all the times I've pictured her here, and I can't help but smile at the idea of knowing she's a permanent fixture in my bed and my space. I picture us sitting on the porch, her drawing in her sketchbook while I strum the guitar as the pigs, Knox, and Carla run around the yard.

When I bought this place, I didn't ever imagine that I'd be this serious about a woman. But as I think back over the last few months, it hits me that I want Lucy Phillips by my side for the rest of my life. I've joked that I've been obsessed with her since we met, but when I think about it, I realize that it's more than that. What I feel for her is more than a passing infatuation or lust for really good sex.

When I moved down here, people kept telling me how well I was handling the accident. And while I never went through a phase of being mad at the world, if I'm honest with myself, part of me thought my life was over when I decided to buy this place. The only thing that was keeping me going was the plans to fix up this house and take care of the farm so that I could live out here alone. But over the last few months, she's shown me that there's so much excitement and life to live outside of the rodeo. And in the process, I've fallen head over heels for Lucy Phillips.

All I want is to share this place with her, but in order for that to work, it has to be furnished. Filled with a new determination, I head inside to set up the headboard and bed frame.

It takes me less than an hour to check that task off the list, and I pull out my phone to send Lucy a text.

Colton: I know it's only been one night away from you, but I'm already over it.

Lucy: I agree. This whole sneaking around thing is for the birds.

Colton: Yeah. As soon as your brother gets home, we'll tell him.

Lucy: Ugh, I'm not looking forward to that.

Lucy: But also, he won't be home until Thursday for Thanksgiving. There's no way I'm gonna last that long without seeing you.

I think about what she's saying and realize she's right. The idea of staying away for almost a week when I've gotten used to spending every spare moment with her feels like an eternity.

Colton: You're right.

Colton: Come over tonight.

Lucy: Hmmm

Lucy: I know you're close to being done with the house, but do you even have a bed?

Lucy: I'm all for a romantic indoor picnic, but I draw the line at sleeping on the floor.

Laughing, I snap a picture of the bed I just put together and send it to her.

Lucy: Well I'll be damned. Looks like we're having ourselves a sleepover.

Lucy: Do you have sheets though? And a comforter? Or pillows?

Pausing, I realize she's right. I grab my keys from the kitchen counter and head to the truck.

I send her the link to a few furniture sites, and as I pull down the driveway, I can't help the smile that takes over my face.

My girl is spending the night at my house, and I have some serious work to do.

"Oh my god, Colton. When did you do all this?" Lucy asks as I guide her to the bedroom. She's been here less than five minutes, but I couldn't wait any longer to show her what I spent the afternoon working on. I'd only planned to buy sheets, a comforter, some pillows, and a few other essentials. But after a trip to the neighboring city, I spent an hour and a half in the home section, trying to make sure everything was perfect. In hindsight, it's safe to say I might have gone a little overboard, but I'm still pretty happy with how it turned out.

I look at the bed I made right before she got here and the string lights I'd hung around the room since I didn't want to pick out lamps and shit without her. I also grabbed two matching nightstands, and on top of them I placed a framed selfie of the two of us that I took during our movie night. Next to it is the small picture of the meadow she'd drawn for me when I first gave her the sketchbook. I'd also picked up a blue rug after remembering that it was her favorite color.

On top of the decor, I made a little picnic after her joke

earlier, stopping by the deli and grabbing sandwiches, chips, and cookies and placing them in a basket on the bed.

She glances around in surprise, taking in all of the details I'd included in the space, before launching herself at me and kissing me hard. "Oh my god, Colton. This is incredible."

"Do you like it?" I ask, desperate to hear her say the words.

"I love it! I know it's not my room, but you're gonna have to kick me out because I never want to leave. It's so cozy."

"Darlin', if you think I'd ever kick you out, you don't know me as well as I thought you did," I murmur, and she turns to kiss me.

I slide my fingers through her soft hair, gently pulling her closer to me. I don't think I'll ever get used to how good her mouth feels on mine.

Forcing myself to pull back, I lead her toward the bed. "Are you hungry?" I ask, gesturing to the basket in front of us.

"I think dinner can wait," she whispers, sitting down on the bed and moving the basket to the floor before leaning over to pull me down on top of her. "I want something else first."

I laugh, slipping my arm around her and turning us so that she's on top of me.

"Oh, is that right?" I ask, slowly sliding my hands up her sides under her sweatshirt.

"Yep," she says, dropping her head to whisper in my ear. "I want you to fuck me, Cowboy. I've spent all day thinking about how much I missed your cock."

As always, her dirty words light a fire under me, and I hurry to rip her sweatshirt off over her head.

"Is my girl feeling needy?" I ask, groaning at the sight of the light blue lace bra she's wearing. Under the glow of the twinkle lights, I can just see her nipples through the light fabric, and I lean in to suck one in my mouth.

She moans on top of me, rolling her hips against my cock. "Colton, please. I promise, you can take your time later. Right now, I need you inside me. Please, please fuck me."

Lust rolls through me as she continues to grind against me, and I pull her mouth down to me, delivering a slow, greedy kiss as my hands trail down to tug at her leggings. Realizing what I'm doing, she leans down and tears them down her legs, throwing them to the side of the bed before grabbing frantically for my belt. She undoes the buckle and unbuttons my jeans, barely breaking the kiss, and she frees my cock. She's wearing matching blue panties, and I groan as she rubs herself against my bare cock, the texture of the thin fabric combined with the heat of her pussy making me wild. Reaching down, I tear them off her, the thin fabric shredding in my hands as I lift her, getting ready to line her up on my cock.

"Colton Harris, you owe me a pair of panties," she whines, but I can tell by the desire in her eyes that she doesn't care that much about the fabric I just ruined.

"I'll take you tomorrow and buy you the whole damn store," I murmur. "But right now, I need to feel this tight cunt dripping for my cock.

I tease her entrance with my finger, groaning in appreciation when I find her soaked for me.

"Such a good girl, aren't you, Darlin'?"

She rolls her hips, desperate for me to give her more as I trail my fingers up and down the inside of her leg.

"Please," she moans, and I grab her hips and line her up to take my cock. As soon as it touches her entrance, she sinks down hard, and I whimper at the feel of her pussy gripping my cock like it was made for it.

"Damn, baby, you feel so good," I groan, pulling her down to kiss her mouth as she fucks herself on my cock.

Reaching up, I toy with her clit the way that I know drives her mad, rubbing slow circles around it as she slams herself down on my cock hard enough that her tits bounce with each motion.

It doesn't take long before her pussy clamps down hard around my cock, and her arousal gushes out of her, covering my lap. The combination of sensations spurs on my own orgasm, and I buck my hips into her coming hard, and covering the inside of her walls with my cum.

She collapses onto my chest, my cock still firmly inside her, as she leans up to press a kiss to my lips.

"The room's perfect," she mumbles, her eyes closing as I hold her. After a minute, she leans back and pulls herself off my cock, and I groan at the sight of my cum running down her slim thighs.

"I can't lie, that was a pretty good way to break in the bed," I tease, standing and grabbing her hand. "Now, let's take a shower, and afterward I'm getting a taste of that sweet pussy."

CHAPTER 32
LUCY

"All right, I think we need another seventy-five of the Saddles and Spruce and maybe fifty of the Candy Cane Lane to be ready for the market next week. Is that what you got too?" I ask Amelia, looking at the mess we've made of the kitchen.

There are candles spread out all across the counters and flowing over to every bare surface we could find in the dining room and living room, and the house officially smells like Santa's workshop.

"Yep, I got the same thing," Amelia says, looking down at our inventory list. "I doubled the most popular scents from last year in our predictions, so I really hope we aren't left with too many extras."

"I don't think we will be. The Christmas markets are always some of our best sales of the year. Plus, I was thinking we should do another one of our movie nights in December. We can show a Christmas movie and sell hot chocolate. And we could open the store for candles and gifts too."

"Oh, I love that idea," Amelia gasps, and I can already see

the gears turning in her brain as she starts to think of all the different ways we could make the event a success.

We work in silence, mixing the wax for the last batch of candles, before I work up the courage to ask, "How are you holding up, Mel?"

My best friend smiles sadly at me as she starts to pour her batch. "I'm okay. Now that I'm really away from it, I'm realizing how much I let him manipulate me. I know I have to take some responsibility for how I acted, but he just had me so confused, Lulu. I don't know how I didn't see it before, but I was just so caught up in my feelings for him, you know?"

I nod, continuing to work as I listen.

"He just had this way of making me believe everything he told me. I don't know, maybe it's just proof that I'm an idiot, but I just wanted everything to work out. And I knew everyone in my life didn't like him, so it started to feel like he was all I had."

"We only disliked him because we saw how he was treating you, babes. I'm sorry we made you feel that way. But when you stopped responding to my texts, I just figured you didn't want to hear from me."

Amelia looks up at me with wide eyes. "What texts are you talking about?"

I blink at her, trying to figure out what she means. "The texts I sent you asking you to hang out or asking how you were. Or the ones asking you for help making candles," I say before adding, "You know, all the ones you never responded to?"

"Lucy, I swear to God, I never got any of those texts. I thought you were ghosting me because I'd gotten back with Mitch. He told me you were tired of having to put up with me and clearly didn't want to spend time with me anymore. I swear, I never would have ignored you that way."

I stare at her, setting down the container of wax I'm using

to fill the canisters in front of me. "Wait, Mel. Where's your phone?" I ask, looking around the room.

"Right here," she says, holding up her cell.

"Can I have it for a second? I want to see something."

She holds her phone out to me, confusion clear on her face, while I tap through her settings.

"Mel, I'm assuming you weren't the one who blocked me, were you?" I ask, holding up her phone to show her my contact on her blocked contacts list.

Amelia stares back at me, confusion and hurt covering her face as she starts to cry.

"What? No! I swear, no matter how mad at me I may have thought you were, I wouldn't have done that. You have to believe me. I don't know how many nights I spent crying to Mitch that you didn't want to hang out with me anymore. I even sent you a few texts, but when I never heard back from you, I took the hint."

"I'm gonna kill him," I mutter, piecing together what obviously happened as I remove my number from the list and hand her phone back to her.

I watch the moment it all clicks for Amelia, her face turning a dark shade of red the angrier she gets. "That lying, cheating, controlling, good-for-nothing, bastard!"

She looks at me, tears still in her eyes. "I'm so, so sorry, Lulu. I know I didn't know, but I hate that you thought I was ignoring you. I know I flaked at work too, but I just felt so horrible being around all of you when I thought you hated me."

I hug her, swearing that if I ever get the chance to punch Mitch in the dick, I'm taking it.

Amelia cries for another moment before pulling back to look at me. "Okay, now that that's over, please distract me from feeling like the biggest idiot asshole in the world. How are things with the cowboy?"

I pause, trying to decide how to respond. "I really, really like him. But I'm scared, Mel."

"Why?" she asks, confusion clear on her face. "It's clear as day that man adores you."

"Well, we have to figure out how to work this out with my brother, for one. You know he's not going to take this well, and as much as he drives me crazy, I don't want him to completely hate me. And that friendship is so important to Colton too—I can't be the reason he loses his best friend."

"Lulu, you can't put that on yourself," my best friend argues. "You and Colton are adults, and if you want to be together, then you should be together. As well intentioned as your brother may be, he has to remember that you're not a little girl anymore. It might be rough at first, but he'll come around. I mean, you're serious about this, right?"

I think back through all the moments that Colton and I have shared over the last few months—the days spent working the pumpkin patch, the slow mornings sitting on the porch watching the animals, the late nights as he made me come harder than I ever have in my life, and the way he makes me feel valued and smart. As I try to figure out how to answer that, it hits me that I'm completely in love with Colton Harris.

"Yeah, I'm serious about it," I mutter.

"Okay, well, you just have to believe it's gonna work out. Now, please, for the love of God, tell me you have ridden that mustache."

"Happy Thanksgiving!" Mom yells as Colton comes through

the front door on Thursday evening. "We're so glad you joined us!"

"Oh, of course. Thank you for having me," he says, making his way over to pull my mom into a hug. "I don't think I'll ever be able to thank you for everything y'all have done for me over the last few months."

My mom pats his cheek affectionately before waving her hand at him dismissively. "No thanks needed, honey. You know you're like part of the family now. You're welcome any time."

Amelia catches my eye across the counter and stifles a laugh at my mama's words. I shoot her a dirty look.

"Hey, Amelia. Lucy. Miss Martha and Mr. Bryce," Colton says in greeting.

I struggle not to meet his eyes. We're so close to being able to tell the truth about what's going on between us, but I know that we can't be caught sharing loving looks across the table today.

Instead, I turn my attention to my Uncle Bryce and ask, "So, you've been traveling a lot over the last few months. How's that been?"

My uncle opens his mouth to respond just as the front door opens, and my brother steps inside.

"Honey, I'm home," he yells, dropping his duffel bag on the floor and holding out his arms wide.

My mom yelps and hurries to hobble over to hug him.

"Oh, Hayesie, I'm so glad you're home," she yells, pulling back to wipe a tear from her eye. "I know I'm being dramatic, but I just worry about you so much when you're away. It's so good to see you!"

Hayes pulls back and pats my mom on the shoulder.

"I'm just fine, Mom," he reassures her before turning to face the rest of us.

"Hey, man," he says, walking over to Colton and slapping

him on the back. "I hate that I didn't get to see you last weekend, but thanks for coming. It meant a lot to me. Oh, and I can't wait to hear the list of corrections I have no doubt you have for me."

"Sure thing, man. It was fun. And yeah, there were a few things I noticed. We'll go over them later."

Hayes laughs. "I have no doubt," he says sarcastically before walking over to hug me.

"Hey there, Lucy Lu. I see you managed to keep everything standing with both Mom and me gone. I was half expecting to come home and find the pigs taking up residence in my room."

"Not this time," I say lightly.

Hayes makes his way around the rest of the room as Mama pulls the rolls out of the oven.

"All right, y'all. Now that everyone is here, I think we're ready to eat," she says, sorting them beside the rows of casseroles, vegetables, turkey, and dressing. "Go ahead and fix your plates before everything gets cold."

The seven of us crowd around the counter, filling our plates with food before we settle in around the dining room table.

"I just have to say, I'm really thankful for every person sitting at this table," my mom says, looking around at each of us. "The last few months may have had their ups and downs, but we've come out on the other side stronger than ever. And Colton, we couldn't have done it without you."

The rest of the table nods as Colton waves her off. "I'm more grateful for y'all taking me in after I got a little overwhelmed with the renovations."

"I tried to tell you," Hayes mutters, and the rest of us laugh before we start eating.

The table falls silent as we dig into the food my mom and Aunt Martha spent the last few days preparing. "Mama, Aunt

Martha, everything's wonderful," I say as Colton and Hayes chat about Hayes's last few months on the team.

I fight to keep my attention from straying to him too often, but it's hard. *Just a few more hours. Then dinner will be over and we can talk to Hayes. You just need to keep the secret a few more hours.*

Dinner feels like it lasts forever, and as soon as my Aunt Martha stands to clear the plates, I shoot out of my chair.

"I'll do it," I offer, desperate to have a minute away from everyone. I gather the first few plates and walk them into the kitchen, sitting them in the sink and blowing out a breath.

"You okay?" Colton's low voice comes from behind me.

I jump in surprise, turning to see we're alone in the large kitchen. He walks the plates he's carrying over to the sink before wrapping me in his arms.

"We can't do this here," I remind him, but I don't pull back, happy to be in his arms.

"You looked upset," he mutters, running his fingers through my hair. "I just wanted to check on you."

"I'm just nervous to tell him," I admit.

Colton drops a kiss to my forehead, rubbing my back for reassurance.

"It's gonna be fine. I promise Hayes is going to understand—"

"Understand what?" a voice comes from behind Colton, causing us both to freeze.

CHAPTER 33
COLTON

"Understand what?" Hayes asks again, louder this time.

Lucy looks around the room before staring at me with a panicked expression. I turn to see my best friend standing in the doorway, the hurt and fury evident on his face.

None of us speak for a few moments before Hayes asks, "Does anyone want to explain to me what the fuck is going on here? Because right now it looks like my best friend, who I asked to take care of my family, is wrapped around my little sister. But I'm sure that isn't true, especially after he explicitly promised to stay away from her."

Lucy opens her mouth to say something, but I hold up my hand to stop her. "I've got it, Darlin'."

Turning to face my best friend, I take a deep breath before admitting, "Hayes, I'm sorry. I really value your friendship, and I'm so grateful for everything your family has done for me these last few months," I start, taking a deep breath.

"But at the same time, your sister has become the most important person in the world to me. We're together, and we plan to stay together whether you're okay with it or not. But we would really love your blessing."

"My blessing?" Hayes asks, looking down at where Colton's arm is still wrapped around me. "Let me get this straight. I leave my best friend— one of the people I trust most in this world—alone with my little sister. I explicitly tell him to stay away from her. He spends the last three months promising me everything here is going well and that my sister is in good hands with him. Only to come home and find out that everything he said was a fucking lie. And after all that, you're gonna stand there and tell me it doesn't matter how I feel about it because you're gonna do it anyway, but you want my blessing!" he yells, his voice getting louder the longer he goes on. "And not only that, but you didn't even have the decency to come and tell me what was going on. Instead, I have to walk in on you two, sneaking around like a bunch of fucking teenagers. So no, you don't get my fucking blessing."

The room goes quiet for a minute, and I try to keep my composure as I say, "Hayes, I'm sorry you're hurt, but—"

"Hurt? Yeah, I'm fucking hurt," Hayes interrupts. "And pissed off, and betrayed, and annoyed, and—"

"Hayes, I'm sorry, but you don't get to do this," Lucy says, interrupting her brother's rant.

"Lucy, I'm just trying to protect you," Hayes starts, and Lucy holds up her hand.

"That's exactly my point. I don't need protection, Hayes!" Lucy explodes, the words pouring out of her. "I know you have good intentions, but I'm an adult. You don't get to judge me for who I want to date or the way I live my life. Now, I've decided that I want to be with Colton. We don't need your blessing, but we're asking for it because we care about you! And for the record, we were planning to tell you as soon as dinner was over and we could talk to you alone. Now, I'll apologize for a lot of things in my life, but I won't apologize for falling for your best friend."

The room goes silent, and Hayes stares at us for another moment before turning and walking out the back door, slamming it hard behind him.

Lucy sighs as she tries to hold back the tears filling her eyes. She drops her head on my chest as she stares at the door where he just left before whispering, "Well, I guess on the plus side, we don't have to keep this thing a secret anymore."

CHAPTER 34
LUCY

Colton wraps his arms back around me as I wipe away at the tears pooling in my eyes. I hadn't really expected my brother to take the news well, but actually seeing how angry he was had hurt my feelings more than I expected.

"I'm so sorry, Colton," I cry. "I should have known this was going to blow up in our faces."

Colton smooths a piece of hair back from my face and drops a soft kiss to my forehead.

"Baby, nothing about what just happened is your fault. We both knew what we were getting into when we started this thing. And I'll be honest, as much as I value your brother's friendship, I'd do this whole thing a million times over as long as I end up with you in my arms at the end of the day."

"But what about—" I start, and Colton holds up his hand to stop me.

"Let me finish, Darlin'," he says, and I nod, wiping another tear from my eye.

"Lucy, I don't know if you even realize how fucking obsessed with you I am. Ever since that first night in The

Watering Hole, I knew I was gone for you. But over the last few months, I've seen just how funny, smart, and incredible you really are. An old bastard like me had no business falling in love with a woman as perfect as you, but it's too late to worry about that now. Because Lucy Phillips, I am completely in love with you."

I stare at him in shock at his declaration while he continues. "There's nothing in this world that could convince me that we aren't meant to be together. And I'll do whatever it takes to convince you that this thing between us is worth whatever your brother wants to throw at us."

He pauses, looking at me expectantly. "So, what do you think? Are you still in this?"

"You love me?" I whisper, my mind stuck on that singular sentence.

"I do," he says, and I don't miss the hint of nerves in his voice. "It's okay if you don't feel the same way yet, but I just want—"

"Colton, I love you too," I admit, interrupting him. "You are everything I didn't know I needed, and you make me so unbelievably happy. I want to be with you more than anything."

Colton smiles, dropping his mouth to mine and delivering a slow kiss that makes my heart race. Our mouths tangle, and he pulls me closer into his arms, letting me feel every inch of his perfect body.

"Well, I'll be. Fucking finally," my mom says from the door, and I pull back, looking at her in shock.

"Mama, did you just curse?" I ask, looking at her with wide eyes.

She shrugs, coming into the kitchen, followed by Aunt Martha and Amelia. "Well, I think this situation calls for it," she says, looking over at her sister. "We've been wondering if you were ever going to tell us about the two of you."

Colton and I both look at her with shocked expressions, and she laughs. "Baby, I'm old, not stupid. And I know you two thought you were being so secretive, but anyone in the world could see the way you two look at each other."

"Why didn't you say something?" I ask.

"I figured when you wanted me to know, you'd tell me," she says simply before adding, "but I'll be honest, I never expected it to take this long."

I cringe. "Sorry, Mom. We just thought it was best to keep it between us until we talked to Hayes."

"Yeah, and we can see how well that went," Aunt Martha says. "We heard all the racket he was making from in the dining room."

"Yeah, it's safe to say he's not happy," I agree. "I'm sorry we ruined y'all's dinner. We were planning to tell him tonight, but he found us in here talking, and well… you know the rest."

My mom sighs. "I understand he's upset, but y'all have nothing to apologize for. You are both adults, and if you want to be together, then that's all there is to it. I do wish you'd felt comfortable enough to tell us, though."

"I'm sorry, Mom. I really am. It just all happened so fast. To be honest, when I met him, I had no idea who he was. We actually met the night you had your accident, but we didn't realize who the other was."

"I know," my mom says, and I stare at her again in shock.

"What, you knew? How?" I gasp, and my mom and aunt both break into giggles at my expression.

"Baby, did you really think you could kiss all over some man in Mills Corner and think it wouldn't get back to me. The waitress there told Miss Audrey, and it hit the group text before you left the bar."

Colton looks at me, shaking his head. "This damn town,"

he murmurs, and I can't help the laughter that bubbles out of me.

"Damn, I guess we weren't as sneaky as we thought we were, Cowboy," I tease, and he kisses my forehead in agreement.

"Yeah, I guess you're right."

"So, what do you think we should do about Hayes?" I ask, turning back to my mom.

She sighs. "That boy… Listen, baby. I know he drives you crazy with how overprotective he can be, but he does it out of love. When your daddy died, he took the responsibility of looking after you so seriously, and I know I probably should have stepped in to stop him. I was dealing with my own grief, and it was easier to just let him than worry about starting a fight with him. But I can see now how that was a mistake. He has good intentions, but he's gotta let you live your life the way you want to."

"I think I should talk to him," Colton says.

My mom nods. "I think you should, but give me a few minutes with him first. I'll go find him, and you can come after I've been out there a little bit," she says, grabbing her jacket and slipping her bare feet into her shoes by the door.

Amelia winks at me and gives me a thumbs up before she and my aunt head into the living room to watch football with my uncle.

As soon as we're alone, Colton turns back to me, dropping another kiss on my forehead. "I'll be back, baby. And after all this is over, I want you to think about spending the night with me. Now that this is out in the open, there's no reason we should have to stay apart, and I'm really tired of waking up without you in my bed."

I smile up at him, pretending to think about it. "Hmm, I guess that could be arranged, Cowboy."

CHAPTER 35
COLTON

All right, let's get this over with. He's your best friend, Hayes. You rode bulls for a living. There's no need to be this nervous about talking to him.

I head out to find Hayes. After searching around, I see him sitting with his mom on the tailgate of the farm truck. Taking a deep breath, I make my way over to where they're sitting, taking my time so that Mrs. Phillips can finish whatever she wanted to say.

Hayes's back is to me, so he doesn't see me approach, and I stand off to the side for a moment, listening to his mom.

"Baby, I know you're doing it out of love, but you've got to let Lucy make her own choices," she says gently, grabbing her son's hand.

"But Dad—" Hayes starts, but Mrs. Phillips holds up her hand to silence him.

"Hayes, your daddy would have never wanted you to take on this much responsibility for your sister's happiness. She was a teenager when he died, but she's grown now. You have to let yourself off the hook a little bit."

"I just want to make him proud," Hayes says, and I don't miss the emotion in his voice.

"Oh, baby. I know you do. And he would be so proud of the man you've become. But don't push away two of the people who love you the most because you're so determined to prove a point."

Mrs. Phillips stands and kisses her son's cheek before turning to head inside. As she passes me, she pats my arm in reassurance, and I take a deep breath before making my way over to the truck.

"Hey," I say, trying to ignore the nerves building in my chest.

Hayes just looks at me before nodding his head in my direction, and I take that as my invitation to sit beside him on the tailgate.

"I'm sorry," I start, trying to figure out how to make him understand how much his sister means to me.

"Yeah, you should be. I can't believe you—" he starts, pausing when he sees me holding up my hand.

"Let me finish, okay? And then you can yell and scream and call me all the names you want," I say, and he nods in acceptance.

"Let me be clear. I'm not sorry I fell in love with Lucy. She's the best thing that ever happened to me, and there's nothing in this world I wouldn't do for her."

Hayes's eyes widen in surprise at my declaration, but I continue. "But I *am* sorry for keeping it from you. I'm sorry for breaking your trust. I should have told you sooner, but I wanted to talk to you in person."

Hayes opens his mouth to respond, but after a moment, he falls silent and lets me keep talking.

"I'll be honest and say that no one is more surprised than me that she wants to be with an asshole like me. But from the moment I met her, she's been under my skin, and I don't ever want her to leave."

"How did this happen?" Hayes growls. "Because I thought I was pretty fucking clear that you were supposed to stay away from her."

"You did. But it was too late. Lucy and I met that first night I was in town at The Watering Hole. Neither of us realized who the other was, and she stole a piece of my heart that night. Now, should I have come clean about it the night I came over for dinner? Probably. But at the same time, neither of us knew where this was going to go. We really did try to just be friends. I swear we did. But the more time we spent together, the more we both realized that it wasn't what we wanted. And now, I'm completely in love with her. I wasn't lying when I said that if it comes down to having to make a choice, it'll be her every time. But I really hope you don't make me make that choice."

Hayes stares at me, and I think he's about to tell me to fuck off, but instead he asks, "So, you're really serious about her?"

"More serious than I've ever been in my life. She's it for me, man."

Hayes sighs and rubs his hands over his eyes. "Listen, I don't know that I like this. I'm still pretty pissed at the way it all went down. Lucy was right when she said she's an adult though. If this is what you both want, then I'm not going to do anything to stand in your way. But if this goes south, just know I'm always going to be on her side."

I nod. "I can live with that. I really am sorry for springing this on you the way we did. But I'm glad you're home. I'd love to show you everything Lucy and I have done with the house."

"I'd like that," Hayes says, reaching out to pat my back.

"But just promise I won't walk in on y'all kissing again or some shit."

"Um, that's a promise I don't know if I can keep," I tell him honestly. "Now, I think you need to go have a talk with your sister."

"WELL, overall, I think that went well," Lucy says, collapsing into bed beside me. "What's Thanksgiving without a little family drama, right?"

"Yeah, I'm not sad that everything's out in the open," I admit, pulling her into my arms. "I didn't get to ask you earlier—what did Hayes say when he talked to you?"

"He just apologized for the way he's treated me since Dad died. I think he finally realized how suffocating he could be. I love my brother, but I don't need him to tell me how to live my life. I think things should go a lot smoother between us from now on. He also said he's okay with this whole thing as long as I'm sure it's what I want."

"That's great, baby," I tell her, wrapping my arms around her and pulling her tighter to me. "God, I've missed this."

Lucy laughs, poking my chest with her finger. "Aww, who knew Colton Harris was such a big softy? It's hard to believe it's been less than a week since we came home from the rodeo and found everyone at the house."

"Yeah, it feels like forever since I had you in my bed."

"Well, now we don't have to spend any nights apart if we don't want to," Lucy says, leaning in and dropping a kiss to my lips.

"I don't want to," I add, pulling her on top of me as I deepen the kiss.

She laughs, and I pull back. "I'm serious, Lucy. Do you want to move in with me?"

She looks at me with wide eyes, trying to make sure I'm serious.

"Wait, really?" she asks.

"Yeah, I mean, if you want to. There's no pressure though if—"

She cuts me off, kissing me hard. "Yes! Yes, yes, yes."

"Thank god," I groan, threading my fingers through her hair.

"Now, can we stop talking and start fucking?" she asks.

Damn, this woman is something else.

I reach up to slide her sweater over her head. "I'm pretty okay with that idea," I whisper, leaning in to drop kisses down her neck, making my way down until I get to her light purple bra. "You and these damn bras."

Lucy smiles, rolling her hips against me in the way that she knows drives me fucking insane. I lean in and lightly bite her breast, making her gasp. "So damn pretty," I mumble, reaching around to unhook the clasp and slide the fabric down her arms.

As soon as she's free, she reaches down and yanks my shirt over my head. "Naked. I need you naked."

"Whatever you want, Darlin'," I mutter, lifting my hips to help her yank my jeans down my hips.

As soon as my cock pops free from my jeans, she leans down, sucking me into her mouth. I groan at the sight of her pink lips wrapped around my length, reaching down to pull her back up to me.

"Sorry, baby. You look hot as fuck with your pretty mouth taking my cock, but there's no way I'm coming until I'm buried in that perfect cunt of yours," I whisper, yanking her leggings down her legs.

As soon as she's bare for me, I flip her over and move to

the side of the bed, lining myself up with her entrance to take her from behind.

"You know you look so damn perfect spread out and ready to take my cock," I say, reaching down to tease her entrance.

She groans in response, rolling her hips to try to force me to hurry. "Patience, baby. We've got all night."

"Please, Colton," she pleads. "Please make me come now."

At her words, my control snaps, and I push into her, whimpering at how tight she feels in this position.

"Damn it, baby. Your pussy was fucking made for me," I tell her.

Leaning down and grabbing her hips, I work myself in and out of her.

I groan at the sight of her cunt taking my cock this way, moving my hips faster. Snaking my arm around her, I start teasing her clit.

"Lucy, you're fucking soaked for me," I tell her. "Did my sweet girl need to be fucked?"

She moans in response, bucking her hips faster against me, and I start to feel her walls tighten around me.

"That's right, baby. Are you gonna soak my cock when you come for me?"

At my words, she detonates, her pussy clamping down around me and making me see stars. Her arousal gushes out of her, drawing a groan from my lips and setting off my own orgasm.

We both gasp for breath, coming down from the high of what we just did. I pull out of her gently and watch as my cum drips out of her. "There's nothing in the world that compares to this view," I mutter, flipping her so that she's lying on her back and reaching down to run my fingers through it. Unable to stop myself, I slide my fingers back inside her, fucking her with my cum.

"Give me one more," I whisper, moving my finger in and out of her faster. She freezes, and I think she's going to tell me to stop. Instead, she starts rolling her hips, moaning as I add a second finger.

"Such a good girl," I praise, moving my fingers faster and leaning down to press a kiss on her clit. As soon as my mouth touches her sensitive skin, she clamps down around me again, riding out her orgasm. After a moment, I pull my fingers free and leaning down to pull her lips to mine. She crawls into my arms, tugging on me until I collapse on the bed beside her.

"I don't think I'm ever gonna get enough of this," she mutters, laying her head on my chest and closing her eyes.

"Me either, Darlin'."

CHAPTER 36
COLTON

"They're here," Lucy yells, watching as her mom and brother pull down the driveway of The Last Lasso later that week.

"Okay, perfect. I just checked on the steaks and they're almost finished," I say, coming in from the back porch and following her out the front door.

In the front yard, Denise, Daryl, and Carla run to meet Lucy's mom as she gets out of the car.

"Oh, my sweet babies. I've missed y'all this week! I still can't believe I let Lucy talk me into letting you three move over here."

Hayes rolls his eyes at his mom, walking up the walkway to join us on the porch. "Well, I guess it's safe to say this place looks a lot different than it did when I left."

I laugh and grab Lucy's hand, leading them inside to show off the house. Her mom stands, following us inside with the pigs right on her heels. Hayes gives us a look of disbelief as the pigs run into the house, collapsing on the small dog beds Lucy bought them in the corner of the room.

"You've gotta be fucking kidding me," he groans, shaking

his head at the sight. Knox runs out from where he was napping in our bedroom, jumping up on his hind legs, almost knocking Hayes over in the process. "How the hell do y'all deal with this shit?"

"It's getting cold, and they love being inside," Lucy say defensively. "And Colton built Carla a little matching house outside since she's getting too big for the house."

Hayes throws his hands up in surrender, focusing back on the house. "Anyway, everything looks good, man. This place really came together better than I thought it would. But wait, did Andy ever come take care of the squirrels for you?"

"Not quite," I mutter.

"What the fuck?" he yells, and Mrs. Phillips and I share a look, both of us laughing as we walk outside, where Lucy is holding the bag of sunflower seeds.

"Dinner time," she sings, and the squirrels pile out of the pink playhouse, crowding around her and waiting for her to drop the seeds for them.

"This can't be real," Hayes mutters under his breath.

"Yeah, welcome to the chaos." I sigh, smiling as my girl feeds the animals at her feet. "I've gotta say, they've kind of grown on me."

"Unbelievable," Hayes groans. "I can't watch this anymore. Is dinner ready?"

"Yeah, just let me take the steaks off," I say, walking up the stairs and piling the steaks on the platter I grabbed for inside. "Let's eat!"

Lucy and her mom follow us inside, the pigs and Knox never letting the women out of their sight as my girl grabs the silverware to set the table.

Hayes walks over to where I'm standing and mutters, "You're really happy here, aren't you?"

"Happiest I've ever been," I admit truthfully.

Hayes nods. "Then I'm happy for you, man. I know I

probably should have reacted to the whole thing better than I did, but if anyone deserves everything they want, it's you."

I nod, clapping him on the back. "Aww, Hayesie, are you going soft on me?"

Hayes flips me off as my phone rings. Looking down, I see Sam's name flash across my screen, and I hit the button to accept the call.

"Hey, man. What's up?" I say, making sure everything is ready for dinner.

"Hey, Colton. I need to talk to you about something, and I want you to let me finish before you tell me no," he says, and I laugh.

"Wow, you're really selling this already, aren't you?"

"I guess. Anyway, I've been thinking about it, and I think I'm ready to retire. I'm pushing fifty, and honestly, staying on the road for a few months out of the year isn't as fun as it used to be. But, that means the Bama Bulls will be looking for a new coach."

My heart rate picks up at his words, and I wait to hear what else he's going to say. "Do you think you'd be interested? Obviously, it would have to go through the owners, so this isn't anything official, but I think you'd be a pretty perfect candidate if you're interested. I'm meeting with them tomorrow, and I didn't know if you wanted me to mention your name?"

I pause, trying to decide how I feel about it. After the accident, I thought my days with the rodeo were over. But maybe there's a way to still have a part of the life I spent the last fifteen years building.

"Umm, let me talk to Lucy about it tonight and I'll let you know."

"Lucy, huh? Sounds like we have a lot to catch up on," Sam says with a laugh. "But that's fine. Just let me know before noon tomorrow."

"Will do," I say, hanging up and turning to Hayes.

"What was that all about?" he asks, just as Lucy and her mom join us at the counter.

"What's going on?" Lucy asks, slipping her arms around my waist.

"Sam just called. He wanted to know if I was interested in coaching the Bama Bulls next season."

The three of them stare at me in shock until Lucy asks, "Well, what did you tell him?"

"I said I'd have to let him know tomorrow after I talk to you. I'm not making any decisions without you, Darlin'."

She smiles at me, pulling me down so she can press a kiss to my lips. "I'm up for whatever you want. If this is something you want to do, we do it. Amelia and I have already been talking about bringing in help around the farm, and I'll travel with you wherever you go, at least through the summer season. But if you don't want to go back to that world, then that's okay too. However, I think you'd be great at it."

"Nothing is guaranteed yet. Sam's going to talk to the owners and wanted to know if he could bring my name up."

"What do *you* want?" Lucy asks.

"You," I say simply, and she laughs.

"Well, you got me, Colton. And you aren't getting rid of me anytime soon. So, is this something you want to do?"

I hesitate, thinking about it for a minute, before I nod. "Yeah, I think it is. You know, everything ended so suddenly for me, and while I don't have any complaints about the way it all worked out in the end, I think it would be nice to say goodbye to that part of my life on my own terms. Is that stupid?"

"Not at all," Lucy reassures me. "I think it sounds like fun."

"Yeah, I think it could be a good time," I agree. "And I'd get to go back to telling old Hayesie here how to ride."

"Great," Hayes says sarcastically, causing the rest of us to laugh.

"All right, now that that's settled, y'all fix your plates," I say, gesturing to the food in front of us.

After everyone has their food, we settle around the table. As soon as we sit down, Knox, Denise, and Daryl stand from their beds and make their way over to stretch out under the table, looking up at us expectantly.

While Hayes and his mom start to eat, Lucy leans over and rests her head on my shoulder. "Did you know that I love you, Cowboy?"

I drop a kiss onto her forehead and smile. "Not as much as I love you, Darlin'."

EPILOGUE

LUCY

SIX MONTHS LATER

"**D**aryl, you get back here right now!" I yell, shaking my head at the mess in front of me. I was working on a new painting in the art room Colton set up for me. I set the paint brush down for one second on the short stool Colton built me so I could check my phone, and somehow my pig picked it up. I looked up to see him dragging the bright pink paintbrush around the floor as he chases his sister.

I'm running behind him, trying to figure out how in the world I got myself into this predicament, when the door opens, and Colton comes in, his eyes widening as he takes in the chaos in front of him.

"Damn it, Daryl," he groans. "Stop that!" Unfortunately, all this seems to do is make Daryl more excited as he takes off back through the living room, leaving a squiggly line of pink paint in his wake.

"Well, hello to you too," I tease, walking over to kiss him. "You can see that today is going super well."

"Yeah, I see that," Colton says, shaking his head. "I missed you today, though."

"I missed you too," I say honestly. "I was almost finished with the last painting for this month's market when Daryl swooped in and stole my paintbrush."

"Yeah, I guess we should do something about that, huh?" he asks, bringing my mouth back to his.

"Uh huh," I say distractedly as Colton continues to kiss me, neither of us making the motion to move.

Finally, Colton drags his mouth away from mine and smiles at me. "Okay, if I don't stop, this is going to get out of hand."

"I'm okay with that," I tease, and he shakes his head at me.

"As much as I'd love that, there's something I need to show you. But when we get back, we're picking up where we left off," Colton says seriously, grabbing my hand and leading me to the front door.

As soon as he opens the door, Daryl, Denise, and Knox all rush from the back of the house, following us outside.

"Where'd you leave the paintbrush, huh?" I ask Daryl, shaking my head at the paint covering his snout.

He looks up at me, his short tail wagging happily, and I roll my eyes. "You three are really something else."

As soon as the words are out of my mouth, Carla and the squirrels run from the side of the house.

"I guess they were feeling left out," Colton says, shaking his head as the squirrels jump on the pigs' backs. "I know they do this all the time, but I'm still convinced that can't be normal."

"Babe, I don't know if you've noticed, but there isn't much normal about this house." I laugh. "Now, where are you taking me?"

"Well, I planned to take you to the meadow, but somehow, this feels right."

I look at him in confusion. "Babe, what are you talking about?"

Instead of answering, he sinks down to one knee and pulls out a small black ring box. I stare at him in shock as he opens the lid, revealing the most perfect teardrop-shaped solitaire diamond I've ever seen in my life.

"Lucy Phillips, you're everything I never knew I wanted. You came into my life when I was least expecting it. Ever since the night you walked into The Watering Hole, you've owned every piece of my heart. And nothing in this world would make me happier than getting to spend the rest of my life by your side. So, will you marry me?"

As soon as he finishes, the animals all run over, thinking that Colton wants to play. Knox barks, and the pigs scramble around him, almost knocking Colton over as they all try to get his attention.

"Damn it, can y'all not let me have this one moment?" Colton groans, causing me to laugh. He stands, shaking his head.

"I can't imagine a more fitting way for us to start our lives together," I mutter, and Colton looks up at me.

"Does that mean you're saying yes? You'll marry me?" he asks, his expression hopeful.

"Absolutely, I will," I cry, reaching my hand for him to slip the ring on my finger. The moment it's on my hand, I sigh, soaking in how perfect this moment feels.

"I love you, Colton Harris," I mutter, looking around at the life we built together.

"Not as much as I love you, Lucy Phillips," he says, dropping his mouth to mine.

We kiss for a moment, lost in the feeling of each other.

"You know, I'm gonna miss this chaos next month when we start touring."

Colton was officially hired as the Bama Bulls head coach just before Christmas, and we leave for the season in less than three weeks.

"I can't believe I'm saying this, but so will I. But you and I both know they'll have a great time staying with your mom."

I nod, knowing he's right. "Also, I need to run something by you," I say hesitantly.

"What's up, baby?"

"Well, I was talking to Amelia, and I think she should come with us. You know she's had a hard time since she and Mitch broke up, and I don't want to leave her. Plus, if she's there, it'll give me someone to hang out with while you're in training.

Colton goes quiet for a second before nodding. "Actually, I think that's a good idea. But I'm getting her a hotel room at each stop, because there's no way I'm going four months without fucking you."

"I think that's a great compromise," I agree, leaning back in to kiss him.

Pulling back, I look down at the ring he just placed on my finger. "We're getting married," I squeal. "You know, there's no take-backs. You're officially stuck with me forever."

"I like the sound of that," Colton replies, planting a soft kiss on my forehead.

Reaching up, I take his hat and place it on my head. Colton smiles, his eyes filling with mischief. "Now, Darlin', you know I only take that hat off for one thing."

"I know," I tell him, grabbing his hand and leading him back toward the house. "Now, come on, Cowboy. I think you have something to take care of."

Want more from Mills Corner? Amelia's story is coming in 2026.

ACKNOWLEDGMENTS

Wow, I am so excited you're finally holding this book in your hands. This book was so much fun to write, and I am so grateful that you took a chance on my story. However, it wouldn't have been possible without some super special people!

First of all, C, none of this would work without you. You are my strongest supporter and the reason I believe so strongly in love stories. You take everything in stride, and you always remind me of the joy I find in these books. You're my favorite happily ever after, and I love you endlessly.

To my parents, thank you always going out of your way to support my dreams. You always remind me that there's nothing I can't do, and your encouragement is always exactly what I need to hear. Thank you for always being down for a signing and pushing me to be the best I can be. To Nonnie and Dah, thank you for being the absolute biggest cheerleaders I could ask for. The four of you are what keeps me going, and I couldn't love you more.

Cassie, all I can say is bless your heart for putting up with all my chaos. You were the first person to encourage me to write this book, and I'm so glad you did. Thank you for every graphic, voice memo, and email that got us here. Truly couldn't do this without you.

To the author besties who sprinted with me and encouraged me to tell this story, I'm so very grateful. I couldn't love y'all more. A special thank you to Ambar for your detailed notes and endless check ins.

To my alpha/beta team—y'all are the real MVPs. Emma, Hunter, Rose, Megan, Mary, Rachel, Katie, Anna, Emily, and Ashley, y'all make writing fun! I'm so grateful for your feedback and all the unhinged reactions.

Emily and Staci, thank you so much for the most perfect covers. I adored working with y'all and can't wait to continue!

Erica and Caroline, you are both a rockstars! Thank you so much for all you did to help this book shine!

Rae, you are the sweetest angel, and I'm so grateful for your patience and feedback during this process.

To my ARC readers, thank you so much for agreeing to take a chance on me and these characters. Every tag, review, and post means so much to me, and I truly could not be more grateful.

And finally, to you dear reader, thank you so much for your support. None of this is possible without YOU, and I cannot thank you enough for picking up this book!

FULL LIST OF CONTENT WARNINGS

Loss of a Parent (Off Page)
Discussions of Grief
Discussion and Depiction of a Toxic/Controlling Relationship
(Not the Main Characters)
Discussions of Cheating (Not by the Main Characters)
Death of Livestock (Natural Causes)
Injury from Bull Riding (On Page)
Medical scenes from injury
Explicit Language
Explicit Sexual Content

BE THE FIRST TO KNOW

Want to stay up to date on all the things? Join my newsletter, sign up for alerts on upcoming signings, and follow my reader group here!

ABOUT THE AUTHOR

Hollie Luckie is a small town girl that wholeheartedly believes in happily ever afters. Between reading and writing romance, she is always getting lost in a fictional world. She resides in south Alabama with her high school sweetheart, her dog Memphis, and her own farm of quirky farm animals. You can find Hollie on Instagram at @authorhollieluckie or on Goodreads.

ALSO BY HOLLIE LUCKIE

Springside Series

Where We Break

Why We Break

What We Build

Deer Valley Inn Holiday Novellas

Matchmaking Under The Mistletoe

Married Under The Mistletoe

Crestbrook Cove

Searching for Sunshine

WTS (Coming Summer 2026)

Mills Corner

Secrets and Spurs

WE
CAN
ALWAYS
TELL

WE CAN ALWAYS TELL

An Anthology of Trans Erotic Horror

THE LAUGHING MAN HOUSE PUBLISHING

This book is a work of fiction. References to real people, events, establishments, organizations, or locales are intended only to provide a sense of authenticity, and are used to advance the fictional narrative. All other characters, and all incidents and dialogue, are drawn from the author's imagination and are not to be construed as real.

WE CAN ALWAYS TELL